ALICE

CLOSE

YOUR

EYES

ALICE CLOSE YOUR EYES

AVERIL DEAN

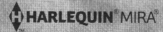

Recycling programs
for this product may
not exist in your area.

ISBN-13: 978-0-7783-1586-5

ALICE CLOSE YOUR EYES

For questions and comments about the quality of this book, please contact us at
CustomerService@Harlequin.com.

Printed in U.S.A.

First printing: January 2014
10 9 8 7 6 5 4 3 2 1

www.Harlequin.com

For my mother.

Every spirit builds itself a house.
—Ralph Waldo Emerson

CHAPTER ONE

I am inside Jack's house.

Rain trickles down the windowpanes and a spring thunderstorm rumbles almost inaudibly in the distance as I drift through the blue window light, in and out of the shadows, tracing the objects in the living room with my gloved fingertips. A queen conch shell reclines on the sideboard, its frilled pale pink lip deepening to a slick rose interior as the shell curves in on itself. I pick it up, hold it to my ear. A phantom ocean soughs inside the empty calcium walls. I imagine the bowl filling with surf, overflowing, disappearing under the sand.

The furniture is low and modern, with square brown side chairs and a kidney-shaped coffee table in front of the fireplace. The living room is arranged around a rag-leather area rug, and at one end of the sofa is a floor lamp made from a piece of gnarled, tiger-striped mesquite, stained and rubbed to a satin finish the color of a cinnamon stick. On the wall next to the fireplace hangs a graphic, ceiling-high painting of a raven on its perch.

I circle the room, opening drawers and doors, careful to leave things as I find them. I search the kitchen cabinets and the top shelf of the coat closet, the blanket chest by the door and the bookshelves against the wall, until I find what I came for: a simple wooden box, the contents of which are of no value to anyone but me and the guy who collected them.

A brass clock sits in the center of the mantel, clicking like an old lady's tongue as I tuck the box under my arm. *Hurry.* I hesitate, my eyes on the back door. *Hurry.*

I cross the room and start down the hallway. To my right, a door is ajar. I give it a gentle push and step through the doorway. The home owner—*Jack,* I think, loving this, *Jack Calabrese*—has turned over the second bedroom to his hobby, ships in bottles. The room is lined with shelves bearing elaborate models in heavy glass bottles of different sizes and shapes, and under the window, a worktable is strewn with tiny pieces of wood and lengths of string. It looks like he's begun work on a new model, and has only gotten as far as laying out the components. I circle the room, running my fingers along the smooth curved glass. I press my nose to the mouth of one of the bottles and inhale. Sawdust, mixed with a briny scent that makes me think he salvaged this bottle from the beach. Together the aromas evoke a shipyard, or a seaside lumber mill. I peer through the bottleneck at the ship inside, its prow aimed right at me.

My thoughts judder to a halt. A key clicks against the front door and slides into the lock.

My heart leaps, stumbles, restarts. Adrenaline flashes through my limbs.

In a second I'm out the door, skidding silently down the hall to the bedroom. I duck around the corner, run to the window and flip the latch. But the sash is fitted with a security lock that prevents it from opening more than a few inches. No sign of the key, and there won't be time to pick the lock. I turn back to the room in dismay. The bed is low to the ground, no space underneath. No shower curtain in the attached bathroom or wardrobe against the wall. And the back door I entered through is at the other side of the house.

Out of options, I cross the room, slip through the closet door and slide it shut. The hangers clatter as I push the clothes aside and sink to a crouch, clutching the wooden box to my chest.

From the hallway, footsteps approach. Heavy, thudding against the hardwood floor.

Even here, I feel exposed. In my closet, there would be places to hide: a raft of boots and sneakers, a curtain of secondhand coats, the blue plastic laundry basket in the corner, full to overflowing with sweaters and faded jeans. I could have buried myself in belongings, hidden for hours until he either left again or fell asleep. But in this half-full closet, only a thin sliding door stands between me and discovery.

A slice of my reflection shimmers on the metal frame. My eye flashes, caught in a chink of light from the bedroom window. I ease sideways and press my back into the corner.

The footsteps get louder and more deliberate. They cross the room to the window I left standing open. A scrape of the window frame, and the whisper of rain outside is silenced. There is a pause. Then three steps, louder.

The grit on the bottom of his boot grinds against the floor.

My heartbeat is crashing in my ears, pounding at the roof of my mouth. Surely he will hear it. I hold my breath, feel my eyelids stretch open, then snap together. I screw them shut and chant a silent prayer.

Please don't open the door. Please please please don't open the door....

The box in my arms tilts a little, shifting the contents. A muffled clunk from inside strikes my ears like a mallet.

Shit. God fucking dammit.

The door begins to slide.

The first thing I see is a claw hammer, raised to shoulder height. Then a fist, wrapped around the handle. A man's face. The knife's edge of his jaw, serrated with afternoon stubble. His eyes, framed in the thick brown rims of his glasses, squinting into the darkness, then widening in surprise.

Jack Calabrese.

He slides the clothes aside and stares down at me.

"What the fuck."

I scramble to my feet, through the rack of jeans and flannel shirts. A lock of dark hair flops over my eyes.

"You want to tell me what the fuck you're doing in my closet?"

"Robbing you." My voice is thready. I clear my throat, jerk my chin.

His gaze falls to the box in my arms. He's taller and more imposing than he seemed from a distance. But as he looks at me, his angry expression melts to a sort of baffled amusement, as though he's waiting for me to explain the point of a joke. Up close, I notice an unexpected dimple that fills with shadow when he speaks and empties when he frowns, leaving only a short, thin crease to mark the place.

I hold out the box with both hands like a guilty child. He takes it from me, looks briefly inside and sets it on the dresser.

"You have odd taste for a thief," he says. "Or poor judgment."

I step toward the door. He shifts his weight, a bare movement, but it stops me in my tracks. I glance automatically at the window. Closed and latched.

"Don't I know you?" he says. "From town or something?"

"No. Look, I'm sor—"

"Is this about Rosemary?"

I look at him blankly. "No."

His gaze wanders down my body as he takes in my Pixies T-shirt, torn secondhand Levi's. Knitted, elbow-length gloves, striped orange and blue.

There is a light thump from the closet. A couple of shirts, dislodged from the rack, have fallen to the ground. To leave them there seems rude, so I gather them up and hang them back on the rail, smoothing the fabric, adjusting the hangers as though I can convey a benign intention by the care I take with his clothing.

When I straighten again and face Jack Calabrese, his expression has softened to that of a cool stepfather dealing with the teenager who's just wrecked the family car. And though I've dressed to inspire that reaction, just in case, his self-confidence unsettles me.

He lays the hammer on the dresser, next to the wooden box. "Want a drink?"

I must have heard him wrong. "A drink."

"Yeah." He speaks over his shoulder as he passes through the doorway. "You look like you could use one."

I follow slowly, my legs weak as water, boneless, loose. Down the hallway, past the ship room. Outside, the rain has picked up, pattering against the roof, the raindrops sliding thick as wax down the windowpanes.

He takes two glasses from the cupboard and fills them with ice. I steal a glance at the door. Now would be the time to run—make a mad dash across the room, out the door, down the road to the main street and the shortcut through the heavy woods to my house. I imagine myself there, safe and warm and locked in tight.

But I don't run. The same thing that drew me here keeps me rooted to the spot.

He crosses the room and hands me the drink.

"So, what were you looking for, exactly?" he says. "Money? Drugs?"

"Neither, nothing." I take a sip of fiery-cool liquid. "Just the box."

"That box of sentimental crap? Why?"

"C-curiosity."

"About what?"

Warmth bursts over my cheeks and seeps down my neck, and that seems to answer his question. And in a flash, I realize he's handing me the perfect excuse—for the break-in, for everything. I see, dimly, the path before us. All I need to do is let his ego lead the way.

He smiles. "I'm flattered. And how did you know about the box?"

"I didn't. At least…I mean, everyone has a box. Usually with men it's a shoebox. Yours is…"

"Mine is what?"

"Nicer than usual."

He crosses his arms, leans a hip against the granite counter. His voice is slow, intimate, as though we're exchanging secrets in a crowded room. The corner of his mouth twitches upward. "This a hobby of yours? Breaking and entering? Stealing men's boxes?" He raises his eyebrows, loading the question with innuendo.

I swirl my drink and stare into the glass.

"Look, I'm sorry."

A white gleam slides along the frame of his glasses when he moves his head. His eyes are veiled by a sheet of window light across the lenses.

"So, what did you want to know?"

What can I say that doesn't seem absurd to the point of madness? *I wanted to know what your house looks like, what's in your fridge and medicine cabinet, where you keep your jack mags and how well-used they appear to be. Whether that accent is Boston or Philly. I want to know what your shampoo smells like, whether you leave your socks on the floor, can keep a houseplant alive, own a cat or a bong or an insulin syringe. I want to see how you rumple the bed.* And the sum of all those answered questions, plus a thousand more I haven't thought of yet:

I want to know whether you'd kill for me.

I set his glass on the counter and head for the door, shuffling sideways to avoid turning my back to him.

He follows, hands in his pockets.

"What's your name?" he says.

The heel of my sneaker hits the step at the entryway. "I'm sorry."

"You mentioned that."

"And I'll be going now."

As I reach the door and twist the handle at the small of my back, he closes the gap between us, stretches one long arm over my shoulder to hold the door closed. I stare straight ahead, watching his pulse flicker in the hollow under his jaw.

"Tell me your name," he says. "I'm guessing you know mine."

I won't look him in the eye. My breath has grown shallow and quick, small gusts over my lips.

"Well?"

I don't know how to answer. None of this is going according to plan. I feel like an actor onstage who's rehearsed the wrong play. I need to get out the door, get away, think it through before things go too far—

Before I can react, he reaches behind me, slides his hand around my ass and into my pocket and comes up with my wallet. I make a grab but he yanks it away, opens it and takes out my driver's license.

"Alice Elizabeth Croft," he reads. "Five-four, one hundred fifteen pounds. Black hair, green eyes."

He returns my wallet, smiling, looking me over. "Sounds about right."

"Can I go now?"

He steps back, hands up. "Who's stopping you?"

I open the door and stumble onto the front porch, pausing at the top step to pull up my hood.

"Hey, do you want a ride?" The amusement in his voice is clear, even through the storm. "It's 336 Signal Road, right?"

I run down the wooden steps and leave him laughing behind me.

I unlock my front door, drenched and out of breath from my mile-long sprint through the forest. My sneakers are muddy and bristled with pine needles. I toe them off, strip out of my gloves, T-shirt and jeans and leave them in a dark, sodden heap next to the door.

In my bra and underwear, I head for the bathroom and

take out my kit: straight razor, ointment, gauze and a large, flat bandage. My hands are trembling and too slippery to hold the razor. I wipe them on a towel and sit at the edge of the tub, my ankle crossed over my knee, and run my thumb over the tapestry of pink and white scars on the sole of my foot—the hard, half-healed ridges and faded round cigarette burns, the deeper, purplish groove from last year's infection. I slide the blade across the arch of my foot. Once, twice, three times. There is a short, shocked pause before the invisible cuts fill into fine red threads, then fat strands of yarn, swelling crimson beads, each one adorned with a square, striped catchlight from my bathroom window. One by one the droplets shiver and burst and drip to the tile, swirling into the rain that trickles from the ends of my hair.

I close my eyes as the fire sets in. The razor blade clatters to the floor.

CHAPTER TWO

On Vashon Island, there is a strange tree. Decades ago when the tree was young, a boy parked his Red Ranger bicycle there, straddling the fork and locked in place with a sturdy chain. The bike was never reclaimed so the tree grew around it, engulfed it, until only the wheels and twisted handlebars remained visible, suspended six feet off the ground like some giant prehistoric insect trapped in amber.

I lived near the tree when I was growing up. My grandmother had a small trailer in a lot across the road, and I would sneak away sometimes, silent on the loamy footpath, to my spot on a mossy stump where I would stare up at the bike and wonder how to extricate it. Something about the preternatural fusion of tree and bicycle distressed me. That horrifying, remorseless consumption—the strangled metal, trapped inside the bowels of the tree.

Recently I read that the bicycle was vandalized and the front wheel removed. I imagine the bike's decapitation, the final indignity. I don't want to see it.

"Mocha decaf," says Midge.

"You're good," I say, easing the café door shut. A rich

aroma greets me: coffee and cream, and something seductive from the huge ancient oven behind the counter.

"What else?" she says.

"Whatever that is in the oven."

Midge smiles, wiping her hands on her canvas apron. She
has always reminded me of a Sesame Street monster. Small,
square, adorably ugly. A huge fierce grin full of crooked
teeth, a tuft of wiry black hair. "You can't have that. It's a
wedding cake."

"So cruel. Thank God there are muffins."

I take my breakfast outside and lay out my notes and
pages. It's early morning, drizzly and cool. Across the gravel
road, two gray horses appear through the mist, grazing in a
ragged field against a backdrop of dark pines. One of them
lifts her head and lets go with a high-pitched whinny that
rips through the stillness and trails away.

Aside from the Red Ranger tree, Vashon-Maury is like
any other island in the Puget Sound, with one utilitarian
commercial district featuring a handful of disorganized grocery stores, interspersed with touristy shops bearing hand-
painted names like Heron's Nest and Treasure Island, where
you can buy mugs depicting the Seattle skyline or salt and
pepper shakers shaped like the island's famous strawberries
(which nobody grows anymore, though the festival lives on).
On Thursdays, we have a farmers' market with lumpy rows
of pumpkin and zucchini, and jars of organic jam covered
by squares of red-and-white gingham, tied around the lid
with hemp twine. At the north end of town, our single-
screen theater shows last season's films in a postapocalyptic
setting; the stoner at the ticket counter will ask if you want
popcorn, and if you do he'll follow you to the snack bar to

ring you up, then trudge upstairs with a hot dog for himself and start the film ten minutes late.

It's a humble town, peeling and briny. So it makes no sense for me not to sleep at night, but the fact is I can't. I haven't slept in the dark since I was thirteen years old. Instead, I spend the nights working on my manuscript—*Zebra Down,* fifth in the series of young adult novels that's been paying my bills since I left high school—and in the mornings I take a walk or ride my bike to the Beanery for a cup of coffee.

I brush the crumbs off my fingers, open a book of writing prompts and choose one at random. This is my daily routine, my exercise, prescribed by an online writing teacher who believes in the importance of keeping the creative muscles loose. Ten minutes, scribble like hell, see what comes out.

Faceless men.

I set the timer on my phone and begin.

At night I dream of faceless men. They move through the architecture of my imagination like spirits, shadowy incubi who wait for sleep to deliver me. They press me into the walls, the floors, and I am trapped here in the structure, with all my ghosts inside me and all my rooms on display. I let them seduce me, reveal me and all the secret places where I simmer and burn, let them lift me up and drag me down and nail me with their need, until I feel the push of everything male against all that is female in me.

My phone beeps at the end of ten minutes. I read my page of scrawled handwriting as I sip my coffee and crumble a bite of muffin over my plate.

Nail me, I think disgustedly. Paging Dr. Freud. I cross it out and write it back exactly the same way. Twice.

I obliterate all three versions with lines that dent the paper, rip the page from my notebook, crumple it and toss it toward the trash can. The paper bounces off the rim and lands on the sidewalk. Before I can get out of my chair, a man on his way out of the coffee shop stoops to pick it up.

Jack Calabrese. He grins and starts to open the page.

I leap up and snatch it away.

"Whoa," he says, laughing. "Check out the reflexes on the little cat burglar."

I back away, the ball of paper in my fist, and begin to pack up my notebooks. My heartbeat accelerates—I feel the pressure rise in my neck.

"Don't go," he says.

"I need to get home."

"Why? Is someone waiting for you?"

My mouth tightens. No one is waiting for me, but his tone implies that he knows this already. As though such a thing is outside the realm of possibility.

"Sit with me for a few minutes," he says.

He is unshaven but his hair is damp, and he has a freshly scrubbed look about him. His flannel shirt is soft with age, drooping over the bump of his shoulders, the cuffs rolled up over his brown forearms. He has a cup in his hand and under his arm a book that he lays on the table as he claims the seat across from me. *Intensity.* Dean Koontz.

In the distance, the tsunami siren blares. We recognize the test pattern and ignore it.

"You're a writer, then," he says.

"Nothing gets past you." I sink into my chair, still collecting my notes and battered index cards. I wind a rubber band around the latter and shove them into my satchel.

"So hostile. You got no time for the guy who caught you breaking and entering?"

His tone is even, but the challenge in his eyes, framed by the heavy rims of his glasses, stops me. I snap my bag closed and lean into the back of my chair.

"I apologized for that. What else is there to say?"

"People do have unnecessary conversations sometimes, Alice."

My name sounds too easy coming from him. Too familiar.

"Look. I get that you feel entitled to mess with me. But unless you've got something to tell them down at Barney's cop shack, you can fuck straight off."

"Got it. But have dinner with me first."

"Yeah. That's not going to happen."

"Why not?"

I don't want to answer. The fact that he's here makes me uneasy. I know his schedule—at 7:00 a.m. he should be at work. It occurs to me that he may have followed me, and I don't like that turn of the tables at *all*.

I get to my feet and sling the satchel over my shoulder. "Let's just say, it seems like a bad idea."

"I can't believe that's something that normally stops you."

Heat rushes up my neck. I pull up my hood to cover it, and carry my dishes to the plastic bin next to the trash can.

He raises his cup to bid me goodbye. "If you change your mind, you know where to find me."

I grit my teeth and turn away. It feels like a long walk

to the corner where I've left my bike, and with every step I feel his stare at my back.

It takes all I have not to turn around.

He is all I can think about on my way home from the café, through my hot shower, as I brush my teeth and hair and crawl at last, at 9:00 a.m., into bed.

At first his face fills my mind's eye. The sharp line of his jaw; the row of even white teeth, flashing like sunlight on water; the double frame of his glasses and thick dark eyebrows, under which his eyes gleam with mischief. But as I lie in my bed with the memory of him, stroking tentatively over the thin, warm fabric of my cotton underwear, his face becomes shrouded, dissolving into obscurity. I know it's him the way you know it in a dream: it's his presence, his name in my mind, but he has become both more and less than himself. In my fantasies, he's an archetype, faceless and almost formless. He is what he does. He is the *idea* of a man.

I remember his house, the doorknob cold in my hand, his long arm stretched above me to hold the door closed. He's angry that I've invaded his space, angry that I want to leave. I have crept deliberately into his den and my curiosity has a price.

You want to know me, he says, and his hand is in my hair. The scent of him fills my mind. He tips my head back and kisses me openmouthed, laying a first easy claim to the inside of me. I feel his attention, all his focus on me. He has tasted me now. He can smell me. His hand moves down the front of my body to my breast, and I feel my nipple gather in his palm. His body stiffens, slows for a moment, and I sense the predatory tension in him.

One of my hands is flat against his chest, the other clutching the doorknob at the small of my back. But I know from his kiss and the boldness of his hand on my breast that I won't be leaving until he has fucked me. The inevitability panics and excites me. This could hurt, it could be awful; I could get pregnant. A procession of frightening conse-quences marches through my mind, but every protest is swept aside by the simple, profound need of his to fuck me. Of my need to let him.

He reaches under my shirt, subduing me with the weight of his body, and unclasps the front of my bra. He moves back, assessing, arrogant, and lowers his head to my breast as he unbuttons his jeans, then gathers my skirt to hitch it over my hips. He strokes me through my underwear, one finger teasing at the hem as if there is a choice in this for either of us.

I open my mouth and he kisses me again, puts words lit-erally into my mouth.

You wanted to get caught.

He drags one knuckle over my clitoris and traces my lower lip with his tongue.

Wanted to get fucked, didn't you.

He slides a finger under my panties, inside me, and I hear the breath hiss past his teeth as we discover together how wet I am. His one finger is joined by a second, and he draws them up my folds, over my clitoris, circling.

He moves back to see my face, my bare breasts, then his mouth returns to mine. His mouth is hotter, more demand-ing. He licks my teeth and bites my lip. His fingers are back inside me, two and then three, his eyes on my face as my resistance dies away.

I begin to move with him, following his rhythm. The tips of my breasts are drawn up tight against the rasp of his shirt. I test him with a twist of my wrists and feel the fingers of both his hands tighten against me. This comforts me somehow. I know he won't let go, will not stop, and the knowledge gathers between my legs like lightning in a storm, and with his mouth over mine I am coming. Pain and desire meet inside me, sharp as a thunderclap. My cunt grabs and releases, clenching hard around his fingers, an undulating ripple moving upward through my body. I am still coming when he lifts me up and open, his hands around my knees, then pulls me down on top of him. He is huge and I feel the invasion of this, but I spread my legs and let him in until he's buried inside me, immediately orgasmic, pounding his need to the depths of me with long, firm strikes against the wall of my cervix. He shudders, and I feel the trembling pulse of his ejaculation—the final evidence of his domination, of my surrender.

Yes, he says, *oh, fuck yes.*

I open my eyes, blink into the morning light with the blood still roaring in my ears. The sheets are damp, my limbs buzzing as though I've just taken a hard electric shock.

Jack's face reforms in my mind's eye. It's his smile I see as I drift off to sleep, my hand still clamped between my legs.

CHAPTER THREE

There was a boy in my third-grade class named Danny Kukal. When they lined us up for the yearbook photo, he was at the tall end, while I brought up the rear as the smallest in class. He ran with a pack of unruly boys with chapped lips and cowlicked hair, easily dominating even the fifth-graders on the playground. Every recess they took over the tetherball courts and the coveted red rubber balls, merciless and loud and endlessly annoying.

I felt myself somewhat protected from the worst of their behavior. I was a girl. A pretty girl, apparently. But as the school year went on and the boys settled on their targets, my distaste for them grew. Danny Kukal was the worst. I resented his popularity, his quick cruelty toward the smaller kids, his arrogance. I detested his wide yellow teeth, too big for his face, and the swaggering upturn of his butt under the school corduroys. Quietly my disgust swelled into a hatred too big to contain. I began to offer a snarky counterpunch to his taunts, under my breath at first, then bolder as others heard and appreciated my childish wit. I felt my power. The power of words, of mind over might.

Danny heard, too, and didn't know what to do about

me. I could see the struggle play out on his face and in his attempts at bluster. I was an unfamiliar target. A girl. Even a kid as charmless as Danny Kukal knew it was unacceptable to punch me in the nose or call me out after school.

In the spring, he came upon a solution at last.

"I heard about your mom," he told me. "A little prostitute, that's what I heard."

Looking back, I can see the word was as foreign to him as it was to me, but neither of us was too young to understand an insult when we heard one. He'd picked up some ammunition and was set to deploy it.

"Should've kept her knees together."

Baffling. But accompanied by howls of appreciation from the boys, along with other words I *did* understand.

"Slut."

"Whore."

"Trailer trash."

My wit deserted me. I ran sobbing to the girls' room and sat in crumpled agony for the rest of the day, trying to make sense of what was clearly a monumental insult. When I got home that afternoon, I told Nana all about it.

I had never seen her so angry. Usually Nana's temper was quick and loud, easily triggered and quickly forgotten. This anger was different. This was slow, deliberate, maternal fury. Her face hardened and flushed a plummy red.

She folded up the dishcloth and sat next to me at the wobbly Formica table. Pulled my chair around slightly to face her.

"Did you start this?" she said.

I opened my face to her, tried to hold my eyes steady. "No, he started it, he—"

She held up a hand.

"I see."

We sat that way for a minute or two.

"Lovey," she said, "when someone insults your mum, when they use that kind of language, you mustn't let it pass. There are some words that... There are things that require a response. You understand?"

I nodded.

"If you were a boy, I would tell you to knock the piss out of him. But you can't very well do that, can you? You'll have to think of something different. You're a clever girl, Alice. Learn to use what you have."

She dismissed me after that, but called to me as I left the room.

"Don't mention any of this to your mother," she said.

The next day, and the days after that, I worried over the problem of Danny Kukal. He was the large centerpiece of a straggling army, and I was a loner, now more than ever. I had no ally, no rebuttal to what he'd gleefully hit upon as a successful series of taunts that the group repeated now and then, with gradual loss of interest, as at a joke that has played out. I kept my face still and thought about what Nana had said.

On my way home from school about a week later, I stopped in front of the Kukals' double-wide. The family dog came rushing up to edge of his pen, broken teeth bared, snapping and growling as he did every day. He was junk-yard ugly, a bad-tempered nuisance with a grizzled brown coat and one missing ear. All the neighborhood kids hated and feared Schultzie. Everyone but Danny Kukal. He was proud to be the only one the dog didn't bite.

"Hey, Schultz," he would croon, tossing down his back-pack after school. "Hey, Schultzie, I saved you a cookie."

Danny really loved that dog.

That afternoon, most of the boys were at baseball practice, so the house stood empty. No car in the driveway, no bikes in the street.

Learn to use what you have, Alice.

I went around the side of the dog pen and sat down in the grass with my back to the fence. The dog made repeated runs at me, barking dementedly, snarling with his muzzle stuck through the chain links. For several minutes I sat quietly, braiding strands of grass like hair, and let him carry on. When the barking turned to grumbling, I took out what was left of my ham sandwich, broke off a piece and fed it to him carefully, keeping my fingers out of reach and avoiding his filmy eye. He devoured it with grunts and wet snorts, slapping his nose with his wide pink tongue. A bite at a time I fed him all I had, followed by a few leftover chips I was saving for an after-school snack.

He ate it all, thinking he'd made a friend.

That night, after my mother and Nana went to bed, I snuck into the laundry room and found Nana's rat poison. I mixed it with a gob of peanut butter, made a sandwich and stowed it in my backpack.

I thought about the sandwich all day. Several times when the teacher spoke to me I didn't hear her, and during the morning's math test I thought I would be sick and had to run without permission to the girls' room, where I stayed until the teacher came to get me.

At lunch I took the sandwich out and looked at it. Sniffed it. Turned it over in my hands.

"You should eat that," Danny called from across the cafeteria. "Maybe you'll get fat. Maybe you'll get boobs like your mom." And then, "Would take a lot of sandwiches, though."

The boys hooted and carried on, chanting. *Eat* it, *eat* it. I didn't look up. Just kept turning the sandwich over in my hands. Eat *it,* eat *it,* eat *it.*

After school I walked alone to the Kukals' house and sat down at the far end of Schultzie's pen. This time the dog didn't bark as much. He put his muzzle through the pen and flapped his tongue at me.

"I'm sorry," I whispered. I rolled up the sandwich and stuffed it through the chain-link fence.

The poison didn't take effect immediately the way I thought it would. At first the horrible old mutt rolled his eyes almost comically, nipped and growled at his stomach as though he was angry at whatever was happening inside him. He was so ridiculous about it that I began to smile, with the beginnings of a sort of relieved remorse bubbling in my chest. The stupid dog was too tough and mean to die. This was a lame attempt on my part. I'd let it go and find some other way to get even with Danny Kukal.

But then Schultzie began to cry. The comical expression on his face became a grimace, freakishly exaggerated with the whites of his eyes unnaturally wide. He limped in circles, tearing at the skin of his flanks, stretching it, letting go, biting again, drawing blood. He flopped to the ground like a fish, stiffly one way, then the other, crying. Crying. At last his body flexed so far sideways that it stuck that way. He didn't roll then, he simply lay there, strangling, a string of sandwich-flecked foam oozing out the side of his mouth.

The filmy eye rolled back and locked on me, and the life dimmed from him like a flame sinking into wax.

I walked into the woods, sat down on a stump and rocked

forward and back, one arm clamped around my stomach, the heel of my hand shoved into my mouth. My teeth dug small blue trenches into my skin, then drew blood.

My mother came in that night and said she'd heard the Kukal's dog had been poisoned.

"Poor old guy," she said. "How could someone do a thing like that? They've had that dog since he was a puppy. I remember when they brought him home from the pound."

Nana was in her chair, watching TV and working on a crossword puzzle. She looked up slowly, looked right at me, and winked.

The gray house sits like a stump in the grass at the end of a long suburban street on the south side of the island, slightly apart from its neighbors and surrounded by a rusted chain-link fence and a tangle of weed-choked shrubs. The miniblinds in the front window are dented; the tumble of bricks in the side yard has not been moved. The house looks the same today as it did when my mother and I moved in a dozen years ago.

In the park across the street, I sit alone in a rubber swing, rocking idly forward and back, forward and back, an exhausted pendulum.

Sometimes I leave the park and walk through the neighborhood, past the small elementary school where Danny and his friends used to torment me, past the salon where my mom and I once got the two most awful haircuts, to the corner where the ice cream shop used to be. Ice cream was our Saturday ritual after my soccer practice. My mom liked to get a scoop of butterscotch and one of bubble gum, which seemed like an odd combination to me. But she always laughed and gnawed on the rock-hard nuggets of gum and said, "Don't judge." And she would dot the tip of my nose with ice cream and kiss it clean.

The ice cream shop was bought by Starbucks a few years ago, its pink candy-striped awnings replaced with ubiquitous green. On rainy days, I go inside and sit at the window with a caramel macchiato, which tastes a little like butterscotch if you try hard enough.

Sometimes, when no one's home, I go up to the gray house and peek in the windows. The blinds are always closed. There is nothing to see. I don't even know what I'm looking for.

The house didn't feel so sinister when my mother lived there. True, it broke our hearts to leave Nana's trailer after she died, but my mom had a new boyfriend who had invited us to live with him.

"I need the help, Alice," she said. "If we stay here, I'll have to go off-island to get a second job. And who will be with you?"

"I can stay by myself."

"You're nine. What if something happened?"

"I could go to Sarah's…"

"Sarah's mom hates me," she said.

"But—"

She sat down on my bed. Her factory uniform was rumpled, name badge askew. The freckles across the bridge of her nose stood out so clearly against her pale skin that they looked as if they'd been stamped on, one by one.

"Trust me. This is going to work out, I promise. There's a school right down the street, and Ray has a good job. You like him, right?"

Wrong, I thought. I didn't like him at all. He was ugly and big, with hard, rough hands and a laugh so loud it hurt my ears. He left tracks in the toilet and distressing smells in the air.

"Sure," I said, because there was nothing else to say.

We moved in with Ray the next week.

A Honda pulls up now at the gray house, and behind it a small U-Haul truck, which ambles past, angling, then reverses and backs slowly into the driveway. The door opens and a man climbs out. He zips up his jacket and waits in the driveway.

A woman gets out of the car, then two young girls. They line up along the fence, looking at the house. The older girl says something to her mother, receives a kiss on the top of her head. She takes her sister's hand and the two of them cross the street to the park where I sit watching, while the man in the driveway opens the moving van and starts to unload it.

As the girls get closer, the younger one, a mop-headed bundle of about three, makes a beeline for the swings, careening forward on stubby legs with her sister in tow.

"Sissy, swing me," she says. Her voice is a bell, chiming in the stillness.

The bucket seat is a stretch for the older girl, who is maybe nine or ten. She wraps a skinny arm around the toddler's middle and tries to lift her into the swing.

I toss away my cigarette. "Want a hand?"

The girls blink up at me with fawnlike eyes, trailing garlands of golden hair that cling to their eyelashes and the matted fleece collars of their coats.

"These seats are really hard to get into," I say, and my throat is unexpectedly tight.

Without waiting for permission, I scoop up the little one and slide her into the swing. Her chubby stockinged legs poke out the holes in the seat and she curls her hands around the chains.

"Swing me," she says imperiously.

This time my smile feels more natural. I give her a nudge.

"Do you want me to push her, so you can swing, too?" I say to the older girl.

Soon both swings are in motion, squeaking gently, sending up rhythmic swirls of cool spring air as they pass. The sun peeks through the clouds and warms our faces. With my eyes closed, the park sounds like it did when I was a kid. Bird calls and rustling leaves underneath, bubbling with children's voices on top.

And my mother, laughing, her eyes full of sky.

After a few minutes, the older girl lets her sneakers skid along the ground. She comes to a gradual stop, spins in place a few times by twisting the chains together and then letting go. The swing gains momentum and carries her hair like a banner in the sunshine.

Little sister thinks this is hilarious. She giggles and chortles, snorts, then breaks into a full-bellied baby laugh until I can't help but join in. It feels strange to laugh, as if I'm tempting the gods. I stop laughing and listen to them instead.

Finally their amusement plays out and they go off to the slide. I resume my spot on the swing, shake out another cigarette and watch them while I smoke it. Big sister is pushing the little one up the slide. They keep tumbling down and having to start over.

When the girls get tired, they amble back across the street and go inside the house. The man comes out and stands in the driveway, hands on his hips. He's looking at me.

I look back, rocking.

CHAPTER FOUR

The next day, I ride my bike into town to the small family games and craft store off Harbor Street, where an internet search told me I could find kits for making ships in bottles. The shop turns out to be a bright, trim little place run by a four-foot-tall Filipino who says his name is Ernie.

I point to the model in the window—a pirate ship in a fat glass bottle.

"Did you make that?"

He beams, inflating. "Yes."

"How is it done?"

Ernie takes the bottle off the shelf and points a stubby finger at the glass. "You see? The masts are on hinges. You put the ship inside, pull the hinges to raise the masts."

I'm disappointed. "I thought the ships were built inside the bottle."

"You can do it that way, too." He grins, his teeth flat and gray as paving stones. "Have to be patient. And careful."

His expression says he doubts I could be either.

"What would I need to build a ship that way?" I say.

"You don't want to do that. Model with the hinges, much easier."

I look at him, unsmiling.

Sighing deeply, Ernie puts the bottle carefully in place on the shelf, then disappears through a curtain at the back of the store. He returns a minute or two later with a long flat box that he sets on the counter. Inside are the components of the ship, neatly bagged in clear plastic, along with several strange, long tools, and a black-and-white instruction manual. I take this out and open it.

"This is in German. Where are the English instructions?"

Ernie shrugs, palms up.

"Seriously?"

"No refunds."

My clothes are damp when I hop off my bike and walk up the driveway to my home, a two-room bungalow lying pale as a trout's belly against a tangle of claw-tipped pines and dense clumps of ivy and ferns. The property is isolated from its neighbors by a strip of untended forest on one side and twenty-five acres of grass crops on the other. It's a perfect house for me, because the days are almost as quiet as the nights, but the town of Vashon is a short bike ride away.

And Jack Calabrese's house is closer still.

The bungalow was crammed with the previous owner's possessions when I bought it. The closet reeked of moth balls and that awful geriatric stink of age and poor health; the carpet was dotted with so many cigarette marks it's a wonder the house never burned down. A tweed couch and rabbit-eared TV took up most of the living room, and the dresser in the bedroom was missing two drawers, giving it a crazed, gap-tooth appearance not unlike its previous owner.

After I bought it last fall, I hired a salvage company to clear the property, swap out the appliances and lay some new flooring. Then I painted the walls and began to fill the rooms with things I like. Now the living room is a riot of color and pattern: a leggy ottoman I recovered in a muted fruit pattern on sturdy twill, trimmed with a row of tiny chenille pom-poms; a low celadon couch, a jumble of down pillows and a striped blanket in yellow, red and dusty-blue. Over the couch is a collection of eight prints by an artist I admire, who creates abstract line drawings in one sitting, his pen never leaving the paper. Each of the drawings vaguely resembles a human eye, so the whole wall seems to stare me down every time I walk into the room. Several times I've taken the prints down, but I always end up rehanging them. They're odd and uncomfortable. They make me feel aware.

I'm proud of this house. It's a fortress that has not been breached.

I lay the box on the kitchen table and unpack it while a pot of coffee is brewing, sorting out the pieces according to the photos in the instruction booklet. Then, one piece at a time, I begin to assemble the ship.

It takes all night. The tools are hard to get used to, and I go through three different glues trying to find one that really works, but by eleven o'clock, I've assembled and painted the hull. I ease it through the neck of the bottle, then spend the rest of the night working systematically through the pieces—masts, rope-strings, other parts I can't name but which correspond to the photo on the box—until at dawn, the sails unfurl at the end of my foot-long forceps.

My neck is cramped and twitchy, but the ship is perfect. I imagine it life-size, tossing on the sea, its prow carving a milk-white swath through the water.

I understand something about Jack Calabrese. He's a patient man. Methodical, fastidious. And probably lonely.

Before I go to bed, I carry the model to the garbage can outside and let it fall to the bottom. There is a loud crash, glass on metal. The mast cracks, and the ship breaks free from its display stand inside the bottle and splinters in half.

I replace the lid of the trash can and lock the door behind me.

When I was a little girl, Nana taught me to make shortbread.

"The trick," she said, "is not to overwork the dough. As soon as it holds together, stop mixing."

She showed me the way the dough was supposed to look, and explained all the things you could do with it. Jam cookies, sandies, bars covered in nuts and caramel, or just plain shortbread, which is how we both liked it best, cut into wedges and warm from the oven. We made it once a week, and sometimes my mom would come in to help.

She wasn't as domestic as Nana, and probably not as smart, but it didn't matter because she was so full of life. She'd enter a room in midconversation, sweeping everyone in like a child playing jacks, jostling us in her hand, then tossing us aside again when she left. There was a stillness I came to associate with her absence—a tense, hopeful waiting. I often imagined her across the Sound and walking among the strange tall buildings of the Seattle skyline, all light and glass. Who would she see, where was she going? I asked her sometimes but the answers were always unsatisfying.

"To work," she'd say. Or, more often, simply, "Out." Sometimes she'd give my nose a playful tweak, to let me know it was okay for me to ask, and also okay for her not to tell me. I am her age now and still don't know where she worked when Nana was alive.

Other times, my mother was definitely "in." She'd sleep all day, lazy and gruff, not eating or bothering to shower or brush her teeth. On those days, Nana would take me to the garden and show me how to tie up the runner beans or transplant the seedlings at just the right depth. We would work peacefully together for hours—or rather, she would work and I'd assemble props for my imaginary games, transforming a basket of vegetables into a cast of characters, the peppers doing battle with the evil eggplant. The world existed in my mind —the objects were only stand-ins to mark my place in the game.

If the weather was bad, Nana and I would read. We went once a week to the library and would come back with a sackful of books about magical places and characters who were more bold and fearless than I could ever be. That was the world I came to understand: *out* was where things happened, but it wasn't a place to live.

But living *in* can be exhausting in its own way. I've forced my body into an unnatural circadian rhythm, dictated as much by my fear of the dark as a perverse desire not to be conquered by it. To cope, I've resorted to enormous cups of tea and slices of buttery shortbread that I bake in the middle of the night and eat right from the pan, perched on the counter next to the warm oven with one foot propped on a cabinet door, pushing it forward and back as I stare into the impenetrable forest behind my house between swipes at the latest draft of my book.

I'm sitting like that now in a tank top and a pair of men's white briefs, with a notebook in my lap and a mug of coffee on the windowsill. I'm working through a rewrite of the fifth book in my series, and I'm behind schedule. My agent, Gus Shiroff, has been sending patient emails designed to keep me on track without freaking me out—he's a paternal sort of guy—but from their increasing frequency I know I need to get a move on. Which means lots of coffee and long hot showers.

As I finish a long passage of dialogue and settle back at my perch with a fresh cup of coffee, I see a pale shape moving at the tree line.

Because of the island's laid-back population and the fact that the property behind my house is vacant and heavily wooded, I have never covered my back windows with anything more than sheer cotton panels, which are usually left open to take advantage of any meager beam of sunlight that filters through the trees. Until now I've never stopped to consider that someone might be looking into my fishbowl the way I have looked into others.

There is no doubt in my mind that the movement is that of a person. The shape is too upright, the motion too familiar. Someone is in my backyard.

I squint through my own lamp-lit reflection into the gloom outside. It takes a minute for my eyes to adjust. Then I see him.

A man. In a gray hooded sweatshirt. He's standing at the tree line, hands in his pockets. Looking right at me.

I jump, half falling off the counter. The coffee cup lands with a heavy clatter in the sink and splashes hot as blood across my chest and bare legs.

The man doesn't move. He makes no effort to hide and he doesn't look away. A spark of fear lights at the base of my spine and rushes upward to the nape of my neck. My mind leaps ahead as I catalog my vulnerabilities: my phone is in the bedroom, I'm in my underwear and there are large holes in the walls between us, covered only with fabric and sheets of glass. I feel like a bird in a cage.

Without taking my eyes off the figure outside, I reach behind me and draw a long, narrow knife from the butcher's block. My fist closes around the handle. I ease down the length of the kitchen to the sliding glass door and check to see that it's locked. My eyes dart to the clock—4:17 a.m.—and catalog that, too, as if the time of day will explain the stranger's presence here. Maybe he's a neighbor. A farmer from the property next door. But this man is too still, too focused. An innocent motive would have him moving along, especially since he has to know I'm scared out of my mind.

For several seconds, we face each other through the glass and the darkness. My reflection lies between us, as though I'm looking through my own ghost at the man who will murder me. Then he takes a few steps forward, stops again at the edge of the porch light and pulls back his hood so I can see his face.

Jack Calabrese.

My breath seizes, then resumes with a whoosh. The familiarity is a comfort only for a few seconds, until I remember the cold anger in his face when the closet door opened. The huge expanse of his chest. His fist, clenched at his side, the outline of the hammer against the wall. And I was rude to him when we met at the coffee shop. He has every reason to be angry.

His face is expressionless now. He crosses the yard and

mounts the steps to the back porch. The wood creaks under his weight. I feel the vibration of his feet on the floor.

He's right there. On the other side of the glass, his head tilted a little to one side. The shadows obscure his eyes. But I feel his stare. The tips of my breasts crinkle under the thin cotton of my tank top, and I am painfully aware that I'm standing here in nothing but my underwear. A prickling heat suffuses my neck and face. My limbs seem simultaneously weightless and clumsy.

I want to tell him to get the hell off my porch before I call the police. But my lips are frozen and my throat is clamped with fear.

He reaches for the door. Pulls, finds it locked. He smiles slowly.

I back away. My fingers tighten around the handle of the knife. A chill races up my arms, followed by a coursing tremor that rattles my teeth.

"You started it," he says. Through the glass, his voice sounds warped, as though we're underwater. He turns and walks away, loose and easy down the steps, through a shaft of hazy window light like a still from a film noir.

The forest closes behind him and he is gone.

In my bedroom closet is an old peacoat. I reach into the pocket, take out a wedge of papers, unfold the pages and spread them out across my bed.

This is Jack Calabrese's life story. I know all about him—what he's done and what he might be capable of doing. He has the sort of mindset I know I can exploit.

I sit down on the bed with a pillow bunched in my lap and the knife on the bedside table. I look at my notes and try to reassure myself. Surely it's all here. I've been watching for months, and writing things down. I've done my homework.

After a few minutes I take the pages to the fireplace and lay them on the embers. The flames lick the edges of the paper and die. I stir them with a fire poker, shove them into the coals until they ignite. In a few seconds, all this careful research exists only in my mind.

The room has grown cold. I add some wood to the fire and warm my hands over the flames.

I can't sleep now, even as the windows blush with early light. I pace around the house, check the doors and windows, turn on the radio and turn it off again. When the sun rises over the trees, I venture cautiously outside. There is a depression in the grass where he stood. I turn in circles on the spot, trying to imagine what he saw and what he thought, what it means that he was here.

Later in the morning, I find a cardboard box on my doorstep. It's sealed with packing tape, but has no shipping label or address on top.

I take it to the kitchen and set it on the counter. With a paring knife, I slit the tape—first at the sides, then down the center. Inside is another box of thinner, white cardboard. I lift this out and set in on the counter. One more piece of tape to slice, and there, nestled in a bed of tissue paper, is a third box.

Jack's box. The one I tried to steal.

I run my hands over the fine-grained cherrywood and trace the inset panels of satiny bird's-eye maple. The brass hinges are so cleverly concealed and aligned that the slightest touch is enough to open the lid. Inside, the box is lined with black felt and filled with his belongings—and on top, a note, written in narrow black script on a square of cream-colored paper:

> *Alice ~*
> *I'll show you mine…*
> *7:00 ~ Jack*

Below his name, he's written his phone number.

I set the note aside and peer into the box, lifting things out one by one and setting them on the counter. A set of spiky metal jacks with a few clinging fragments of blue and red paint; a business card, embossed with the name of an architectural firm in bold letters over the faint design of a blueprinted floor plan—Taylor & Fitch; a pair of heavy, unmistakably authentic handcuffs; a key on a plastic Motel 6 key ring; a piece of wax paper, folded into a square, and inside a perfect four-leaf clover; an old pair of eyeglasses with a crack in the lens; a black-and-white photograph of a dark-haired woman on the beach, winsome and laughing behind heavy sunglasses; a folded-up piece of paper with part of a handwritten Neruda poem; a man's wedding band, which I slip over my thumb; and on the bottom, facedown, a last photograph. I pick it up and turn it over. A square of yellow window light on a dark wall, softened by a sheer, wavy curtain—and behind that, a wraithlike figure peering out from the space between the curtain panels. I recognize the tattoo on the girl's arm before I know her face.

It's me. Looking right into the camera without seeing it, as if at something very far away. He must have taken the picture from the forest behind my house. He must have been there, watching, for a long time. In fact, seeing the top I'm wearing in the photograph, he must have been there more than once. I haven't worn that shirt in three days.

Awareness swells inside me. My skin is shivery-thin, barely able to contain me.

This is a language I understand. The language of secrets.

I'll show you mine.

My gaze trails away, over the countertop and past the entryway corner, where I see my reflection in the hall mirror. The photo is pressed to my lips, and the expression in my eyes, caught in a wedge of late-morning sunlight, seems suddenly, vibrantly alive.

I smile, and my reflection smiles back.

CHAPTER FIVE

"How did you find this place?" I ask.

It's 8:30 p.m., and we're seated at a tiny table inside an equally minute Thai restaurant in Seattle, across the Sound from Vashon Island. The restaurant's narrow facade is deceiving. Inside, the ceiling opens to a second-floor dining room with space for only six tables. We have a bird's-eye view of the kitchen below, where a cloud of steam rises from an ancient hammered pot as the cook ladles up two bowls of soup.

"I came here with a friend," Jack says. "And left with the waitress."

A young woman appears at the top of the steps and deposits our dinner on the battered wooden table. When she's gone, I give him a look.

"*This* waitress? She looks about sixteen."

"Different one, actually."

"And is this safe to eat?" I lift a spoonful of soup. "You know better than to piss off the person feeding you, I hope."

"What makes you think I pissed her off?"

"Seems likely, let's say."

He lowers his head with an amused twist of his lips and begins to eat.

"It wasn't like that. Her father was the cook. He went down on the job. Right there." He points the top of his ceramic spoon at the kitchen below. "Had a stroke apparently, and fell into the wok on his way down. Spilled hot oil all over himself. The ambulance came for him and I gave his daughter a lift to the hospital."

His expression doesn't change, but I sense the reproach.

I drop my gaze to the table. "You do have a way of making me feel like an asshole."

"Eat your soup."

The liquid slides down my throat, tangy and unctuous. Slices of sour cucumber float in the broth.

"What happened to the old man?"

Jack pours out some fresh tea. A thread of steam rises from my cup.

"Dead," he says. "Probably never felt the burns at all."

He seems to consider this for the first time.

He didn't ring the doorbell when he arrived at my house earlier this evening. By tacit agreement, we've already abandoned the notion of privacy. I left the door unlocked, and he simply walked in and came looking for me as if he owned the place, as if his previous visit had not been an illicit one.

I was at my dresser, clasping a fine silver chain around my neck.

He came to the bedroom doorway, leaned his shoulder against the wall, his sweater pushed up over his forearms. Clean jeans, clean work boots. I wondered what he thought of my clothes, which an old boyfriend described as having been "put together by a twelve-year-old gay boy with a boot fetish and twenty bucks to spend." Lots of vintage and secondhand. Little discretion.

I cut my own hair, too. With the straight razor from my kit.

"So what's that about?" he says now. "You follow guys, break into their houses and steal shit that has no value to anyone but them. Why? What's so interesting?"

"Everything."

He leans back, waiting.

I set down my spoon and cup my tea in both hands, prepared with my story this time, set to deliver it on cue with a face full of rueful honesty.

"Have you ever been in a crowd—at a concert, maybe, or on the street—and noticed the way all the faces seem to blend together? But when you pick out a single person, suddenly he's not this anonymous guy anymore. He's somebody. An individual. You know?"

Jack nods.

"Well, I became sort of fascinated by that. I'd ask myself questions about the guy. Like, I wonder where he lives. I wonder what's in his refrigerator. Or his sock drawer or DVD collection. What's his name? How strong are his glasses? What's in his medicine cabinet? It was a game. But after a while, I started to wish I could check my guesses to see if they were right."

"So you started breaking in."

"Yeah. I knew this girl once who taught me how to get into houses. Where people hide their spare keys, how to break a window quietly. She could get in anywhere."

"Who was this?"

"Just someone from the foster system. I roomed with her at the Center for a while. She's a wizard, smart as hell.

Anyway, I discovered that it's actually really easy to get in and out, provided no one's around."

"You never got caught before?"

"No." I raise my chin. "And I wouldn't have with you, either, if you hadn't picked that day to forget your phone or whatever."

He looks at me skeptically. It's impossible to tell which part of my story he isn't buying. I pretend not to see the doubt in his eyes. I'm locked into my bluff now and need to ride it out.

"And is it only men who interest you?" he says.

"Yes."

"Never followed a woman?"

"No."

"Why not?"

"I already know about women."

"Hmm. So what did you find out?"

"That most men are perverts. That they collect weird things like agates and toy race cars and Asian porn. That every guy has at least one picture of his dick—God knows why."

He laughs, and I find an odd, sagging comfort in the sound.

"That they always hang their pictures too high—present company excepted—are strangely attracted to futons and can't keep their houseplants alive."

I take up my chopsticks.

"That's it?" he says.

"Pretty much."

"And what do you leave with?"

"Just the box."

"Not the stereo, not the TV. Just the box?"

"Right."

He tips back in his chair, watching me eat.

"You're an odd little chick, Alice Croft."

I shrug. "Everyone's odd."

"So how long were you following me before I found you in my closet?"

"I don't know. Two or three weeks, maybe?"

The corner of his mouth twitches. I feel his gaze on me and a tumbling fullness in my stomach.

"So for three weeks," he says, "I've had this gorgeous little thief following me around, just dying to get into my bed, and I didn't even know it."

I set down my chopsticks and wipe my mouth. Take a sip of tea.

"Your bedroom, maybe. Not your bed."

His gaze slides from my face, down the front of my Pink Panther T-shirt and up again.

"My mistake," he says.

By the time we leave the restaurant, the ever-present clouds have dissolved into rain. Jack opens his umbrella and pulls me underneath, his arm around my waist. His sweater feels comforting against my cheek, a nubbled cushion over the firm bump of his shoulder. The city around us vibrates with the energy of a million lives, with ten million boxed-up secrets. I feel myself at the center of them, small but protected, my feet slapping the rain-sluiced sidewalk and Jack's falling into step as he shortens his stride to match mine.

"My friend has a boat," he says. "Would you like to see it? We could walk there."

A warm, fragile bubble of happiness swells inside my chest.

"Yes, I would."

★ ★ ★

The boat turns out to be a small motor yacht, moored in a slip at the end of a long wooden dock. With a long sleek nose and shining chrome rail, it bobs on the dark water like a shard of wet ice.

"You have some fancy friends," I say as Jack reaches out to help me on board.

He grins. "This one thinks so. I keep having to remind him about the time he pissed his pants in second grade, just to keep his ego in check."

I turn in a slow circle on the wooden deck, looking around. The rain has subsided, leaving a blanket of fat raindrops over the seats and metal railings. Jack unlocks a metal box under one of the benches and takes out a rag. He wipes down a seat and part of the railing, then tosses the rag back where he'd found it.

"I have some weed," he says.

"So do I."

He laughs and pulls a plastic-wrapped joint from his pocket. "Well, make yourself comfortable."

We settle on the vinyl seat, half facing each other. The seat is too high for me and my feet dangle, so I curl one leg up and tuck my foot behind my knee. He gives me the joint and lights it with a yellow Bic. We pass the weed back and forth as we talk.

"Where did you grow up?" I ask.

"Upstate New York. My dad owns a chain of liquor stores in the city. I came out here to go to school."

"Do you have brothers and sisters?"

"A brother. Much older than me. He was already in high school when I was born."

"You were an afterthought."

He squints at me through a curl of sweet-scented smoke. "Yeah. Thanks for noticing."

"I'll bet you were spoiled."

"The hell I was. My dad was a hardhanded son of a bitch."

"But your mother stuck up for you, didn't she. A middle-aged Italian lady with a baby? Don't tell me."

He leans back, drapes an arm over the back of the seat.

"You've had a head start. You've already been in my place, sniffing around. What did you learn?"

"Not much. I wasn't there very long. I found the ships, the blueprints. Are you an architect?"

"Used to be."

"So what are you now?"

"A carpenter."

I frown. "That's kind of a step down, isn't it?"

"You could say that."

"Did one of your buildings collapse or something?"

He smokes the last hit and tosses the roach overboard.

"No, actually I was a very good architect. Everything I designed is still standing, as far as I know."

"Then what—"

"Curiosity killed the cat," he says. "Something you might want to consider."

"She had eight more lives if I remember right."

I get up and move to the end of the rail, letting the buzz wash over me. The waves slosh languidly against the side of the boat.

"I looked you up," he says. "Alice Croft, author of *Zebra Crossing*. 'A beguiling, gripping read.' 'Dark and dazzling.' Very impressive."

I shrug. I hate talking about my work, and especially

about reviews of my work. No one ever asks the right questions, and my answers always seem stilted and inadequate. As soon as the books come out, I stash my copies in the closet and try to forget about them.

The *Zebra* series was a fluke as far as I'm concerned. Something about the motley collection of boys—albino, meth addict, freerunner, clairvoyant, all trapped inside a Scottish neo-Gothic boarding school—captured the public's attention. So much so that Gus Shiroff has signed not only the foreign rights but film and TV, as well. Nothing has been done with them so far, but there is talk of a cable series and wild speculation about who might be cast in the lead roles.

For me the whole thing is bewildering. Before the *Zebra* books I had never written for anyone but myself. I sent out my original queries on a whim, expecting a much longer apprenticeship before any of my writing became publishable. But Gus liked the first book right away, and suddenly I found myself with a career and what seems like a never-ending procession of deadlines—all good things, but for a loner with a serious lack of business sense, it's a bit much. On Gus's advice, I've tried to isolate myself as much as possible and concentrate on finishing the series.

"A lot of loneliness in those books," Jack says.

I accept this in silence. It's a common observation.

"What about your family?"

"Dead." The word seems flat, so I keep talking to fill the silence. "My grandmother died when I was nine, and my mom a year and a half later."

"And your dad?"

"Don't know him."

"So who do you hang out with, then? What do you do?"

"Write."

"That's it?"

"Pretty much. Very glamorous, this lifestyle."

"No boyfriend?"

"Not at the moment."

He is quiet, looking at me. When he speaks, his voice sounds different, lower in pitch.

"Not at the moment," he repeats, as if to himself.

He gets to his feet and moves toward me, hands in his pockets, his face lost in shadow. For a second I forget what he looks like. His features won't come together in my mind.

He stops, leaning against the rail.

"Last night you had a knife in your hand. Now look at you."

I glance around at the deserted docks, where rows of boats bob silently in the inky water.

I don't like this, I want to say. *Take me home, I want to go home.*

My empty fingers curl into a fist, pressed to my thigh.

"You wish you had one now," he says softly. "Don't you."

He closes the distance between us, lifts his hand and traces the column of my neck, down the front of my T-shirt—the barest brush with the tip of his forefinger.

A bone-deep shiver breaks inside me, as though my gears have slipped and are juddering for purchase.

He turns away and disappears through the cabin door. I close my eyes, waiting. A minute later, a familiar song seeps into the cool night air, a haunting, languid groove, and he's back, his hand outstretched toward me. He pulls me into his arms.

My home feels very far away now, across the water and another divide I have not yet measured. Jack's heartbeat is more than idea or even a sound—it's a vibration under my cheek, a relentless drumbeat driven by something I don't understand. More than sex, darker than seduction. This is pure male impulse.

On the last thread of music, he begins to undress me, his fingers cool and rough as stone against my skin. He unbuttons my sweater, slips it over my shoulders and drops it to the deck. He pushes me before him, a step at a time, down the narrow staircase to the tiny bedroom. I feel the mattress behind my knees, and he puts a hand behind my head to keep me from bumping it as he lowers me to the bed. This small kindness blooms at the base of my throat and burns my eyelids and the bridge of my nose.

Silence closes around us, broken only by the hollow sound of the waves lapping against the side of the boat, and the eerie flow of the music around us.

He reaches under the hem of my skirt and runs his hand up my thigh until it comes to rest on my hip. With his other hand, he takes off his glasses and sets them on the bedside table.

You wish you had that knife now. Don't you…

What would happen if I asked him to stop? Would he take me home? Apologize? Get angry and call me names? Would he stop at all? I've told no one about him, or where I would be tonight, and he knows it. He could hurt me, kill me, carry my body out to sea and no one would ever know what happened to me. I would be the face on the milk carton.

My train of thought stops there.

No. I could never be the face on the milk carton. Those missing people have families to search for them. No one would look for me.

I would be gone. Gone.

He strokes me, down my thigh and up, sliding his palm along my waist. He tugs at the strap of my underwear and winds it twice around his thumb, pulls it tight until the fabric nips and pinches between my legs.

I close my fist around the front of his sweater. He leans over this obstruction to kiss me again, one hand cupped around the back of my head, one between my legs, slipping along the edge of my underwear. His kiss is firm and insistent, slanting to stroke the inside of my mouth with his tongue. He tastes like burned marshmallow on a young stick, toasty and green.

His teeth close over my lower lip as he traces me through my underwear. I twist and clutch at his shoulder, trying to catch my breath. But his mouth is demanding, and he has found, with his thumb, the bump of my clitoris. I choke back a moan of anxious greed, and raise my hips to meet him, sinking my fingers into the damp fringe of hair at the nape of his neck. I trace his stubbled jaw and the edge of his lip, feel the muscles below his ear bunch and release as he kisses me, the steady strength of his pulse against my thumb.

He tugs my underwear aside. My thighs tighten reflexively, but he's already kneeling between them; he's got his foot in the door. His back stiffens, two fingers slipping through my folds. His tongue moves past my teeth, deeper, seeking, and I know he's worried, the way all men worry when they get this close to the prize.

Don't stop me. Don't pull back, don't take what I need. Don't get in my way.

He eases my panties down to my ankles and slips them off. Sits back on his heels and looks at me, with my skirt around my waist and my underwear crumpled in his fist, pressed to his nose. His gaze never leaves me.

"Take off your shirt." His voice is quiet and direct.

I peel off my T-shirt, trembling from the blast of adrenaline and the force of him. The room swims around me. The bobbing floor beneath us feels insubstantial and unsafe, as though we might suddenly sink beneath the water and never realize it had happened. I want him to hold me and give me something solid to keep me in place.

But he wants to look at me.

"And your bra," he says. "Take it off."

The music has changed. The singer chants an impatient bridge, punctuated by a pop-slide in an eerie minor key as the bra straps stutter down my arms. The chorus rises, driving and sensual, a low hum of synthesized bass guitar buzzing underneath the melody. A breath of night-chilled air drifts over my breasts, crinkling the tips, tightening my skin.

A slow smile creeps across his lips when he sees the hoop in my left nipple. He rises and strips to his boxers. And this time he doesn't have to speak. I shimmy out of my skirt and sit with my knees pressed together, shivering, untethered, enduring his long visual exploration. His face is half-hidden, divided down the center by shadow and light.

Now look at you…look at you….

I let him ease my thighs apart. His gaze falls, locked between my legs. A groan rumbles in his chest when he sees the tattoo low on my abdomen, just above the smooth mound of my pubis: ~ *Make it hurt* ~ He passes a thumb over the letters, then dips again into the slippery heat between my legs, his fingertips circling, deepening, nudging at my cunt. He kisses the tip of my breast and flicks the silver hoop with his tongue.

"What are you about, hmm?" he says, and sucks my nipple into his mouth. The metal ring clicks against his teeth.

But I can't answer. I arch my back and turn my face aside. A coil of desire constricts at the base of my belly.

He eases me back, lays a chain of kisses around my breast, down my ribs, into the shallow dip beside my pelvic bone and finally to the liquid heat between my legs.

Our floating room begins to spin. I am strangely disembodied, as though all my senses, all my pain and pleasure and naked want, are concentrated under the warmth of his mouth. I claw at the blankets and bunch them in my fists. But when I sink my fingers into his hair, he catches my wrists and pins them at my sides, muttering under his breath, his teeth grazing my clitoris. With the anchor of his mouth to hold me in place, I wind around him like a tetherball on a rope, in dizzying spirals that lift me to his mouth.

"Come on, baby," he says. "Right now..."

His voice vibrates against me, and in the last moment it is his breath, the lightest touch of cold and heat, that topples me. I leap under his mouth, my wrists still pinned to the bed, my cries sailing into the night. He follows me, groaning with pride and dark male glee. His tongue flattens over me, dips inside me, drinks me in so thoroughly that I soar up again, simply from the idea of being consumed this way.

As the room spins to a halt, I realize my eyelashes are wet with tears.

Jack kneels between my knees and rolls on a condom. The light skims across his body, painting long, striped shadows in the grooves of his abdomen. He slides inside me without a word, without preamble, driving his hips forward, pulling me to him with one hand splayed against the small of my back. A breath snags in my throat at the size of him.

He stops, the muscle in his jaw flexed and quivering. "Jesus," he says. "So fucking tight. Be still."

After a moment, he begins to move, his hips rolling to the undercurrent of music and the elemental motion of the water beneath us. I wrap my legs around his narrow waist and pull him closer. We fall into a deep, slow rhythm. Each gliding thrust is an incantation in a language I don't understand. My whole body strains, listening. And from the back of my mind, from some small and lonesome and untouchable place, I seem to hear my own voice chanting in time.

I want to go home, I want to go home.

It rains again that night. Jack turns off the music so we can listen to the drops on the roof and the surface of the ocean. The sound forms a soft cocoon around us, a background noise to the steady thrum of his heartbeat under my ear.

"Tell me a secret." His voice rumbles as if from the inside of a bass drum. "Something no one else knows."

"I like to keep my secrets," I tell him.

He slips out from under me and raises himself up on one elbow. He pushes the covers aside and runs his hand down my body, brushes the tip of my breast with his knuckles.

"I can't figure out if you know what you're doing," he says. "But you want to be careful with me. I'll fucking eat you alive."

He lowers his head to my breast. His mouth opens over my nipple, warm and demanding. His erection hardens like a newly forged sword against my thigh.

We stop at a café near the marina for breakfast. We are both starved, and devour plates of eggs and pancakes and large cups of coffee in silence, as though we've been lost at sea for days. Then we go across to the corner market, where we buy cigarettes and a pack of gum. And condoms, which Jack purchases without comment while I pretend to admire a rack of key chains.

He pulls up in front of my house and walks me to the door. I stand on the step and put my arms around him, press my lips to the stubbled underside of his jaw. He takes my face in his hands and kisses my cheeks and eyelids and the tip of my nose.

I don't ask him inside.

I know he'll call before the day is out. The phone rings four times. On the fifth ring, I pick it up.

"Baby," he says. "What have we started?"

CHAPTER SIX

I have always liked cemeteries. There is a calmness about them, a purposeful tranquility. I like the names, carved in marble or set in brass, the dates still visible after a century or more. My favorite headstones are embellished with epitaphs written by the family left behind, which seem a humble and endearing attempt to sum up a life like the log line of an epic novel: *The heart of man is restless until it finds its rest in Thee... Now twilight lets her curtain down and pins it with a star... Little Boy Blue has gone away.*

One of the first things I bought when I received the advance on *Zebra Crossing* was a matched pair of gravestones for my mother and grandmother, to replace the cheap brass plaques that had been set in the ground to mark the places where their ashes had been interred. My mothers deserved proper headstones; they deserved to stand upright, not laid like pavement in the grass.

I have brought my scrub brush and thermos of soapy water. I kneel before my grandmother's grave and scrub away the dirt and bits of moss that have accumulated in the crevices since last month. I pour water over the granite surface, watch it gather into tiny pools at the bottom of her name, then trickle away and disappear into the grass.

At the edge of my mother's grave is a spider on a half-formed web. It's a beautiful thing, pale gold, with long delicate legs and a slender body covered with fine hairs. I put my face down close, peer into its many glassy eyes. Its front legs pluck gently at the dew-jeweled threads. A single drop of water falls to the rung below and hangs there, clinging to the corner, where the cells of the web are joined by a tiny silken knot.

With the back of my scrub brush, I destroy the web and smash the spider into the grass. I pour water over the brush to clean away the bug's remains, then more water over the headstone. When I am finished, I run my fingers through the carved letters, over the cold arc of granite and the carved stone rose at the center.

Later that night, Jack comes back for me. We head north, straight up the boulevard, past the tiny Vashon Theater crouching beige and humble on the left, and the much larger vine-covered brick yoga studio on the right, past the auto shop and the Episcopal church, until the town peters to an uncertain end and we leave it behind. After a few minutes, Jack turns onto a narrow dirt road fringed with pines, through which the Puget Sound shines in the twilight. He doesn't stop until we've reached the empty mouth of a trailhead, where the moon sits like a pearl on a sheet of hammered pewter.

Below us is the beach my mother took me to about a month after Nana died. The weather was chaotic that day, blustering and weeping from a swollen sky. Holding hands, my mother and I wobbled through the high loose sand, then turned our shoulders to the sea.

For a while, we walked in silence, bundled into our hoods, hands buried deep inside our pockets.

"Things are going to be a lot different now," my mother said.

I nodded. Things were already different. We came up against the bewildering absence of Nana every day. Breakfast was cold now, and late. My braid had unraveled to a ponytail, and the week before the batteries for my favorite doll had died, leaving her with an open, frozen mouth where she used to chew from a little plastic spoon. Now the doll's mouth seemed to be screaming mutely, endlessly. I had put the doll under my bed, then in my toy box, before finally wrapping her in a rag and burying her in the garbage can on the curb outside.

"Nana was good at this," my mother was saying. "For me it's harder. We're—I'm going to have to figure out what to do about money. Maybe get a second job. I don't know."

"I can get a job," I piped, aware this was childish. But Nana would have expected me to find a way to help.

My mom took her hand from her pocket and laid it on top of my head. "You're a little young for that, squirt."

She took my hand. Hers was cold and thin as a bird's wing. She smiled down at me, her face dewed with raindrops, melted somehow, as if all the bones under her skin had dissolved. It was the expression of the smallest on the playground, the soft, malleable face of directionless fear.

Jack and I get out of the truck and stand together, blinking at the moon's smug roundness, listening to the clicks of the cooling engine.

"Makes you feel small, doesn't it?" he says.

"And alone."

"You're not alone, you're with me."

I look up at him. His face is all planes and lines, and skin like a tarp stretched over the bones. He lights a cigarette, holds it between two fingers while he plucks a strand of hair from my cheek with his thumb and ring finger.

"First star," I say. "Let's make a wish."

He smiles from inside the cage of his glasses.

"Careful what you wish for, little box thief. You might get it."

"What do you imagine I'm wishing for?"

"Comfort. Same as the rest of us." He peers at me through the smoke. "Or maybe not. Maybe it's something else for you."

He produces a stack of blankets from the backseat, lets down the tailgate and makes a nest in the truck bed, between the wheels of his pickup. I wait, smoking his cigarette, tracking a satellite across the sky. Nana used to worry that satellites and meteors could come down and crash on our heads. *You'd never see it coming,* she would say with a shudder and a sidelong glance at the sky.

Nana was pretty superstitious all around. Not only didn't she step on the lines and cracks in the sidewalk herself, she kept me from doing so. No black cats, no number thirteen. As if she always knew the end would come at her fast.

When he's finished, Jack helps me up and we settle together against the wall of the cab, our legs tangled on the blankets, my head resting in the hollow of his shoulder. The moon rises and retreats as though pulled by an invisible string into the starry sky.

"I like your house," he says unexpectedly.

"Yeah? You're the first person to see it inside."

"It looks like you."

"A hot mess."

"Emphasis on hot."

"I'm surprised you'd like it. Being an architect and all. It's not exactly an original."

"Not outside, no."

"Have you ever lived in a house you designed?"

"No. I'll build one for myself one day. I'm making payments on a plot of land south of Portland, near the coast. Waiting for zoning to approve the plans."

"I'd like to see them."

"Yeah? They're in the truck."

"Well, break them out."

Prompted by my interest, he lays out the blueprints and describes the design—a modern Craftsman, with a wall of windows overlooking the sea, which will extend all the way through the bedroom, to open that side of the house to the ocean breeze and the patio. Lots of golden wood, he says, lots of glass. But for all the house's delights, it's the kitchen that enchants me most. A long soapstone counter faces the open window without obstruction, inset with a deep, wide sink and built-in cutting board.

I run my fingers over the delicate lines of the blueprint.

"You did all this?"

"You sound surprised."

"Shocked. I can't imagine where you'd even begin."

"With an idea. Like writing a book, I'd imagine."

"That's not at all the same thing."

"No? Why's that?"

I shake my head, spread my fingers wide. "Well, because a book is only ever an idea, and then a refinement of the idea.

What you do requires mathematics, physics, logistics. Books are just an arrangement of words, anyone can do that."

"Bullshit. I couldn't."

He rolls up the blueprints.

"I've been reading *Zebra Crossing*. It's more than an arrangement of words."

I'm surprised, and touched. I've never known a guy who's read my work after meeting me. It's usually the opposite: the minute a man hears I'm a writer, he'll bolt in the other direction to avoid having to read a book in which he has no interest.

"I think that's the first time I've seen you smile," he says, watching me.

I resume my poker face and clear my throat.

"This house looks expensive."

"Yeah, it will be. But a lot of the materials will be repurposed and I can do most of the work myself. It will take a while, obviously."

I want to know where a carpenter will find the money to build a house like this. It feels intrusive to ask, but Jack reads my mind.

"My family has some money," he says. "My dad owns a chain of liquor stores back East. He settled me fairly well."

"He's still living?"

"Yeah."

I frown, trying to get the lay of the land.

"We had a falling-out," Jack says. "He basically shoved some money at me and told me to get the fuck out."

"But if you have money, why do you work as a carpenter?"

"Well, it's not Hilton money. And a man should always work, whether he needs to or not."

"Only, not as an architect."

He takes off his glasses, folds them and sets them aside. Then he slips one arm under my legs, the other around my shoulders, and shifts me in one fluid motion so I'm flat on my back.

"Carpentry is good for upper body strength," he says.

He stretches out next to me. Twines our fingers together and turns them this way and that to see the effect, a herringbone pattern in brown and white. His hands are rough with calluses, wide and flat and strong. Mine seem like a child's in comparison.

He tips my face to his and kisses me. His mouth is firm against mine, but supple, seeking. He catches my lower lip between his teeth, nuzzles into the ticklish skin under my jaw. Goose bumps blossom on my neck, and I tuck up my shoulder to make him stop. Smiling, he smooths them away with the palm of his hand and begins to unlace the neckline of my peasant blouse.

"Beautiful," he says as he uncovers me. "Like an anime doll that fell into a rag bin."

I can't help laughing.

"Why does no one like my clothes? This is style."

He draws the fabric aside and runs a finger along the lace edge of my bra. "I like your clothes just fine, so long as they're on the floor."

He unhooks the front of my bra and pushes the cup aside. Then he settles over me, his warm tongue curving around my nipple, his dark hair curling around my fingers. I watch his mouth, entranced by the contrast of his darker, stubbled skin against the pale swell of my breast. He takes my silver hoop in his teeth and tugs gently as he gathers slow handfuls of my skirt and finds the bare curve of my hip, grinning at my thigh-high striped socks.

"I take it all back," he says.

I get to my knees and take off my blouse and his shirt, my skirt and underwear, run my hands over his chest and the hard slope of his shoulder. I unbutton his jeans and reach inside, wrap my fingers around the solid, dew-tipped length of his cock, and move down his body to take him in my mouth. His skin tastes clean, faintly salty, like the back of my hand before a shot of tequila. I weigh his testicles in my palm, run a thumb across their wrinkled surface and follow the fat speed-bump under his dick with my tongue as I take him to the top of my throat. We fall into a natural cadence, his hand at the back of my neck.

He leans against the cab of the truck, holding my hair aside, watching. His face is impassive, but his body begins to shift. His breathing picks up. The texture of his skin feels smoother and more taut. I want him inside me and worry that he'll finish in my mouth, but he stops me, pulls me away with one hand tangled in my hair.

He digs a condom out of his wallet and rolls it on, motions for me with his fingers. I straddle him and ease down the length of his cock. I close my eyes. I have never had sex outdoors before, never felt the night wind on my bare breasts or felt this cool lick of air on my clitoris as I am spread apart. It's electrifying. The heat between my legs crackles like molten lava spilling into the sea, hot meeting cold.

Jack groans and holds me in place. "Jeeeesus," he says. "Wait, baby..."

I am still, imagining what distraction he turns to at times like this. Work, maybe. Measurements and angles, building codes and deadlines and the drying time of a slab of concrete. I wonder what this feels like to him, how wet, how tight I am around him. Already my cunt is clenched like a fist, contracting in upward ripples as if to draw him deeper inside me.

I open my eyes and he opens his. His gaze sweeps over me with dark appraisal, a fierce masculine pride, proprietary and urgent, and my body answers with an almost painful thrill from someplace low and deep inside my belly. He lifts me up and presses me down, fixated on the connection point between us, his hands splayed wide over my hips.

I lean forward to brace myself on the rim of the truck bed. The tips of my breasts graze his bare chest. He guides my nipple to his mouth, pulls me closer with one hand around the back of my neck, the other stroking my ass, sliding between my legs.

My breasts grow heavy, tingling, wet from his tongue and cold from the night air. My breath whistles past my teeth. He flexes his thumb against my clitoris and lifts me with each thrust of his hips, up and down. I feel him growing thicker inside me. I open my legs, arch back, leaning on my hands with my breasts raised like an offering to the sky. The stars seem to circle overhead. The night air moves over my skin like a cool cotton sheet, catching at my breasts, sliding across my thighs.

He turns his thumb so the tip is pressed right into the cleft of my clitoris, and that feels so good, unbearably good, as though he's tripped a wire inside me, cut me loose and catapulted me into a rush of pleasure that shoots through my limbs and right to the top of my head. I come and he is chasing me with long hard strokes, clutching at my hips as if he can find more of me if he tries. A deep groan stutters from the back of his throat. His abdomen contracts under my hand.

It takes a few minutes for him to soften, for me to get my bearings and enough strength in my thighs to crawl away. He wraps the blankets around me and we share a cigarette as the moon beams down upon us and the crickets resume their song.

"Watch yourself," Jack says.

"Watch your own self," I tell him, picking my way across a cluster of damp rocks. "You keep watching me, you're gonna wipe out."

It was Jack's idea to go hiking today, up the Chulapai Trail where the flat, loamy footpath wanders through an undergrowth of ferns, and gradually upward between slabs of mossy granite, rising like the ruins of a long-dead city in the forest. He is sure-footed as a mountain lion, graceful and swift, with an inaudible loping gait that makes it difficult to tell where he is when he follows behind me.

"Stop shaking that ass at me," he says. "It's distracting."

"Go around. Problem solved."

"Oh, hell, no."

A few minutes later we reach the end of the path, a slender waterfall that twitches like a mare's tail in the sunlight. The sound is soothing, steady, punctuated now and then by the squeals of a group of young children who are splashing in the cold pool below.

Jack and I set down our backpacks and settle on a low, flat rock. He digs out a bottle of water and tips his head back to take a drink. The knob of his Adam's apple slides under his skin, framed by sleek ropes of muscle on either side. His hair is ruffled, curling around his ears, falling into the space between his eyebrows and the frame of his glasses. His hand, big and easy around the bottle, is dusted with shimmering strands of dark hair.

His attention is on the family below us. "You like kids?"

I take the water bottle. "Yeah. I like them a lot, actually."

"Hmm. That surprises me."

"Why's that?"

"I don't know. You don't strike me as the motherly type. You said you were raised in foster homes?"

I begin to unpack our lunch.

"Yeah, but not until I was ten. I lived with my mom before that."

"And she died?"

"Yeah."

"How?"

"Does it matter?"

"To me it does."

I lay out the cherry tomatoes, the sliced-up salami, cheese and crackers. Olives and apples.

"Asthma attack."

"I'm sorry."

"You and me both."

"So then—"

"So then, nothing. Fast-forward twelve years, and I'm all grown up."

"That's—"

"Yeah, I know."

"Fast-forward twelve years."

"Right."

"And you never met your dad."

"No. My mom was fifteen when she had me. I think he was sixteen or seventeen. He went off to college."

"And you lived with your mom's parents?"

"With my grandmother and my mom, yes. Nana died when I was nine."

"What was she like?"

I pop a green olive into my mouth and bite through to the almond inside. "She was a country girl from Australia. Five feet tall, really frail-looking, but she was tough. She had all kinds of stories about things she'd survived—tornadoes and drunken husbands, things like that. She was a great story-teller. She raised me, really, my mom was way too young."

He doesn't say anything, but I hear a question in the silence.

"She took me to the library the day after my ninth birth-day. It was rainy, middle of winter, and the sidewalks were icy. And Nana had a shortened leg, from a car accident when she was young. So at the top of the steps she's juggling this stack of books and hurrying me along, fussing because I had my nose in a book and she thought I was going to fall on my head. She was so busy yelling at me, she missed the top step herself. And she just sailed, in slow motion, from the top of the steps all the way to the bottom without touching down. Coat, purse, books, everything flapping… I think I laughed, she looked so Mary Poppins, sailing that way. I thought it was a joke."

He lays his chin in the palm of his hand, shakes his head.

"But she landed headfirst at the bottom of the steps with this horrible thud, and her feet on the stairs but the wrong way, like the world had turned sideways and she was walk-ing up the risers."

I pause, remembering the soft quivering swell of her belly where her blouse had ridden up, looking down the steps and up her skirt at the crumpled triangle of her underwear.

At her face, foreshortened, slack-jawed with surprise. I still can hear the dense mechanical gurgle of her breath, breaking the silence after my laughter died away.

"As soon as I heard her breathe I knew she was gone. Her body was just catching up."

He looks at me, squinting in the sunlight. "Jesus."

I reach for another olive. He reaches, too, then waits for me to choose first.

"I had a friend in foster care," he says. "He said the foster families always had some dark reason for wanting him around. To work in the family business, or watch the younger kids. Once he ended up in the hospital with a couple of broken ribs."

"Did you think there was some altruism involved?"

"Well, no, but—"

"The foster system is completely fucked. Any kid who falls into it is fucked. There's no fine motive, no one gives a shit. The kid is the state's responsibility until he's eighteen. It's nothing more than that."

He doesn't look at me. "My friend said he was glad he wasn't a girl. He—"

"You know, one of the first things I learned as a writer is the value of negative space. Some stories don't work when you jam them with facts."

"You think we won't work if you fill in the blanks?"

"I don't know. But if you really want to find out, you can start by filling in some of your own. This falling out with your parents. What was that about?"

He builds a sandwich with a cracker, a slice of salami, cheddar, then another cracker. He eats the whole thing in one bite. Swallows, wipes his mouth.

"Did your dad want you to go into the liquor business or something?"

"No."

"Your mother wanted you to marry her best friend's daughter."

He smiles. "No. Nothing like that."

I peel the paper from a disc of sausage, wondering whether he'll tell me the truth.

"I got into some trouble," he says. "Spent eighteen months in prison."

I raise my eyebrows. "Really."

"When I got out, I went to see my parents. My old man had a fat check already written. Told me to take it and never come back. Said I had broken my mother's heart."

"Wow."

He shrugs. "There are worse things in life. Think if he'd been a poor man."

"So this is why you're not working as an architect?"

"Yeah. No firm's going to take me on with a prison record."

"But you could work independently—"

"Yes, I could. And I will. Let's say I'm trying to get my bearings first."

We eat in silence for a few minutes. The children have quieted, as well. They are bundled into towels and gathered in a semicircle around a young blonde woman and a man I guess to be her husband.

"Shocked?" Jack says.

"No."

"Concerned?"

I look at him. "Should I be?"

He doesn't answer right away. When he finally speaks,

his voice seems different and his eyes are fixed on the family below.

"Probably."

"So what was prison like?"

"Loud. Crowded. Pretty fucking scary, if you want to know the truth."

"Because of the other inmates?"

"Yeah, that. And also just the concept of being trapped in a room with no way out. I used to have nightmares about the prison being on fire and all of us left in there to burn."

"A therapist would have a field day with that."

I pop a tomato into my mouth and burst it with my tongue. The warm juice gushes over my tongue and trickles down my throat.

"Aren't you going to ask what I did?" he says.

"I don't need to ask. I can look it up online."

"Yeah, I guess you can."

I wet a napkin and wipe my hands. "But brownie points if you want to save me the trouble."

He digs out his pocketknife and begins to peel an apple. The blade slides like a scalpel under the skin, around and around without stopping, until he holds the flayed apple in his hand and the whole peel dangling from the tip of his knife.

"Sexual battery," he says. He hands me a slice of apple. "Now let's talk about those brownie points."

CHAPTER SEVEN

"She deserved it, I suppose," I say.

He tosses the apple peel to a couple of chipmunks who are squabbling over an empty peanut shell.

"Oh, she deserved it, but just to be clear, I didn't rape her."

"You were convicted, though."

"I pled out."

"I see."

"I'm not a rapist."

"So then why did she accuse you?"

He leans back on one elbow and lights a cigarette.

"When you get into a long-term relationship, things change. For some people, the changes are good. You have a steady job, a couple of kids, a house in the suburbs, and you settle down. That's what I thought I was getting."

He drags on his cigarette.

"For Rosemary, marriage was a power play. She got what she wanted—the house, the new car, me, all of it. But nothing I gave her was enough. I started working long hours to keep up with all the shit she needed. The clothes, the vacations to Paris and Costa Rica and fucking Amsterdam.

Jewelry, salon, God knows what else—it's all a blur at this point. Anyway, about three years into our marriage, she starts with the drugs. And I'm not talking about marijuana. I'm talking crack and heroin, whatever else her boyfriend would give her."

"Her boyfriend?"

"Yeah. This douche bag she took up with. A friend of a friend. She was running with another crowd by that point. I didn't know them."

"How long did this go on?"

"About a year. Finally this dude convinces her that she'll get a better divorce settlement if she accuses me of hitting her. He figures I'll pay up to get her to drop the charges."

"But she didn't drop them."

"No. Because I refused to pay. I told Rosemary to go fuck herself and I filed for divorce."

"So she accused you as payback?"

"Yeah. The next thing I know, I'm under arrest and she's telling everyone I raped her."

"But you didn't. What kind of proof did they have?"

"Nothing. It would have been her word against mine. But my lawyer thought it was a risk, so I took the plea."

His eyes are level and hold mine a shade too long. He hands me the cigarette and I take a slow drag.

"What was the boyfriend like?"

Jack raises his eyebrows. "What was he like? A fucking crackhead, that's what he was like. How the hell do I know?"

"You've never been curious to find out more about him?"

"Why should I?"

I shrug. "If it were me, I'd want to know who screwed

me over. You've never wanted to investigate? How do you even know it was his idea?"

"My buddy knew him. He said this guy told him all about how he was planning to make money off Rosemary's rich father-in-law."

"What happened to them? Your divorce went through, I assume?"

"Yeah, it did. Rosemary was long gone by the time I got out. I heard she left the boyfriend, too, but apparently he's still on the island."

"You never went looking?" I'm strangely disappointed in him, that he's allowed himself to be made a fool of this way and has done nothing about it.

He sits up, takes off his glasses and begins to clean them with his shirt.

"I'm not a complete pussy, if that's what you're thinking. I did go see the guy while I was out on bond." He glances over at me, his lips twisted in a wry smile.

"And?"

"I went to his house—this miserable piece-of-shit little place—and when he came to the door I more or less barged in. Rosemary was there. Strung out, clearly. Looked like she hadn't seen the inside of a shower in days. And her hair…I don't know what happened to her hair but it used to be glorious, really long and shiny and thick. That day it looked like she'd cut it herself with a pair of poultry shears, right to the scalp."

A muscle twitches in his jaw.

"I lost it. I would have beaten that cocksucker to death with his own fucking fire poker. Actually had it in my hand, as a matter of fact."

"But you didn't."

"No. Because a fire poker's not much of a weapon when the other guy's got a gun." He pauses, holding his glasses up to the light.

"And now?"

"Now, I stay away from him. Only a goddamned idiot would get caught up in that shit again. And besides…"

He looks at me. His eyes trace the line of my hair, over my neck and shoulders.

"Rosemary wasn't really worth killing for."

I watch his fabric-covered thumb swirl across the lenses. Around and around, a methodical circular motion from earpiece to nose. A shadow plays along the curve at the base of his thumb, and I sense the power in his hands and remember the scrape of his callused palm up the contours of my waist, across the sensitive tips of my breasts.

There was a moment when we were together this morning, with my hair twisted around his hand as I rode his lap at the edge of the bed. He looked down my naked body, between my legs as I took him, back again to my face. And there was something in his eyes. A fierce need, barely contained. Beyond a normal man's desire. His fingers tightened in my hair until I put both hands up to stop him, and with the climax building in his eyes, he drew back his hand and smacked me, hard across the ass.

I don't know what he saw in me, the way the pain brought me to him, the contraction of my whole body around him as I whimpered into his open mouth. But he slapped me again as he pulled at me, again as he came. Harder each time. And there it was, his singular kink—in the wild light in his eyes and the sheen on his brow and the way he swallowed up my cries as he dragged me down on top of him.

He wants to hurt me.

I wonder what Jack would look like if he ever got really angry. He's got to be at least six-three, with the lean, hard build of a soccer player and a soldier's no-nonsense economy of movement that makes each motion seem choreographed. I can't imagine him being clumsy. I can't imagine him ever losing a fight. No matter the opponent, Jack would find a way to win, and he'd have no scruples about keeping it fair.

Rosemary wasn't worth killing for.

But I'm not Rosemary.

I collect our trash, stow it in the backpack and get to my feet.

He rises, as well, and stands eye level to my perch on the rock. With one graceful shrug, he settles the backpack over his shoulders, then wraps his arm around my waist and pulls me closer until we are nose to nose. His eyelashes are thick and dark, almost as long as mine, curving toward his brow.

"Did I lose you?" he says.

I lay my hand over his heart and he covers it with one of his.

We stop for dinner on our way home. I've never eaten so much in my life as I have since meeting Jack. My body has never felt so hollow.

Afterward, in the passenger's seat, I watch the scenery flash by and think about Jack's story, and the level way he held my gaze as he told it.

I look at his profile with the light sliding over it, his arm stretched out to the wheel.

"Lean the seat back," he says.

I lift the lever and push with my shoulders, until the headrest is practically in the backseat. Jack looks over as we stop at the last red light before we leave town. A neon sign is reflected in his glasses, the letters inverted like a child's handwriting. His eyes are obscured for a second, then he turns back to the road and the truck starts to move. He curves his hand around the inside of my bare thigh and pulls my legs apart.

"Unbutton your shirt," he tells me, and I do that, too, letting the thin cotton plaid fall aside in the breeze from the open window. I slide a hand into my bra and lift my breast free of the cup. He reaches past the hem of my shorts and strokes me through my underwear. I prop my right foot on the dash and lean my knee against the door.

He adjusts himself in his seat, then unsnaps my shorts. His fingers are cool, slippery. He glances at me, then the road, back and forth. I watch his wrist moving as the streetlights glide over my bare skin and the silver hoop in my nipple. I move under his touch, thinking, *He wants me, he wants me.*

He explores me that way, unhurried, and because I know what he wants I don't try to come. I just let him look at me, dip inside, taste my liquor on his fingertips. I know when we park in his driveway that he will follow me up the walk and pull me through the door, and he'll take off my pants and bare my breasts to his mouth. He'll kick my feet apart and bend me over the sofa or the dining room table, or he'll push me to the floor and bury his face between my thighs. He may even pull me on top of him right here in the truck, or fuck me standing up against the door that he held closed when I tried to walk away. I will wait and see. He can do whatever he wants.

I watch him and let the pressure build under his fingers. The question echoes in my mind:

Would you kill for me?

CHAPTER EIGHT

A strange thing is happening. The world around me is breaking into fragments, as though I'm looking through a sheet of broken glass. Each shard reveals a clear but separate piece of the view, but when I try to put them together it seems the picture is distorted and obscured by the cracks.

The sensation is vaguely familiar. In the days and weeks following my mother's death, as I was moved from my home and into the foster system, it seemed as though the days were made up of a series of jagged and unrelated images. The visuals stand out in sharp relief, though the larger story—where I went, what decisions were made on my behalf—has never been clear in my mind.

Instead, I am left with individual pieces of the scene: a bubble in the paint next to my bed at the Seattle Children's Center, a small run in the carpet where the cement showed through, a frayed bit of curtain. Above each bed was a cartoon figure made of tufts of faded plastic like a hooked rug. Mine was Cinderella, which struck me even then as a cruel sort of joke to play on a child.

There were faces. Big faces, pressed too close, and big hands. The damp odor of children, like crayons and wet chicken feathers, with a lid of disinfectant over the top. The clammy pipe-metal handrail on the stairs. A laminated sign in the bathroom with a cartoon picture of a frowning toilet, reminding us to flush.

I went to live at the Center even before my mother's funeral, processed and ushered along by a succession of adult authority figures who eventually deposited me at the Cinderella bed, in a room I would be sharing with another girl my age.

She stood between the beds as my caseworker, Carla, made the introductions.

"Alice, this is your new roommate, Polly Jinks."

"*Molly,*" said the girl in a thin exasperated voice. "*Molly* Jinks."

She was fantastically ugly. An albino, with long white hair that trailed over her shoulders in two lumpy braids, and boiled blue eyes that flashed a rabbity pink when the light shone in from the side. Her body was like mine: unformed, narrow, exactly my height. She was wearing a sundress with a safety pin at the waist and a pair of grubby foam flip-flops to which her pale toes clung like roots.

"I stole you a feather pillow," she said after Carla had gone. "You should probably keep it under the bedspread, just in case."

In case of what, she didn't say. She sat down on her bed, legs crossed, plucking at the hem of her dress. After a moment, since there was nothing else to do, I sat, too.

"Your mom died," she said. It was a simple statement, repeating what she already knew. But the three words twisted like wringing hands inside me.

I am an orphan, I thought. *Little orphan Alice.*

Molly began to unravel one of her braids.

"Mine is still alive. Somewhere. I mean, I guess she is."

She thought about this as she reached the top of her braid and started over. Her silvery hair twined around her fingers and the inside of her wrists.

Molly must have braided her hair fifty times a day, minimum, each side. She was a chain-smoker on training wheels, who unfastened her rubber bands with the weary anxiety of an adult flicking a cigarette lighter. This was her thing, everybody had one. Some kids would zone out on video games or TV; some would eat too much, or not enough, or they ate small bits of themselves like finger-nails and scabs; the older kids fought with the adults, the young ones trailed around after them like puppies. We were twitchy or preternaturally still, as if we'd each short-circuited in some specific way as a result of the missing connections in our lives.

I became a cutter that summer. It was my thing.

"You won't be here long," Molly said comfortably. "They'll want to put you with a foster before school starts. Your soc will start bringing people over for you to meet. If you like them, smile a little and start talking about how much you miss your mom. Or cry, but not too much or they'll think you're a head case. But you probably won't like any of them. I never do. The last place I went, they didn't even have a TV. Can you imagine? I was there a week, and only because it took that long for my soc to come pick me up." She tied off the end of the braid and started on the other one. "I didn't tell her it was because of the TV, of course, or she wouldn't have come."

She smiled. "You'll learn."

It was summer when I went to live at the Center. The

staff had activities for us, I suppose, sports and books and all that, though I don't remember much of it now.

I remember Molly, my self-appointed mentor. Ten years old, and the most accomplished thief I have ever met.

"Watch this," she would say. And she'd sidle up to some unsuspecting adult, pointing to a splinter on her palm. When they leaned over to look, Molly's other hand would dart nimbly sideways to a purse or pocket. She never came away empty.

"You need a distraction," she told me, clicking her new pen. "But it can't be the same thing every time or people will catch on."

I was in awe. "Don't you ever get caught?"

"No," she said. "Nobody notices. Don't you think that's kind of funny?"

Not funny, exactly, but I saw what she meant.

Molly could steal anything. Mostly she lifted odd little things: a penny that had been pressed into an oval with the Disneyland castle on the front; a barrette made of pink plastic beads; papers from her own file that she never let me read. Sometimes she took expensive things like the magnifying glass she'd snagged from an elderly foster mom, but she never seemed to care about the object's value. She said money wasn't the point.

I didn't have to ask what the point was. I knew it already. Molly's stealing was a form of emotional scavenging, a way to creep a bit closer by carrying off a person's belongings. It didn't take me long to work that out; I was sneaky in my affections, too.

Growing up in foster care had made her something of a philosopher. She had an opinion on every topic and seemed to feel it was her duty to educate me.

"The problem is," she said as we played cat's cradle with a loop of frayed green yarn, "everybody tells you to be good, but they all mean something different. Mrs. Drummond means be quiet and remember to flush."

We were sitting cross-legged on her bed, our nightgowns tucked up, bare knees bumping. I pushed my fingers into the loops and pulled them through hers.

"Teachers mean be quiet and do your homework. And don't cheat." She lifted our hands and gave me a sly smile through the lines of yarn. "I bet *you* don't cheat."

"No, I don't."

"Then you're stupid. Smart people cheat all the time, everybody knows that."

She shook out the yarn and we started over.

"Foster parents mean be quiet—everyone means be quiet, ha!—and *smile*. A smiling kid makes them look good."

"Why?"

"Means the parents know what they're doing," she said. "Grown-ups are always watching each other. You don't get to stop pretending just 'cause you're old."

We were silent for a moment, trying to make Jacob's ladder, a complicated pattern consisting of several steps that always fell apart before we could finish.

"You'll see. Fosters have weird sets of rules, and they think everyone else's rules are stupid. I lived in one house where they kept a lock on the refrigerator and the cupboard doors. The dad did that, to keep the mom out of there 'cause she was fat. It didn't work, though. She would get back from the grocery store and hide food all over the house. I mean, everywhere. Under the sink, in the garage, inside the bins full of Christmas decorations." She giggled, and our ladder collapsed. "Anytime I needed a snack, I could go right to my laundry basket for a bag of chips."

I looked at her uneasily. Molly talked about foster care like she was telling ghost stories. "Did the dad ever find out?"

"Oh, sure," she said. "But he didn't hear it from me."

Mrs. Drummond came to the door. "Lights out," she said.

Molly gave her an angelic smile and leaped up to turn off the lamp. But a moment later she also opened the curtain, and we resumed our game by the light of the moon.

"Rule number one for how to be good," she whispered. "Don't tell the secrets."

Her fingers slipped through mine inside the loops of yarn, her eyes flashing mercury-silver in the moonlight.

We understood each other from the beginning, and Molly was nice to me. She didn't seem to mind that I was quiet, and I took comfort in her slippery conversation, in the strange pale presence of her. Her oddness was reassuring somehow, a constant visual acknowledgment that the world around me had shifted and everything ordinary had been left behind. A more commonplace friend would have unnerved me.

Because we were the same height, people started referring to us as Salt and Pepper, and later simply as the Shakers: me with my black hair, Molly white as salt. Opposite yet exactly alike.

Molly was a prostitute's child. She had come into the world completely unattached and, with her goblin's face and queer, knowing smile, she made adults uneasy. Every attempt to place her had come to nothing. She was a changeling; no one wanted her for very long.

What she thought of this, I didn't know. Molly kept her

secrets well. It was only now and then, when I'd glance up to see her watching me, when she'd offer to braid my hair or help me untangle a knot in my shoelaces, that a glimpse of her feelings would show through. We would stand side by side at the bathroom mirror, gazing at each other's reflections.

"You're going to be beautiful," she said once.

I could think of nothing to say in response; I wasn't sure I wanted to be beautiful, but answering that way to Molly would have been like refusing an expensive gift.

"You're going to be Lex Luthor," I said finally, and we both laughed, a dangerous moment averted.

Late one night, weeks after my mother died, I lay awake in my Cinderella bed and started to cry. The crying began from someplace deep inside my chest, as though my tightly held grief had begun to unravel, to release the tears from my body with a pain so intense I thought I was dying. My breath came in sharp, knifelike gasps. My limbs tightened and curled inward. I felt my mother standing at the other side of an uncrossable chasm, too far even for me to make out her features, too far ever to touch. She was gone, truly gone, and I was and would always be alone.

Molly crawled from her bed into mine, shivering down under the covers. She wiped the tears from my face with the sleeve of her polyester nightgown, and patted the top of my head until the spasms subsided. Then she kissed me, tight girlish kisses over my lips and face. She reached up my nightgown and stroked me through my underwear.

Molly said this was what grown-ups did. To make each other feel better, she said.

★ ★ ★

I think of her sometimes when I'm with Jack. When his jaw scrapes my skin, when he pounds and pushes too hard, I remember the smoothness of Molly's young cheek, her tentative fingers and tongue, her secret wish arising from a grown man's perversion.

Same as mine.

CHAPTER NINE

The first time Jack leaves his clothes at my place, I think it's an oversight. I wash them and leave them folded on a chair in the bedroom. But the next day he brings more, in an old canvas gym bag, and leaves those behind, as well, crumpled next to the bed. Later, a shirt, an odd pair of boxers, one sock. A pair of muddy work boots drying on the front porch. Gradually the stack of clothes on the chair seems to be saying something, so I clear out a drawer and put them away. I brush off his boots and set them next to mine in the closet and think, *There you are, Daddy,* and wonder where that came from.

I don't leave my clothes at his house, though he's been trying, I think, to make me feel at home. He asks me to stay while he's sleeping, so he can see me in the morning before he leaves for work.

"Bring your work with you," he says. He buys me a chair for the ship room and clears off the table so I can use it as a desk. It's surprisingly easy to work in this room, surrounded by the silent, vacant ships tossing on imagined seas—an idea in a bottle, a world inside the glass walls. Like me with my pages, trying to pin the whole thing down. I feel safe in this house, with Jack sleeping like a guard dog down the hall.

In the morning, long before dawn, he wakes without an alarm and pads barefoot to the ship room where I'm working out the latest plot twist. It's been a long night and I'm at the point in my draft in which the whole thing resembles the ramblings of a nine-year-old. My eyelids feel like sandpaper.

"You look tired," he says. "Why don't you come in and lie down."

My heart turns over like a sleepy child at the sight of him, rumpled and radiating blanket heat across the space between us. I lay my pen aside and rub my eyes with my knuckles.

"I should probably get home."

He moves up behind my chair and lays his big hand over my chest, his thumb stroking my neck.

"How about I run you a bath, make you something to eat and you can sleep here until I get home from work."

Since the day we met I have not been alone in Jack's house or left him alone in mine. I haven't showered or slept here. I'm tired and hungry, but the bath makes me nervous. I've been careful to keep my bad foot covered. The scars could only have been made by a cutter—the assortment of old and new, all on one foot, all suspiciously symmetrical— all unmistakably deliberate.

Jack sees my hesitation and unknowingly delivers the best argument of all.

"I have bubbles," he says.

Concealment.

So he runs the bath and I light a candle, smoke some weed, brush my teeth. When the tub is full he undresses me and I slide into the water, let it close womblike over my head and come up gently, the waterline at my lips. I blink at him in the candlelight.

"You don't even know," he says. He sits outside the tub, his chin propped on one arm, free hand snaking under the surface to find my breast.

"Will you tell me something?" I ask.

"Probably."

I lick the water from my lips. "What was prison like? What was it like, really?"

"Is this for the book?"

"No."

He doesn't answer at first. His hand is gentle, his thumb passing back and forth over my nipple.

"People throw the word *nightmare* around," he says. "A crowded store is a nightmare. A wait in line. A tax audit, whatever. But in a real nightmare there's a sense of unexpectedness. Nothing makes sense. You're going along and suddenly your house is not your house, or the person with you is not that person. And you're still applying waking logic, you're trying to make it make sense. You want to wake up, not just because you want to get the fuck out, but because you're looking for order in the chaos. You want things back the way they were when you were awake."

His hand travels down my body, his fingers slide between the folds of my labia.

"Prison is that kind of nightmare. Anything can happen and nothing makes sense. It's a circus of freaks. And you're locked inside."

His fingers circle my clitoris, and he finds a steady rhythm, up and down, his eyes on my face. I know, and am comforted by knowing, that he'll bring me off.

"I thought about women all the time in prison," he says.

"We all did. Alone at night. All of us jerking off, you could hear the mattresses. The cursing. Everyone dying for a woman. Pussy was all we talked about."

I lean back and let my legs spread open as if in sympathy, thinking of the men he describes, the need in them, the rotation of power from male to female. I feel the echo of that pent-up desire in the gravitational force of my body. The idea moves me. Excites me. There is a difference in the glide of his fingers as he draws the fluid from my body.

"Not even just the way it feels to get laid," he says. "Not even the fucking blissed out ride. We missed everything."

His eyes are on my breasts, which rise and fall with my breath and the tidal pull of his voice and fingers that draws my body like the ocean to the moon. I lift my feet from the water and brace myself on the edge of the tub. My head tips and I arch back. The water eddies around my nipples.

"The way you look when you come, the way your mouth opens. The sounds you make. The way you taste when I've got my tongue inside you."

Orgasm approaches from a distance, a wave on the horizon, building in size and weight. His fingers have not left my clitoris and his voice is low and calm, but underneath is the relentless physical force of him, heavily in orbit around me. I am fluid. I am the sea, rising to the shore.

"So hot and wet, you can't imagine. You don't know how much I think about it. You don't know what it feels like, watching you come."

A note of tension creeps into the seductive cadence of his voice. He wants me. He wants to see me come and I want to watch him while I do. His gaze moves over my breasts and mouth, to the water where his hand is submerged. He slides his fingers inside, curved upward, and presses hard. He sees my surprised response and murmurs encouragement. This is like nothing I've felt before. He's uncovered a secret my body has been keeping even from me. His fingers pull me into a rhythm and I begin to move with him.

"Let's see it, baby, let me see...."

He nudges me from the inside, the tip of his finger fitted like a key into a hidden lock. A wave of pleasure overtakes me, sweeps up my body and lifts me to his hand. My lips part and I let go with a sigh. I watch him, watching me, my clitoris in the palm of his hand. He looks as if I've given him a gift.

"Oh, fuck, yes," he says. "You don't even know."

I close my eyes. My vagina contracts around his fingers as he draws the last retreating ripples from my body. When I am still, he smooths his hand down my thigh, around my calf and ankle. I remember my ugly foot and drop it quickly back under the bubbles. I see a flash of puzzlement in his expression; to distract him, I rise out of the water to kiss him full on the mouth.

"*You* don't know," I tell him, tracing his lips with the pad of my thumb.

He helps me out of the tub and dries me with a beach towel, tucks me into bed. I lie naked between the sheets with the scent of his hair on the pillow beneath my cheek.

"Lie still, baby," he says. "I'm going to make us something to eat."

He kisses my forehead and I roll to my stomach and close my eyes. I am swollen, heavy with sleep, warm and tranquil as a sunbather on an empty beach. I hear the distant clatter of pans and dishes, the friendly shush of rain outside the window, and I am asleep.

★ ★ ★

My foot.

Something is moving up the sole of my foot. In sleep, I imagine a dog's nose snuffling. Then awareness rushes me upward. I open my eyes.

Jack is at the end of the bed. He has the covers pushed back and he's bent over my foot, frowning. His thumb is the dog's nose from my dream.

I scramble up the bed, swatting him away. With one hand I draw the covers to my chin, and as I do there is a crash. He must have set a plate on the bed and I've sent it overboard.

He doesn't look away from me. His eyes are steady, his mouth an uncrossable line. He takes a fistful of the covers and pulls gently, evenly, one hand over the other. I can hold the sheets in place or I can let go—either way is just the same with Jack.

I am naked and trembling against the headboard when his fingers close around my ankle. He straightens my leg and I look away, more exposed than I have ever been. *Don't look at me.* I want to scream and fight, bloody his nose with my heel. *Stop looking at me, I'll hurt you, leave me alone.*

He doesn't say a word. He presses a kiss to the unwilling sole of my foot and lays me back on the barren expanse of the fitted sheet. His voice when he comes makes me want to cry.

"Don't," he says. "Don't…"

CHAPTER TEN

The loss of the secret of my nicks is a heavy blow. Since I started laying them at the age of ten, no one other than the occasional doctor has seen them. But my initial dismay has faded, has shifted to a strange exhibitionist thrill, the almost-sexual release of knowing he's uncovered my secret. He's pushed farther into me than anyone has before.

Something is changing in him, too. I can see that he believes he's found some sort of key, something he's been looking for, a missing piece to the puzzle of me. He's harder on me now. He pinches me; he bites and pulls my hair. He demands all the space inside me when we fuck. He watches my reactions, catalogs the things that get us both off.

Outside of bed he's become tender, even doting. He's working his way around my rickety bungalow, fixing the leaky plumbing, replacing the screens and faucets. He arrives one Saturday with two friends and a truck bed full of lumber, and together they rip up my old porch and replace it. The next weekend he shows up with brushes and buckets of paint, and we work our way from one end to the other, with the music turned up and a hash pipe glowing on the steps. The next day, when the paint is dry, he bends me over the sturdy new bannister. I come twice, the scent of sawdust and turpentine in the air, and leave a row of half-moons with my fingernails in the fresh paint.

"Truth or dare?" Jack says.

I hesitate, weighing my options.

We're in Jack's living room. Midnight has long since come and gone, in a haze of sex and weed and lukewarm wine. I'm wearing his linen shirt and nothing else, having lost my panties in a bet two hours before.

"Truth," I say.

Jack starts making chicken noises that end in a burble from the candy-striped bong on the coffee table.

"Bite me," I say. "Truth."

He exhales, slouches back against the cushions. His bare chest gleams in the firelight, the skin wrinkling over his abdomen like folds of thick velvet on a table. He takes off his glasses and cleans the lenses with a corner of the blanket we've dragged in from the bedroom.

He's working on a pirate ship. The pieces are laid out neatly across the coffee table: masts like matchsticks, delicate twine for the ropes. He has tossed out the "faggoty" skull-and-crossbones decal, saying that the shape and color are enough to indicate its rogue status.

"Give me a number," he says. "How many men have seen that tattoo on your pussy?"

I roll my eyes and drop a tiny ball of weed into the cup of the bong.

"Seriously? Why are men always so obsessed with statistics?"

"We like to know our place in the batting order."

"You're up, stud, isn't that enough?"

"No."

I flick the lighter and set the weed aflame. Smoke begins to fill the chamber. I breathe it in, hold it, let it go. "Well, as it happens, the tattoo is a fairly new addition and you are the only man to have seen it. Other than the guy who put it here, that is."

"Fuck. That's not what I meant."

"Then you should've said what you meant."

"How many men have fucked you?"

"Sorry, your turn is over."

He smiles lazily. "What was it like, having a male tattoo artist do that piece?"

"I don't know. Kind of surreal…"

"Did it turn you on?"

His deep, quiet voice melts through my buzz.

"Yes."

"Did it make you wet?"

"Yeah. I could feel his breath on my hip."

"Mmm-hmm. Did you wish he'd bend you over and fuck you, right there on the table?"

I lay back, prop my legs over the back of the couch, angled so that Jack won't be able to see between them. With my head tipped over the edge of the seat cushion, I watch the upside-down flames and the flickering yellow light on the ceiling, as though a super-8 movie is about to begin.

"No, I wanted him to finish my tattoo."

"Liar."

"It's my turn, anyway. Truth or dare?"

"What do you think?"

"I'm running out of dares."

"Not my problem." He runs a hand up my thigh.

I mull this over. He has already collected his mail from

the end of the driveway, naked, singing "California Girls" at the top of his lungs while I watched from the doorway, wrapped in a blanket, shaking with helpless laughter. He's shameless and cannot be humiliated. I decide on a different approach.

I open my legs, let one foot rest on the top of his thigh. His back grows rigid and his hand begins a downward slide from my knee.

"Don't touch," I say. "And don't look. Not for thirty minutes."

He groans. "Thirty stoned minutes, those are like dog years—"

"Hands in your lap."

"Fuck."

At first I think he won't take the dare. Then he tears his gaze from between my legs and sits in mock chastity on his side of the couch, fingers interlaced, knees together.

"Truth or dare," he says. "Goddamn, I want to look at you."

I unfasten the button between my breasts to let his shirt fall away.

"You're doing great," I tell him, nudging his swelling hard-on with my toes. "I think I'll take the dare, since whatever it is, you won't be watching."

"Aren't you clever."

He leans forward to pack another hit. I blink up at the ceiling, watching the patterns of light through half-closed eyes the way you'd watch clouds go by from a picnic blanket. I imagine the gurgle of the bong as a creek running nearby. I close my eyes, then remember that Jack's dare will need to be monitored, and open them again.

"Here's the dare," he says, exhaling. "You're going to

find someone. A guy, whoever you want. You're going to break into his house, and you're going to take me with you."

"No."

"Can't say no. You agreed to the dare."

"That's not—"

"That's the dare."

"Jack. If I get caught in some strange guy's house, it's bad but sort of ridiculous. We know that, right? But if you get caught, or we get caught, that's another thing altogether. No one is going to laugh it off and send us on our way."

"So you're afraid."

"I'm cautious."

"I thought you had balls."

"Yes, well, if you turned your head, you'd see that I don't."

"Fuck. Is it thirty minutes yet?"

"Not even five."

He leans back, staring straight ahead of him. I follow his sight line and realize he can see our reflection in the glass door. Our images float like spirits on the night sky, dancing orange and purple, our pale skin warmed by the firelight. A ribbon of gold highlight flows across his shoulders. My torso is a horizontal slash on the couch, which is sunk in the shadows so that we appear to be levitating over a murky abyss.

Our reflections gaze at each other.

"Take the dare," he says. "And have another hit."

I blink. The dimensions of the room feel strange, as if the walls are closing in.

"Fine," I say. "It's my turn. And I'm gonna need a truth."

Jack is silent. I wait, unable to judge the passage of time, floating in the moment with only the last feeble pops of the dying fire to penetrate the buzz in my ears.

"What do you want to know?" he says at last.

I get the impression that any question would be unwelcome, but I'm full of courage.

"What really happened with Rosemary?"

His face remains hidden in the reflection, so I turn to watch his profile. His nose has a small bump along the bridge, as though it's been broken—possibly more than once.

He turns to face me. A muscle in his jaw twitches.

"That's thirty minutes. Time for your next dare."

"That's not even close to thirty minutes. And what if I want truth?"

"Forget it. Come with me."

"No, I'm comfortable."

Jack gets up and stands for a moment looking down at me. I begin to feel self-conscious; I press my thighs together and pull his shirt across my breasts.

"Get up, Alice."

But he doesn't wait for me to move. He bends over and scoops me off the couch. I watch us leave the room through the scattered reflection in the window, and turn the corner to his bedroom.

He tosses me on the bed and goes to his chest of drawers. When he turns back, I see what's in his hand.

"No no no." I'm scrambling up.

But Jack is right there, blocking my path. He won't let me get to my feet.

"Shh," he says. "You'll be fine."

"Jack—"

"Don't you trust me? Look where you are."

I blink and try to clear my head. I'm drunk, annihilated on weed. I have been alone with Jack for hours now. He's been all over me. Inside me. It's too late to worry about shifting the balance of power, too late to parse degrees of control.

He begins to slide the sleeves of his shirt down my arms.

"You don't want to do this for me?"

I try to improvise.

"No, it's just that I read that Stephen King story, you know the one, where the guy dies and the wife is handcuffed to the bed, and—"

Jack smiles.

"I'm thirty-two. Swear to God, I won't die on you."

My heart races, and fear begins to burn through the weed and the wine. "Please, Jack, let's do something else."

"This is a dare, baby, you don't negotiate a dare."

"I didn't ask—"

He reclaims his shirt. I shiver and cross my arms over my chest.

"I don't need you to ask. Give me your wrist."

He stares down at me. I felt so in control just minutes ago. Ordered him to look away, teased him and made him wait, enjoyed the power of my body over his. But now the tables are turned and I realize it was only a trick of the mind. He's been in control all along.

He dangles the handcuffs by one thumb.

"Don't make me say it again."

Something in his expression silences me.

I hold out my wrist. The handcuff closes around it with an ominous click, like the bars on a prison cell clanging shut. The steel feels hard and uncomfortably heavy against my bones. My cheeks burn and a treacherous prickle creeps into my eyes and nose.

Jack gives me a gentle backward push. He fastens the other cuff around the bedpost and snaps it closed around my left wrist. I press my face to my arm and fight back the rising claustrophobic panic. He drapes a scarf over my eyes and ties it behind my head.

Just like that, I think wildly. *Just like that, and I'm helpless.*

I twist my arms, feel the weight of the steel. The metal clatters against the bedpost. When I pull harder, the cuffs bite into my skin. I squeeze my hand together and try to free myself.

"Shh," he whispers against my ear. "Don't fight it."

He lays his hand over my heart.

"Are you afraid?"

A screw tightens in my throat. My voice is a choked whisper.

"Yes. Please—"

"I know, baby, shh."

He sits up and I feel him look me over. His presence seems to grow in my mind. The things I worried about— being left here, being exposed or hurt—seem both amplified and unimportant. My mind is swollen with Jack. Why does he need to see me this way? What does he want that I can't do with my hands and eyes and mouth?

I press my knees together.

"Jack," I whisper.

"I just want to look at you," he says in a low voice.

My breath rushes past my lips. My head swims; the room is filled with Jack. I'm drowning in him, trying to keep my head above water.

He bends to kiss me. His cheek scrapes my skin. He nuzzles into the crook of my neck and draws his nose along my jaw.

"God, you smell good," he says. "Spread your legs, I want to see."

He backs away and I hear him at the side of the bed.

Somehow all the things we did before seem a lifetime away. I don't want to open myself that way, let him stand beside me and stare. I want him to cover me with his body, to distract me with sensation. I can't make myself do what he wants.

His hand closes around the back of my knee, and he pulls me apart. One leg, then the other. This is easier, this passivity. Still, when he circles the bed, it takes all my will not to close my legs, curl my body, scream for him to stop looking at me. My heart rolls and gallops; air sweeps past my chilled lips in swift, quivering gusts. My skin flashes hot and cold, damp with anxiety.

He stops at the foot of the bed.

I turn my face into the pillow and choke back a hysterical sob. The handcuffs seem unnaturally heavy and confining and cruel. I want to beg him to fuck me, if only for the sake of being covered. Anything, *anything* would be better than this. A hard shudder courses up my flank. My mind floods with an incoherent, all-encompassing plea.

Please please please...

I think I hear him laughing. Then a zip and the shush of his pants dropping.

The bed sinks under his weight. His fingers close around my ankles, slide up my calves to my inner thighs. I hold my breath and feel his body's reaction to my scent. The stiffening of his fingers, the long slow inhalation followed by a stuttering groan and an incantation of muttered profanity that draws an unwilling contraction from deep inside my body, as though he has summoned some mysterious female archetype asleep inside me.

A bead of moisture rolls down the crack of my ass, tickling.

He settles over me. His tongue sweeps slowly up the crevice of my body. His voice is a rumbled murmur that I feel rather than hear, a vibration against my labia, a tightening of his lips. His stubbled jaw scrapes my thighs. He sucks my clitoris, plucks with his teeth, circles with his tongue.

Now I can't be still. I twist my arms, wishing they were free so I could twine my fingers in his dark hair and hold him to me, make him fuck me with his tongue and relieve this hollow ache in my belly. Heat springs up under his mouth. I arch my back and he covers my bare breast with his hand, rolling my nipple between his fingers. And it doesn't matter that I can't get free, because his freedom is enough. He knows where we're going and how to get there.

The heat and pressure begin to break me. I moan and raise my hips to his mouth.

"That's right," he says around me. "I want to taste you, baby, come for me, that's it...."

He bares me with his fingertips and pinches my clitoris between his forefingers, with his tongue between them and his hands holding me open. That is unbearable, a pleasure so intense it draws hot tears from my eyes. My climax zips like a fuse from the tips of my fingers and toes, up my thighs, down my ribs and explodes under his mouth with a force that lifts me right off the bed. He braces my hips, following relentlessly, not satisfied until he's drawn a second shattering orgasm into his mouth, until I am broken and trembling in his arms, and begging with all my mind to be filled.

He leaves me then, and I wait through the reassuring crackle of his condom. Then he's back, settling between my legs. He slips off my blindfold.

"Look at me," he says.

He pushes forward, an inch at a time, and I can't help but close my eyes against the pressure, the immense, thick maleness of him inside me. He drags his fingers through my hair. His lips move over mine.

"Open your eyes."

He holds me still, withdraws and comes slowly back, watching my face. Then he lowers his head, his sandpapery cheek against mine, and begins to thrust in long, elliptical strokes, a gradual acceleration. Each rotation of his hips drives us on.

It feels safe now, to be under his control. The harder he pushes, the more securely I am held, the more relaxed I become. I am inside his space. He's strong and lethal and he is all around me and he is mine. I want to get as close to him as it's possible to be. I want the weight of him, the anchor. I want to live under his skin, inside his heavy bones, with all of Jack around me. I wrap my legs around him and pull him closer, following his rhythm, rising to meet him with each long stroke, until he grows too fast and strong to keep up with, too ragged to follow, and I can only let myself be carried by him into a last blinding surge of pleasure. His cock throbs like a heartbeat and his teeth close on the underside of my shackled arm, and he comes silently, shivering, buried inside me.

When the last pulsing convulsions have stilled, and he's

begun, finally, to soften, he unlocks the handcuffs and rubs my wrists, kisses the angry red marks and apologizes.

"I don't know, baby," he says, laying my hand across his eyes. "I don't know."

But he never explains what he means.

CHAPTER ELEVEN

I keep the box Jack gave me on a shelf in the far corner of my closet. It contains my treasures now, too, separated from his by a wooden divider down the center. It's a beautiful object, too pretty to be set aside this way, with this motley collection of battered shoeboxes and boot boxes and one flimsy pie box full of odd bits of writing that I'll probably never use. But when I leave it out on my dresser, the box seems to reproach me.

Secrets are nothing to be careless with. Molly taught me that.

She taught me many things. We spent that summer at the Center in a strange groove, immediately more intimate than I had ever been with another person. The impermanence of our friendship was one of its draws; I knew she'd carry away my secrets as I would carry hers, and there might be a measure of relief in letting them go.

Not that we thought of it that way. We were kids; we moved and played as children do. Most days we went next door to the Pax Nursery, a family-run business with flow-ers and herbs at the front of the lot and inside the main building, then shrubs and rows of ornamental saplings running out to the edge of the property, behind which was a peach orchard and a slow-moving river. It was something of a haven to the Center kids—a safe, cheerful place that smelled of orange blossoms and clean soil.

Lyle Pax worked there with his father, restocking the plants and transferring the seedlings to bigger pots. At thirty years old, his body was thin and strong as wire, but you could see the disability plainly in the rubbery wetness of his mouth, the way his lower lip hung and twitched as he repeated things over to himself. We learned from his father that Lyle had been in a car accident when he was fifteen and had spent over a year in rehab before his family was able to take him home.

Years later, this disability was stressed by his lawyer. Medical records were produced, showing the extent and location of the brain damage, and expert witnesses were called to explain how little he was to blame for what happened that summer.

No one had the heart to argue. Blame was assigned to those soft white spots on the MRI, those dead little pieces of Lyle Pax's brain where conscience and self-control should have resided.

Watching him with the late-summer flowers, so gentle with the water on their blossoms, you'd never think he could hurt anyone. Even right afterward, after what everyone called "the incident," with his spade still dripping blood, with blood on his hands and splattered on the ground, he seemed baffled and as docile as ever. He kept saying tearfully that he didn't know what had happened; it was something about her eyes.

He was ruled mentally unfit to stand trial, and died several years later in the state psychiatric hospital.

★ ★ ★

Molly and I used to go to the nursery sometimes, for something to do. This was deemed a healthy activity, and since the nursery was right next door to the Center, they left us to it. We liked to push our noses into the gardenias and make little puppets of the snapdragons, and Mr. Pax indulged us. He'd give us ice cream sometimes from the freezer behind the nursery counter, and he'd let us eat our fill of peaches, right off the tree. The little Shakers from the Center, he'd call us. We thought we were loved.

If you ate that ice cream too fast, it would stick at the back of your throat and explode in a sudden agony, through the roof of your mouth and like a steel blade to the base of your skull.

"Brain freeze," Molly would scream, and she'd smack herself between the eyes. "Eat it faster, Alice. Feel the paaain...."

She'd dare me to swallow big mouthfuls, delighted when my eyes began to water.

We used to play hide-and-seek at the back of the nursery, where the saplings and young pines stood in their wooden boxes, going down to the orchard and almost to the river. It was Molly's game, really. I would have stayed inside with my books if left to my own devices, but Molly couldn't be still that long.

Instead, I ran and dodged through the trees, tucked myself behind shrubs and inside wooden crates, made myself a secret for Molly to find.

"Hide someplace better," she'd say when she uncovered me. She refused to be impressed with my hiding places, even when I'd crawled to the middle of a drainage pipe under the road. I crouched there in the mossy puddles, waiting, sure this time she'd pass by and I'd be safe.

It took her about two minutes.

"I've hidden here lots of times," she said, peering into the darkness. "Come out, it's your turn to be It."

"No fair," I said. "You were peeking. You didn't go all the way to fifty."

"Whatever. My turn to hide, start counting."

She would never admit to cheating. It was part of the game as far as she was concerned.

Lyle Pax would sometimes play with us, but I didn't like being found by him. When the branches parted and the sky showed behind his smiling face, I would jump up and run away, my heart banging like a kettledrum in my chest.

Molly said I was a chicken. She was not afraid of Lyle.

"He's just slow," she said.

But I understood that word literally, and knew that Lyle Pax was fast enough.

And I knew something else about Lyle. One day I had gone alone down to the river, not from the nursery but from the back gate at the Center. I found a half-buried tree trunk and sat down near the water, watching the patterns of light as the river eddied and flowed around the rocks. After a few minutes, Lyle Pax came up the path from the nursery, right to the water's edge. There was something furtive in his movements, in the glance he cast over his shoulder toward his home, that froze me in place; when he unzipped his jeans to reach inside, I was sure he was unloading some bit of stolen merchandise to hide it in the woods. Instead, he knelt down, shifting, and I saw what was in his hand.

Until that day I had never considered the ways in which men were different from us. If I thought of them at all, it was in terms of facial hair and flat chests and deep voices, and strange soft bulges in the front of their pants. The concept of a male erection had never once occurred to me. When Lyle took his in hand, I wasn't even sure at first what I was seeing. But as his arm began to move, I felt the response from my own body, the faint, dreadful tightening between my legs, the distressing fascination of seeing something adult and being unable to catalog the experience in a way that made sense. I sat transfixed, barely breathing, a silent witness to what looked to my eyes like an act of criminal desperation. His shoulders were hunched forward, the muscles in his hand and forearm tense, straining, as if to rid himself as quickly as possible of something he was not supposed to have.

A strand of milky liquid shot from his fist. He slumped back on his heels and watched the river carry it away. Then he wiped his face with his shoulder, zipped up his jeans and went back to work.

Molly was surprisingly uninquisitive when I gave her a halting version of the story a couple of days later. But I saw the cunning slant of her eyes and knew she'd acquired something she considered valuable.

She began to follow him around, asking questions:

"Why are you putting the geraniums back here with the roses?" We were hanging around outside the greenhouse, hoping Mr. Pax would offer us some ice cream or a soda. "Wouldn't they look better around the entrance?"

Lyle's expression was placid. "Dad told me to."

"Do you always do what your dad says?"

"Sure."

"Really? *Always?*"

"Sure." He smiled.

"But you're grown, you don't have to follow orders, do you?"

Lyle didn't answer. His mouth twitched as he thought this through, sensing a trap.

"Sometimes you do what you want." Molly's voice dropped almost to a whisper. "Don't you, Lyle?"

"Sometimes."

"By the river, sometimes. Am I right?"

He picked up a bag of mulch, tossed it over his shoulder and hurried back into the building.

Molly stood looking after him. Then she turned to me with an expression I couldn't fathom.

"Why did you tell me about that?"

I was startled. "I don't know. It freaked me out, I guess."

She gave me that same wily glance and went away.

We never spoke about it in the days after that. Molly didn't seem to want to play, so I went without her to the orchard. Sometimes I saw her with Lyle, laughing, helping him carry the little flats of seedlings. She'd look up at me and grin, one finger tracing a circle next to her ear, and she'd whistle like a cuckoo when he was out of earshot.

I asked Molly why she wouldn't leave him alone.

"Why should I?" she said. "I'm the kid. He can leave if he doesn't want to talk to me."

"Well, he can't really. He works here."

"His dad owns the place, he can throw me out."

"Yeah, but you know he's not responsible—"

"*I'm* not responsible." Her voice rose and broke over the words. She slapped her chest with both hands. "*I'm* the kid."

He is, too, I wanted to say. But Molly's pale eyes had brimmed with tears and I was too surprised by this to speak.

I heard them nearby the day before the incident. From

my seat in the cool damp soil behind the ornamental maples, I watched the two of them at the mouth of the tunnel of trees and I listened to their conversation. Lyle had a pair of pruning shears in his hand, and Molly an oily sack full of her treasures. She opened this and they bent their heads to look inside.

As they talked, I wondered about Lyle, what his life was like, what he thought about. What might a thirty-year-old man with the mind of a child have on the walls of his room? Where would he go when he wasn't with his family? I couldn't picture it; Lyle clung to the place, he never talked about anything but the nursery.

"I collect things," Molly said, reaching into the bag. "Look, this is from yesterday."

She placed a small object in Lyle's muddy hand.

"What is it?" he said.

"A kaleidoscope. You hold it up to the light and look through, and see, this part twists...."

Lyle set down his shears and held up the cardboard kaleidoscope. The plastic beads inside clattered softly as he turned it.

"Look-it there," he said. "Flowers!"

Molly smiled and slid closer to him. She was holding something up to her face, the magnifying glass, which made her eye seem huge and monstrous.

It was nasty of Molly to tease him, but she was like that. She didn't care about hurting someone's feelings, even if the person she was teasing had been kind to her. And with as much torment as Molly took from the kids at the Center—goat-face, they called her, and whitehead and freak—it was easy to understand her glee at being on the other side. Someone else was getting the jab. It moved her up a rung.

When Lyle saw the magnifying glass, he let out a frightened shriek like a bird call.

Molly laughed. "You should see your face. Oh, you should see your face."

He began to tremble. A long sound came up from his throat, *ah ah ah,* and a dark spot spread like ink down the front of his jeans. He dropped the kaleidoscope and stumbled away with his arms crossed in front of him, down the row of saplings toward the house. As his voice trailed away, I crept out from my hiding place.

Molly shook her head, wiping tears of laughter from her eyes. "Did you see his face?"

"He peed himself," I said reproachfully.

"Hey, man," said Molly, who had once been made to sleep in a foster's garage after throwing up on the bedroom carpet. "Things are tough all over."

The next day I was angry at Molly.

She had stolen from me. I had been given a strand of shiny beads, and when it came up missing I went straight to Molly and found it hidden at the bottom of her bag.

I confronted her with the beads, dangling them in front of her nose.

"These are mine," I said, stung at the betrayal. "You stole them."

She was sullen and unapologetic.

"There's no place to hide *anything* here," she said.

It was because of me that Molly went to Lyle Pax to ask

him to hide her things. It was because of me, because I threatened to tell her secret.

There's nothing worse one person can do to another.

Some things you don't need to see. Some things you know.

Molly went alone to the nursery that day with her crumpled bag of treasures. All the small pathetic objects jostling around, a collection that anyone would glance at and toss in the nearest garbage can. But she left the Center and went to see Lyle Pax, to ask if he would hide them for her.

She didn't realize how afraid he still was, or how unstable.

She walked up the shoulder of the road, pebbles pressing up through the soles of her shoes, the bag rattling gently beside her. She entered at the wooden gate, silently moving up and down the rows of trees.

She didn't understand how gnomelike she would appear. How strange with her bulbous head and crooked smile, that rabbity pink light in her eyes.

When she laid her hand on his arm, she thought she was meeting a friend.

From my room with the window open to the balmy day, where I sat with a book across my lap, I heard a high-pitched cry. It began as a sustained whistling note, then broke and deepened to a frantic, throaty wail like something from an animal. The kind of noise you don't realize that particular animal could ever make.

It took me several seconds to realize what I was hearing.

Screaming. And underneath, a deeper male voice: *ah ah ah.*

Some things you see without witnessing.

When I close my eyes, I see a thin man at the end of a

tunnel of trees, a spade like a dagger in his hand. And Molly sobbing on the ground beside him, two red pools where her eyes used to be.

When I get home from Jack's house, I set down my purse and head straight for the closet. I take my box down from the shelf and carry it to the living room, set it down and arrange my treasures in a row along the edge of the twill ottoman: a picture of me with my mother and Nana, happy and whole, sitting together on a driftwood log with our feet in the sand and our hair blown by the sea breeze into an intertwined mass of black, blond and auburn; an Arbus photograph clipped from a magazine, of twin girls with pale braids—on one twin, I had colored in the braids with a pencil, and on the other I had blacked out the eyes; my birth certificate and my mother's death certificate, folded together; the brooch Nana used to wear, an onyx raven with a bizarre crook in its wing and a bloodred ruby for an eye; a ticket stub from *Les Miserables;* a small plastic pack of razors that can be ejected one by one like the candy in a Pez dispenser; an Indian-girl key chain made of beads that my mother bought at a Seattle street fair, because she said it looked like me; and a page of handwritten dialogue from act three of *Othello:*

She did deceive her father, marrying you;
And when she seem'd to shake and fear your looks
She loved them most.

Slowly I repack the box. I fold the scarf Jack tied over my eyes and place it on top, shut the box, give the wood a quick polish with a bit of lemon oil and place it at the far end of the shelf behind a stack of clothes.

It's an inadequate hiding place, but I can't think of a better one.

The box is just too big.

CHAPTER TWELVE

One of the cuts on my foot is infected, swollen and angry red, and it won't heal. I've gone too deep; it happens sometimes. I drive to the quick-care clinic and am seen by a tall gray-haired physician with an aquiline nose and an unexpected West Virginia drawl. He unwraps my foot and raises his eyebrows.

"What happened here?" he says.

"I stepped in some glass on the beach." My face is open wide.

He cleans it with a piece of gauze and I avoid his eye, knowing he sees the older scars, the telltale crazy-quilt of white and pink and angry red.

As he wraps it, he says, "You want to talk about this?"

"About how to dress a cut? Absolutely."

He sighs. But the clinic is busy and I am a stranger to him. He gives me a supply of gauze, bandages and ointment, and tells me to wait.

I put on my boot and wrap myself more closely with my sweater, rocking back and forth to keep warm. The exam room is covered with laminated posters of the female reproductive system and flyers urging patients to have their flu shots and pay their bills. The counter is chipped around the edges, lined with jars of paper-wrapped swabs and instruments, everything scrubbed clean and reeking of disinfectant.

One of the cupboard doors is ajar, and inside I see a rag doll on the shelf, peering out with one button eye.

Carla had a doll like that. Black yarn hair and a green dress sewn onto her muslin skin. You couldn't move that dress, it stayed right where it was on the doll's flat chest, and under the skirt was a pair of green panties that seemed to be part of the doll, ensuring her everlasting chastity. An odd choice, given the circumstances.

Carla sat next to me on the sofa at her house and pressed the doll into my hands.

You don't have to say, you can point and show me where…if you were touched, Alice… You can talk to me… I'm here to help, I'm on your side…

As if she hadn't sent me to that latest un-home in the first place. As if she hadn't urged me to stay when things became uneasy and assured me that I would learn what it was like to be in a *normal* house, with a *normal* family—decent people who only wanted what was best for me.

As if her rescue had not come months too late.

I just sat there with the doll in my hands, refusing to close my fingers. The green dress was an insult, a way of telling me, as if I didn't know it already, that something unsayable had occurred.

But I was thirteen years old. I knew better than to confess to something that had not been proven.

It was the doll that convinced me to keep my secrets. The doll, and something else. Some venomous snake of shame and fear that had come upon me in the night had risen up inside me and bitten so deep and so hard that I remain to this day anesthetized by its poison.

Alice, close your eyes. Be quiet now, shh....

I get down from the exam table, shove the doll to the back of the shelf and close the cupboard door.

The doctor returns a few minutes later with two pieces of paper: a prescription for antibiotics and a referral to a mental health clinic.

"Think about it," he says.

"Think about what?" I say, because I'm embarrassed and my foot hurts more than I want, and because I can see he's trying to be kind when all I need from him is a fucking prescription.

He gives me a tired look and I am instantly ashamed. He tells me a nurse will be in to give me a tetanus shot. At the doorway, he pauses.

"Top of the thigh is better," he says.

And he smiles—a real smile—which draws a reluctant one from me.

"You're a good man, Charlie Brown," I say as he leaves.

Jack wants to talk about the men I know. He hasn't forgotten my dare.

"I don't know anyone," I tell him.

"Bullshit. Who turns you on? A stranger, you know what I mean."

We are in bed. He's stroking me idly from neck to belly. Sometimes he stops with his hand over my breast, a perfect fit.

"No one. I'm done with that, anyway."

"No, you're not. We're going to do it together. It'll be a trip."

"I don't want—"

He raises himself up on one elbow and looks at me—not at my face but at my breast in his hand. His pupils are wide and dark.

"Tomorrow we're going shopping."

We end up at a street market in Seattle. It's Saturday and the place is packed. We wander around with skewers of chicken satay and cups of peanut sauce, share some warm cinnamon almonds from a paper cone. Jack tosses them in the air and catches them in his mouth; he never misses. He buys me a silver ring made of two pieces that fit together like a puzzle. When I pull the pieces apart, they won't align properly, but Jack sorts them out with a twitch of his fingers and puts the ring on my thumb.

I am beginning to relax and forget why we're here, when Jack takes me by the arm and says, "I need a new belt."

He steers me to a wooden display stand, with three tables in the shape of a horseshoe and a rack of belts that hangs down like a curtain from the pegs overhead. On the other side of the table, the vendor in his canvas apron is helping an old lady choose a leather purse. I browse through the selection, picking things up and setting them down. All handcrafted items, notebooks and wallets and cell phone cases, and tough little coin purses that open with a zipper.

"Perfect," Jack says. He's found a belt, black and supple, with a plain brass buckle. He loops it around and around his hand.

The vendor has left the other customer, still dithering over her purchase. He's about thirty, tall and pale, with a straggling beard and a strange, shapeless hat like an empty beanbag. The top button of his shirt is open and a few threads of brown hair reach up to the hollow of his throat.

"Good choice," he says.

He's talking to Jack but looking at me, and I am unsure whether he's referring to the belt or the journal I'm holding. I run a hand over the embossed cover, murmuring something about the softness of the leather. He shifts his attention to Jack, and I flip through handmade pages, trying to decide whether to spring for the purchase. Finally I set it down and wander a few steps along the display, bored for the moment and ready to move on.

"Nice work," Jack says. "Are you the craftsman?"

"One of them."

"Must be tough to make a living these days."

The man shrugs, grinning. "Wanna help me out?"

"I think so," Jack says, unwinding the belt from his hand. "I just want to try this on first."

"Yeah, go for it."

But Jack is looking at me, and for a second I am disoriented. There is an odd shift, as of a pause in the middle of a play, with the audience uncertain whether to applaud or wait for more. He walks a few steps to where I am standing.

"Put out your hands," he says.

His voice reverberates in the warm summer air. There is an intimacy in his tone, in the way he's turned his focus to me. I glance at the leather man and know from his face that Jack has given our secret away. Here in plain view, Jack wants me to show myself and what I am to this stranger, to anyone else who happens by. He wants to expose me.

Jack is waiting, the belt stretched between his hands.

I start to turn away, as if I haven't heard. As if I don't understand what he wants.

"Alice," he says. "Give me your hands."

It's an adult voice, like he's talking to a recalcitrant child. And suddenly I am sliding from this happy bustling scene where people are laughing and items around us are being bought and sold, from this shining ordinary day to a dimly lit room at the end of the hall, where I am accountable to no one but Jack.

I hold out my hands.

Jack winds the belt three times around my wrists. He threads the end into the buckle and slowly pulls it tight.

The edge of the leather is sharp; it's digging into my skin. I imagine myself as he wants to see me, bound and quiet on his bed, slowly opened and held that way, all the decisions and the power in his hands. With the image comes a second sensation, a surprised rush of excitement that drains all the strength from my legs. I take a half step toward Jack, stumbling, blinking the water from my eyes.

Jack lifts my hands with the tail of the belt as if weighing them. Then he releases the buckle, unwinds the belt, runs his fingers over the red marks crisscrossing my wrists.

The man behind the curtain of belts doesn't say a word. His body is rigid, frozen, but a deep red flush swarms up his neck and he's looking at Jack like he's found the new messiah.

"This *is* a good choice," Jack says, watching me.

Four days later, Jack says we've got a date. His face is alight but he is calm, dressed in a black T-shirt, jeans and sneakers. He's freshly shaven and his mouth tastes like peppermint.

"You'll need a pair of gloves," he says.

★ ★ ★

We've crossed the Sound and pull up now in front of what looks to be a converted warehouse. The brick front bears the last peeling traces of the original sign: Holsum Bread Co. Below, a modern font in cerulean neon: HOLSUM LOFTS.

"Noah will be out tonight," Jack says.

"Noah?"

He hooks a thumb under his leather belt to remind me, and I feel an echo of heat between my legs, and a single, dense pulse.

"How do you know he's not coming back? He could—"

"He's got a hot date. And from the sounds of it, he'll either be occupied with her or propped up with his friends at the back of a bar. Either way, he won't be home for hours."

I'm mystified. "How do you know all that?"

"Eavesdropping. I had no idea the amount of information people give away when they think no one's listening. Kind of fascinating."

He opens the driver's side door.

"Come on, baby. This is your dare."

The road is quiet and empty, lined with dark-windowed cars that crouch in the damp night like fat, shiny beetles. My heartbeat thuds in my ears; my skin is alive, coursing with electricity. Fear has lightened me. I can hardly feel my feet touching the ground.

In the center of the building is a pair of stripped metal doors. Jack opens one for me and I step inside. We are in a small vestibule, where several bikes are piled together as though one of them fell over and took the others with it. I peer up the aluminum staircase and hear two or three heavy footsteps, the opening and closing of a door.

Jack is watching me. He grins, makes a spooky face with his eyebrows raised. I have to laugh as he leads the way up the narrow aluminum stairs.

The bread factory has been divided into three stories. At each landing, a hallway stretches the length of the building, suspended by chains and steel beams. We go all the way to the top, our footsteps echoing against the concrete walls. Jack turns right at the walkway of corrugated metal. I am right behind him, staring through the hexagonal holes to the floors below, thinking what a stupid design this is; anyone below could see right up my skirt. He stops in front of a blue door marked 3B, reaches up to the light fixture, a circular lamp on a long metal cable that drops from a steel beam. He pats around and comes up with a key.

"People are so unoriginal," he says, and starts to put the key in the lock.

I stop him. "Jesus. Knock first, will you?"

"Good manners for breaking and entering?"

"Common sense."

I knock instead, hoping we will hear footsteps from inside and see the leather man's face appear at the door. But there is nothing. No sound at all. When I raise my fist to knock again, Jack shoulders me out of the way and puts the key in the lock. He opens the door and we step into a stranger's house.

The apartment is smaller than I expected. It's a studio loft, with a glazed cement floor and a high ceiling. The facing wall is of worn brick, the same as the outside of the building, with two small windows covered inadequately by a make-shift curtain made of sheets. The other walls are covered with cheap posters of foreign cities in plastic frames, and in the corner is a small kitchenette adorned with a desiccated spider plant and a plate covered with crumbs.

The air is filled with the scent of leather—and leather is everywhere. Bits and pieces, scraps of half-formed bags and book covers and belts without buckles. Every surface is covered with this kind of debris, and with small, sharp utility knives, hole punches and awls of varying sizes. Buckles, clasps, buttons and snaps. The tools of the leather man's trade are everywhere.

Jack moves first and I follow, drawing deep full breaths. I circle the coffee table and pick up a small pouch made of fine kidskin; it will be a change purse, maybe, or something to carry jewelry. It feels like a warm rodent in my hand.

"Talented guy," Jack says. He's thumbing through a sketch pad—not one of the expensive ones the leather man is selling, but the cheap kind like they used to give us at school, of thin gray paper that disintegrates when you try to erase something.

I move to Jack's side, and see that the pages are filled with delicate sketches and notes for his work. Purses, mainly, and elegant satchels with attractive shaded folds in the center. I don't remember seeing any of these items at the booth. They are his plans, the designs he's not yet executed.

Jack puts the pad back and I move to the window and part the curtains. There is nothing to see. The apartment faces the vast, blank side of another warehouse. Now I understand why the leather man is not worried about his privacy.

Jack laughs softly behind me. He's at the entertainment center.

"An ass man," he says, flipping over the DVD in his hands to see the back.

"Can we go? If he comes back…"

Jack replaces the DVD and looks at me.

As at the leather man's cart, I am aware of a sliding sensation, a frightening sense of moving from one place to another without taking a step.

"Come here," he says. And I do, as though he's pulling me on a string, a step at a time, until I am in front of him. Though we're alone, I feel the leather man in the room, watching, as if we are inside his mind by being in his home. We're the voyeurs, Jack and I, but that's not the way it feels.

Jack tugs off my cap. At his request, I'm wearing the same outfit I had on the other day at the market: denim miniskirt, ankle-high tennis shoes, a T-shirt screen printed In-N-Out. He pulls me forward with one hand at the back of my head and I lift my face to him, but though my lips are parted he does not kiss them. He slides his hand to the top of my head and presses straight down. With his other hand, he's unzipping his jeans.

"Jack," I whisper, because I don't know another way to protest.

"Do it," he says.

"Let's go, we can do this at home. Or—"

"Right now."

He puts his hand on my shoulder and pushes until I sink to my knees. He's got his dick in his fist and gives himself a couple of firm strokes. I begin to tremble, my jaws locked together. He gathers a handful of my hair.

"Open your mouth."

I obey out of submission more than desire. The scent of unfamiliarity is too strong here, and the knowledge of what we're doing is too great to overcome; I can't just blow my boyfriend in another man's apartment. Jack seems to sense this and it pisses him off. He pulls me forward and presses into my throat. It's too hard, too soon. I begin to gag and pull away.

He hauls me up and pushes me ahead of him to the bed. He's behind me, my hair still wrapped around his hand. I hear the hiss of the leather man's belt, sliding through Jack's belt loops.

"Take these off," he says, tugging at my underwear. I do what he says, though he has pulled me against him so tightly that I can't bend down. I wriggle them to my knees and let them fall to the floor. His cock is rigid and warm, pressed upright at the small of my back.

"You want to be quiet, now." He reaches behind me and pulls up my skirt. "Bend over."

And I do, falling forward as he releases me, my hands flat against the mattress. With one foot, he kicks mine apart, spreads his hand over the small of my back to hold me in place.

The belt lands with a sharp bite across my ass. I realize at once that this is not like any of the slaps or pinches he's given me before. He wants it to hurt; he's using everything he has. The leather tears at my skin like the teeth of an animal; the two halves of the belt fall as one with the snap of a whip.

A gust of air precedes the next blow, a whisper of apology over the sting. I jump, breathless with the pain, but don't make a sound.

I don't make a sound the whole time. I count, waiting, staring down at the leather man's rumpled sheets. Each strike is like a step from land into water, from gravity to buoyancy. My body shifts from a stiff and unwilling resistance to a state of liquid, almost orgasmic obedience, and my mind becomes sluggish with the narcotic effect of the pain. The burn is so intense that it smears my consciousness into a low-frequency buzz. I stop flinching, close my eyes and wait.

At number twenty-nine, he stops and runs his palm over my burning skin, tracing the ridged welts with his fingertips. My arms are trembling. A drop of fluid trickles down my thigh, and I can feel each downy hair in its path.

"You think you deserve that? Look where you are."

He tosses the belt down next to me. I hear the heavy flop of his jeans hitting the floor. I drop to my elbows, my nose enfolded in the leather man's sheets.

"Yes." My voice sounds thick, drowsy.

"Mmm-hmm," he says. "I think so, too."

My legs are numb with exhaustion and relief, but I tilt my hips for him, offer my whipped ass like a prize. I feel connected to him, to both of them, to some primal part of myself I don't understand, to the part of me that accepts and endures and seeks balance on the edge of a straight razor. The pain absolves me. Whatever I have done or will do is being made right, and for the moment I can say, *It's out of my hands.*

I sprawl over the leather man's bed, my hands straight out to my sides, my cheek pressed to the mattress. Jack push-pulls me down the length of his cock, and groans when he hears me finally cry out.

"That's right," he says.

He slips a hand between my legs, circling, slapping at my clitoris.

My body has gone slack, my strength of will swept away by the ineluctable rightness of being taken this way, with the scent of the leather man filling my mind. Softened by my lover, fucked in another man's bed. The beating has made me pliant and acquiescent, delivered me to a place I never suspected I would want to see. Jack rides me faster and harder, charging down his own dark road—but I've become unbreakably soft, melting around him, until at the liquid-hot center of my body, my pleasure overflows. Heat floods my skin, bursts inside me like a balloon full of warm oil, pours into my limbs and makes them heavy, clumsy with the weight of my climax.

I don't make a sound.

"Oh, good girl," Jack says.

He clasps a handful of my hair and cranks his hips until there is nothing left of him to take. He comes then, with a deep grunt and a hard shudder that shifts the bed under my cheek. The legs scrape along the concrete with a small, metallic shriek.

He collapses on top of me, his warm, wide chest covering my back. His heartbeat hammers against my shoulder blade, rolling like a timpani, then gradually slowing as he softens inside me.

My arms are still outstretched. Under the pillow, my fingers encounter something hard and heavy and cold. I don't need to see it to know what I've found.

Before we leave, Jack says he has something to show me. He pulls me into the bathroom and flips on the light. My face is pale, my eyes huge and dark. He turns me gently by the shoulders to face him, kisses me lightly on the mouth. He slaps me, one solid crack, then moves behind me so we can watch as the outline of his fingers blooms on my cheek.

I trace the shape with my thumb.

I am a warrior. Or a child, misbehaving.

The night sky is growing pale as Jack guides the truck onto the ferry for the return trip home. My denim skirt feels rough against my welted skin. I rest my cheek against the cool glass window and close my eyes. The rocking motion soothes me.

Jack wanted me to leave my underwear behind, in the leather man's bed. But though I pretended to, after he turned away I wadded them up and shoved them into my pocket. If the leather man does come home with his date, I don't want to fuck it up for them. So we left the apartment as we'd found it; the only thing we took away was a scrap of kidskin. I lay it in my palm and my palm in my lap, and caress the buttery surface with my thumb, thinking of the gun under the leather man's pillow.

I had no place to hide it tonight, no purse or satchel or heavy coat. Tomorrow while Jack's at work, I'll go back to the Holsum Lofts, upstairs to apartment 3B. I'll be in and out of there in fifteen seconds.

"Alice."

I open my eyes. Jack lays his hand over the top of the steering wheel and points at the car in front of us and one row to the right. The passenger is climbing into the driver's side. I can't see her well in the darkness, but from the way she's turned around, backward in the reclined seat, it's clear that the two occupants of the car are having sex. Her hand is clutching the headrest of the passenger's seat, and she begins to move, a slow, rhythmic shadow within the shadows. Her bare breast dips in and out of the light as though she's swimming, up and down, her throat arched. The windows gradually cloud over and her other hand appears, pressed flat to the glass like a starfish in the surf.

When the ferry arrives with a bump at Vashon Island,

she climbs off and returns to her seat. For a second our eyes meet and there is exchange, an understanding between us.

Then she looks away.

I feel Jack next to me, his eyes on my face.

CHAPTER THIRTEEN

The break-in is a turning point. We both understand now that we are willing to venture into dangerous territory. And with the realization comes a growing division between who we are in daily life and the alchemical reaction of us, together.

Writing has never come more easily. I cover every horizontal surface with words, many of which are hot, usable, the fine-tuned distillation of what I learn from Jack. Previous struggles with scenes and character are magically resolved.

The days when he is gone, the night when he's asleep, I exist in a fugue state, though on the surface nothing has changed. I have coffee at the Beanery and chat with Midge. I send my drafts to Gus Shiroff and accept his suggestions for revision with none of my usual fury and fight. I am easy, languid, drifting around Vashon, noting the crumbling cement where the sidewalk ends, the spiked blades of grass bejeweled with dew, the flattened hair of the passersby and their pale, scrubbed faces, bland smiles, rows of teeth. I am only resting, taking a breather. Waiting for Jack.

When we're together, the two halves of me slide into

focus like the image inside a camera lens. Everything is sharp, defined. Everything is fire or liquid pleasure: the crack of his hand or the deep thump of his dick at my cervix; his fingers tangled in my hair; the muscles in my neck and chest stretching as my arms are bound behind my back; the delicious pull of his belts around my ankles, spreading me apart. I see myself in a series of still images that slither through my mind as I move through the innocent town.

Now when I step out of the bath and wipe away the foam that clings to my nipples and the curve of my hip, I uncover small bruises, ridged welts. I collect them, covet them like badges. I feel a sense of loss when they heal and disappear.

Tonight I'm back at the park, watching the gray house across the street. The lamplights in the windows beguile me. I want to see the inside and find out whether the girls are there, whether they're okay, what they're doing.

The homes in this neighborhood are fairly close together, but I walk up the driveway in a straightforward way; if anyone sees me, they'll assume I've been invited. As I near the front door, I turn and continue around the side of the house and silently through the gate to the backyard.

A window is open at the back of the house. I hear the girls inside, and crouch under the window with my knees pressed to my chest, listening.

Big sister's voice is exasperated.

"Put your arm through, Sarah," she says.

"Don't like these jammies." The smaller voice is muffled.

"They're your favorite."

"They too little," Sarah says with the beginning of a whine in her voice.

Big sister must hear it, too. A small scuffle ensues.

"Let's be quick," she says. "Mommy's putting *Rugrats* on. Do you want to watch it with me?"

"Chucky!"

I smile and lean my head back against the house. I used to watch that show with my mother, curled up on the couch in the living room of Nana's trailer. Nana had the world's tiniest TV, but the living room itself was so small that you were close enough to see the screen no matter where you sat. And my mom loved TV. She kept it turned on all the time, listening to the news or game shows or documentaries about the space program. She said TV kept her smart.

"Imagine," she would say. "When you see a star, you're seeing the way it looked billions of years ago. Think how far away a star would have to be, if it takes a billion years for the light to reach us." And together we would scan the night sky for the faintest star. She said it made her feel bigger to imagine that our bodies are made of stardust, that every molecule is ancient and comes from someplace far away.

"We're part of it all," she'd say, looking up.

About six months after Nana died, I came home from school and found the living room full of boxes. My mother was stacking the dishes between sheets of newspaper, her hair tied back in an old bandanna.

"We're moving out," she said.

"What?" My stomach dropped. She had told me about the move the week before, but many of my mother's promises and predictions failed to materialize. I had hoped this was another possibility that wouldn't come to pass.

"Ray's house."

"What, now?"

"Yeah. I can't afford the payments here. We need to get out before we're kicked out. We're going to Ray's."

"But we don't even know him."

She tucked back a strand of hair and wiped her forehead. The newspaper ink left streaks like charcoal across her skin, and her breath was tight and dry in her throat. She wouldn't look at me. She sat down in Nana's chair and puffed her inhaler, shook it, tossed it on the floor and started rummaging in her purse. Her hands were shaking.

I took the purse, found a fresh inhaler in the corner at the bottom and handed it to her.

"*You* don't know him," she said between puffs. "I've been dating him for five months."

I felt my throat close up. I looked around the room, at the shabby green carpet, the cracked linoleum counters, the beaded curtain in the doorway that I used to drape across my head to pretend I was an Egyptian princess. Through the beads I could see Nana's bed, covered with stacks of folded clothes, and through another door, my bed, covered with the lavender blanket she'd bought me years ago. My face filled with tears, burning my eyes and nose, so that the boxes seemed to be reflections shimmering on the surface of a pond.

My mother resumed her packing with uncharacteristic efficiency—folding clothes, filling boxes, loading them into Ray's pickup truck. When she'd finished, she loaded me in, too, and we left. Just like that. I turned to look back and saw Nana's forlorn yellow trailer swallowed up by the pines, disappearing around a bend in the road.

And we came here, to the gray house on Cooper Street.

The backyard looks different than when I lived here with my mother. Someone has been making an effort. The junk has been cleared away, and there's a line of potted plants from the nursery, still in their black plastic pots. Some are already in the ground, and there are two shovels propped against the fence, as though the work is still in progress. A young tree has been planted in the center of the yard, its limbs reaching up to the pale gray sky.

I sink to the ground, my back to the house, leaves prickling my right cheek.

If I close my eyes, I can almost hear my mother's voice. I was here, in this very spot, the night she died. Same shrubs, same wall at my back. She was angry at Ray. Her voice floated out like cigarette ash, weightless and dry, scattering in the air.

"All you ever want…spend half your time stoned…I thought…I thought…we could be…"

And Ray's voice. Deeper, irritated, every word clear: "This is *my* house. You're under *my* roof—and your kid, too. You're not gonna tell me what I can and can't do in *my* house."

"…always need to remind me…I thought…"

"I don't give a shit what you thought. I made it clear. So you can think what you want, I don't give a fuck."

My mother, sobbing, her voice rising an octave: "You wish I was dead!"

"You know what? You're right, you crazy bitch."

There was a loud thump, something heavy hitting an inside wall. Glass breaking. A door slammed at the other end of the house.

I crept in through the back door, into my room, into bed. And listened to my mother cry.

No one is crying now, no one's fighting. The girls leave the room and I move farther along the back wall, past the back door to the last window before the corner, the master bedroom window. It's covered with a curtain, but when I press my face to the glass, I can see a bit of the bedroom through a chink in the middle. My nose is level to the dresser and I'm seeing the back side of it. Behind the lamp and a ceramic basket is a small dish with a lump of white powder and a glass pipe.

From the window at the other end of the house comes the cartoon theme song and the familiar voices of the *Rugrats* characters:

"Tommy, I got a problem...."

Later I drive to the Roadhouse Bar and Grill, where Ray used to work. Someone's left a couple of plastic chairs by the back door, next to an old coffee can full of cigarette butts and rainwater. Beyond that is a wide alley and a parking lot, and a row of weed-skirted warehouses striped with rust. Several men have come and gone over the past hour since I got here. I stare straight ahead and don't acknowledge them. I keep smoking, waiting.

An oily breeze slides through the alley, and from the parking lot I hear a female voice rise over the rumble of a motorcycle engine: *Come on back, honey, come on back inside.* A chill sweeps up my body. I shiver and hug myself through my coat.

The back door opens. A small, dark-haired man steps outside, wearing a grease-stained apron with the Roadhouse logo on the front. With him comes a draft of warm air, carrying the stench of stale grease and smoke and the earthy scent of fried potatoes. The man sees me and grins.

"Jenny," he says, arms open, head tilted. "Hey, baby, where you been?"

I stand and embrace him, let him kiss my cheeks. His are soft, sticky, like a child's.

"Here and there. Are you off work?"

"I look like I'm off?" He gestures down at his apron. "Some of us got to punch a clock."

"Shit, that's too bad," I say as if this is news to me. I remember Amado's schedule well, and have timed my visit accordingly. "I've got a little smoke, thought you could help me burn it."

He clucks his tongue. "Don't need to be off the clock for that. I got fifteen minutes—you can get me right for the rest of my shift."

We go across the lot to my car, push the seats back and light up the joint. He turns toward me, propping his arm on the seat and his head on his fist, his brown skin tinged blue from the light of my dashboard radio. The strands of his hair pick up the color like optical fibers, straight and flat across his brow. After spending so much time around Jack, Amado's body seems formless, his fingers smooth as a young girl's. But I know from past experience that Amado's appetites are as insistent as any man's, and I see from the way he's eyeing me that he hasn't given up the dream.

"So how've you been?" I ask. "Still playing games?"

He launches predictably into a long, involved tale about his online gaming life. I have no idea what he's talking about and I'm too keyed up to keep track of the complicated rules and anonymous opponents, but it doesn't matter. I listen, keep him smoking, make sympathetic noises. Amado is a puppy, a forty-year-old puppy who lives for his mother and the occasional scratch behind the ear.

I met him more than a year ago when I first followed Ray to the Roadhouse. I feigned a shy and distant romantic interest in Ray, and to keep me from losing my heart, Amado revealed all the dirt he could find on his coworker.

He told me about Ray's drug habits, his skirt-chasing, the sleazy way he'd managed to get Jack Calabrese thrown in prison. It was Amado's gossip that got me thinking hard about Jack.

"So," I say as we get down to the roach, "do you happen to know where I can find Ray?"

He blinks at me. His eyes are glazed, and filled with sudden disappointment. He leans his head against the headrest, and something in the gesture reminds me of my mother.

"You still hung up on that dude, *nena?*"

I smile and shake my head. "He has something for me."

Amado groans. "You, too? Every chick I know is a crack head now."

"Yeah, well. Where's he working now, A?"

He sighs, gazing at me across the small space between us. The need in his eyes is palpable, transparent, as he means it to be. But behind that is something vulnerable. I think of the men Jack described in prison, always dreaming about pussy. Jerking off alone every night, remembering how it felt to be next to a woman. Inside her. Watching her come. *You don't know, oh, you don't even know....*

I take Amado's hand in mine and lay it upturned on my knee. There is a burn mark on his wrist and another on the side of his thumb. I stroke his palm, trace the creases and lines. His fingers flatten and open out, his breath accelerates. I raise his hand to my mouth, press a kiss into his palm, slide his whole hand inside the neckline of my shirt, under my bra.

He sighs out a stream of Spanish words. His fingers curve around my breast, and my nipple stiffens against his palm. He strokes the slope of my breast with his thumb, reaches lower to nestle the side of his hand against my ribs. His gaze moves up to mine.

"We all need something," I tell him.

I can't give him more than this. He will go home to his mother's apartment after a night of grease burns and barked orders and he'll think of my breast in his hand, the texture of my skin. He'll take his dick in his fist and stroke and move and come, thinking of me—of how much more he wanted that I wouldn't give him, maybe, but it could be that I'm the trigger for him to get the hell out in the world, meet a woman, have a life beyond the one he's built inside the playground of his internet games.

I hope so. I've always liked Amado.

The next morning, I drive to the range with the leather man's gun in my purse.

My palms are sweaty. I rub them on my thighs and walk up to the wooden huts, where two groups of men are shooting. One group is older, three guys in plaid I take to be hunters practicing for the season, maybe trying out some new equipment. They each carry a rifle. The two younger men at the hut to the right are shooting handguns.

I sit on the hood of my Chevy, watching the way the young men load their revolvers and get them ready to fire. I notice how they hold the guns. Arms straight, one hand cupped around the butt, one finger curled around the trigger. A slow squeeze, a loud bang that makes me jump.

The report is much louder than I expected. A dangerous whiplash of sound. I imagine the bullet hurtling through space, too fast to see, ripping into flesh with a small explosion of blood or brain matter. The thought of it nauseates me. My mouth waters and I swallow hard to clear it. I need to try.

I go to the end of the row, into the last shack, and set my gun on the wooden shelf. I wipe my clammy palms again, and fumble in my pocket for a bullet. After a moment, I figure out how to open the cylinder, slide the bullet inside the chamber, close it and disengage the safety. I cock the hammer.

My hands tremble as I raise the gun and point it at the tree stump with a crude plywood target nailed to the center. A wave of nausea rises in me. I fight it back, hold my breath and pull the trigger. The gun kicks in my hands. For a moment I can almost see the blood—the soft, fragile, human insides. The thick wet splatter, lumped with tissue and shards of bone.

My mouth fills again with hot water, and this time there is no swallowing it back. I stagger around the wall of the shack and vomit into the soft green grass at the edge of the forest. Gagging, upended, my stomach heaves again and again, until there is nothing left inside me.

The men down the way are concerned, calling, "Hey, are you okay?" But I can't answer. I'm too ashamed. This was my last hope and I can't do it, no matter how much it needs to be done, no matter that it's my responsibility. I think of the little girls and the gray house and my mother and everything Nana taught me, and still it's not enough. I can't do this.

I lean my head on the rough wooden siding and close my eyes.

Jack…

When my stomach settles, I put the revolver in my purse and drive to Jensen Point. It's a cloudless day and the sand is dotted with children. I stand for a few minutes at the edge of the pines, watching a potbellied toddler collect shells in an old tin bucket. With each addition, he peers over the rim as if he can't believe the wealth he's accumulated. Finally the bucket becomes too heavy and he drops it. The shells spill out and he plops down next to them, sobbing, his cries like that of a strange young bird.

It's hard to believe Jack was once this small, that all grown men were babies at one time, then toddlers, and knobby-limbed boys on the playground, with outsized teeth and cowlicked hair. They used to cry, their cheeks ruddy and glazed with tears. I look at the toddler's sand-dusted roundness and try to reconcile it with Jack's gridded abdomen and the solid heft of his shoulders, the thick pad of muscle at the base of his thumb, the depth of his voice. That this little boy will someday be a grown man seems an alien concept today.

I adjust my canvas purse over my shoulder and stroll past the silvery driftwood to the piled-up outcropping at the far end of the beach, where low tide has bared the mollusk-encrusted rocks and left pools of flat, still water in the crevices. I wander among them, stopping to investigate a fat, four-armed starfish and a pair of crabs that face off like tiny duelists, thrusting and parrying, feinting and scurrying along the barnacles. I put a finger between them but the combatants ignore it, determined to continue the squabble.

I shake the droplets off my hand and watch them scatter across the surface of the tide pool. As the ripples melt together and smooth away, I see my face reflected, shimmering on the water—and over my shoulder, Jack's.

I flinch, my thoughts darting immediately to the gun in my purse, and almost fall into the water. Jack catches me around the elbow and helps me to my feet.

"Jesus." I turn to him, moving gingerly over the rocks. "You scared me."

He steadies me but does not apologize.

"What are you doing here?" My voice is too high and too fast. "Shouldn't you be at work?"

He backs up a step, takes a pack of cigarettes from the pocket of his dusty flannel shirt, taps one out and offers it to me. I shake my head.

"Why are you worried about where I should be?" he says. "Are you where you're supposed to be?"

The weight of my purse is dragging on my shoulder. I switch the strap to the other side, farther from him. My chest feels strangely hollow. The sea air sweeps into my lungs but doesn't seem to fill them.

He squints at me sideways as he lights the cigarette, cupping his hand around the flame. "You have something you want to tell me, Alice?"

His expression makes me uneasy. This is an odd place for either of us to be, alone in the middle of the day. Guilt makes me rise to the attack.

"No, Jack, I don't. How about you tell me why you followed me here?"

He smiles around his cigarette. "You really need me to spell it out?"

"You don't trust me."

"Sure I do. What's not to trust?"

I glance around at the innocent beach full of small children and pointedly back at him.

"Living a blameless life, aren't you, sweetheart," he says.

"Except when I follow you."

"Mmm, but who's following now?"

He drags on the cigarette, half smiling, gazing at me

down the line of his cheekbone. Clearly he knows or senses some deception. But I won't be trapped. If he knows something about where I've been today, he's going to have to say it out loud. I'm not going to hand him the information.

I brush past him and pick my way across the rocks, through the tangles of bone-gray driftwood, and retrace my steps across the beach. When I glance over my shoulder, I expect to see him close behind me, or watching from the rocks.

But he is gone.

CHAPTER FOURTEEN

I'm dreaming of Nana.

We're back in the trailer with the beaded curtains, but in my dream it looks more like my house or Jack's. I know it's Nana's house because she is at the stove, stirring a pot of soup. She turns to me and smiles. I'm on the other side of the kitchen counter, waiting for my bowl to be filled.

What kind of soup is it, Nana?

She smiles, a stranger's smile that frightens me. She dips her ladle into the pot and sets a bowl in front of me.

Floating in the broth is the hairless, grinning head of a dog, its lips pulled back over pale pink gums, its skin boiled and ragged, like a pig fetus in formaldehyde. Its eye is clouded and blue, rolling freakishly in the socket.

My stomach turns. I recoil in nausea and dread.

Eat your soup, Alice. It will make you strong.

But I recognize this dog.

It wasn't fit to live, Nana says. She has poisoned it and boiled it in a pot.

I can't eat it, Nana, the poison will kill me, too.

No, lovey, it will make you strong.

In the bowl, the dog's eye stares through the oil-smeared broth. And I know it's somehow alive—and can see me.

The eye blinks.

I run out the door and into the street, where I stop to look back. Nana's window frames are filled with spiderwebs instead of glass. Behind them, the house is burning. Nana is trapped inside. I see her face at the window, engulfed in flames.

I wake up screaming, clammy and nauseated, the sheet clinging like wet cobwebs to my skin.

Jack is there, awake but disoriented. He thinks at first there's an intruder in the house and reaches for the crowbar he keeps by the bed. I'm clawing at the sheet, my feet bicycling, kicking the covers away.

He pulls me into his arms. I try to push him away but he won't let go.

"Shh, it's just a bad dream. Shh…"

I turn and bury my face in his shoulder. He holds me that way until I've stopped shaking. Then we share a small bowl of weed and he settles me into the bed. He goes back to sleep, but I lie there listening to him breathe, watching the pine trees take shape against the brightening sky.

After he leaves for work, I scoot to his side of the bed and bury my nose in his pillow, thinking of the way he looked at me yesterday as we stood beside the tide pools, the easy suspicion, eyes narrow and mouth smiling. He took me out to dinner last night as if nothing had happened, but followed me into the ladies' room and locked the door behind him, lifted me to the counter and fucked me right there, with the faucets turned on and his lips at my ear.

"I'll always find you," he said.

Whether he meant it as a threat or a promise, I don't know.

Finally, I give up on sleep, get dressed and into my car and drive up-island, to the suburban neighborhood where Nana's trailer once stood. Now the land is covered with a cluster of pastel-colored houses with neatly trimmed lawns and squared-off boxwood. But the trailhead is still there. I park my car and start up the path, where as a child I used to walk looking down, seeking out snails and iridescent beetles on my way to the Red Ranger bicycle in the tree. Here in the forest, nothing has changed. The path turns and switches back under a canopy of moss-draped branches and spiked fingers of pine, where the scent of loam overwhelms the briny scent of the sea. I pass a grove of small trees and stop in front of the Vashon bike. Two young boys are looking up, circling the tree.

The bike is smaller than I remember and not as far off the ground. Someone has replaced the front wheel. The new one is the right size and shape, but too shiny. The bike is a patchwork now, a revisiting of the original injustice, an insistence on keeping the tragedy alive. I wonder how long it will take before the bike is vandalized again, and how long after that before someone reassembles it.

The boys are arguing about why the bike was left here.

"My dad says the kid went off to war and never came back," says the blond boy.

"That doesn't even make sense," says the boy in the cap. "It's a little kid's bike."

This is inarguable. The bike is small enough to be ridden by a five-year-old.

"Maybe he died," says the blond wistfully. "Maybe he got run over at the tracks, and now he haunts the bike."

There is a silence. Then one of them says, matter-of-fact:

"Or maybe he just forgot where he left it."

★ ★ ★

At noon, I pick up some deli sandwiches and go to Jack's work site.

He's on the roof when I arrive, silhouetted against the chalkboard sky, moving nimbly along the spine of the skeleton house that someone else designed, where someone else's dreams will live or die, where children will be born and grow and where they'll sit for hours, staring out the windows. Where secrets will be kept—because what is a house, after all, but a very large box?

I get out of my car and navigate the gauntlet of scrap lumber and mud and knowing looks from the crew, to stand on what will be someone's front lawn. The ground sinks under my feet, squelching around my shoes.

I call Jack's name.

He's surprised, and gratifyingly pleased to see me.

I hold up the lunch bag. "How about a date?"

"Mick's gonna be so disappointed."

He climbs down, and we sit on his tailgate with my picnic. I turn my face to the sky, wishing for some warmth from the sun. Summer has come and gone in a flash, hazy and fleeting as it used to be when I was a child. Now the days are shortening and the nights are chilly.

"So what was that dream about last night?" he says.

I shake my head. The dream left me with an inexplicable but overwhelming sense of shame; the last thing I want is to relate it to Jack.

"I can't remember. Something about work, maybe."

"You haven't said much about the writing lately. How's it going?"

I light a cigarette and shrug. "Well, there's no shortage

of words, but a definite lack of coherence. Gus keeps saying I should take a break. So I'm taking one."

"For how long?"

"No idea. Until inspiration strikes?"

He points a corner of sandwich at me. "Thought it was
you who said there's no such thing as a muse, that it's all
just a lot of hard work."

I wobble my head. Writing is unexplainable, one thing
today and something else tomorrow. I need to finish the
final book in the *Zebra* series and send it to my editor so I
can move on to something new. The ideas are coming at
me fast and hot, but even as I write them down, I'm con-
scious of a deeper story brewing underneath.

"How about this," he says. "We'll take the motorcycle,
drive down the coast and find a place to stay for the weekend. By the time we get home, you'll be walking funny
and so ready to get me off you, writing will seem like the
easiest thing you've ever done."

"You're always trying to put something big and fast between my legs."

"Who said anything about fast?"

The motel is small and trim, perched like a sugar cube
on the rim of a rocky cliff. The wind rises around us, a
cool shock on my face when Jack parks the motorcycle and
we take off our helmets. While he goes to the front desk
to check in, I wander down the path to the cliff's edge and
stand looking over the sea and the creaming surf below.

I wonder what it would feel like to fly. To see the cliffs
and the hotel disappear behind me, to dive like a kingfisher
into the crumpled sea. The wind makes me feel light, as
though I could sail away on a current of air. I close my eyes,

stretch out my arms like wings, cup the wind in my hands and let it carry my arms up and down.

I imagine what I might look like from a window of the motel, poised here like a crippled bird at the edge of the sky. It's so easy to perforate the membrane between what's acceptable and what is not, between normalcy and deviance. My perforations are literal. Every nick is an attempt to make solid that shimmering altered consciousness, to get through and behind the curtain of pain, into that shining world a-spin on its axis where everything that hurts is suddenly liquid soft and warm.

The reality, of course, is ugly. Bloody. And misunderstood.

Which is how I came to be admitted to the Parker-Nash Mental Health Center at the age of fourteen. Suicide had never entered my mind, but explaining that I'd gone too far and laid my nicks in the wrong place was not a satisfying explanation to the big concerned faces around me. The incident would not be taken lightly, I was told. I would be helped.

And so began the conversation. Or attempts at conversation. Shrinks have a way of waiting for you to speak—legs crossed, arms open, aggressively silent, letting the vacancy consume the patient's inhibitions. This probably works in paid therapy. After all, who would fork over two hundred dollars to sit in a chair for fifty minutes and refuse to speak? But I found in the silence another blade to play with. I didn't correct anyone's assumptions about me or answer any question more than once. I collected the most painful statements and replayed them in the silence; I let people know that I heard what they were saying about me and didn't give a shit.

How long I would have played this new game, I don't

know. Because after about a week, Molly Jinks was admitted and took up residence in the room down the hall. She told me later that she had awakened one day utterly convinced that she would die if she left the Center, that it would have been like stepping into outer space. She'd suddenly felt as if gravity would not exist for her, that without the protection of four walls and a roof she would simply lift off the ground and float away. When her soc tried to coax her out of the room, Molly dug in and refused to move. Apparently things went downhill from there, with Molly holding on to the doorframe with both hands, screaming and biting at anything she could reach.

"Intellectually," she would tell me years later, "I knew I was being irrational. But you become disconnected from your body when you can't see it. You begin to drift." She thought about this, and her voice became petulant. "I just wanted to be left alone. I couldn't understand why everybody kept pulling at me."

For two days I watched the people around her at the PNC. The patients were afraid of her. An eyeless albino. A freak. Most unfit of all the misfits. The nurses were kind and professional, but they tended to approach her slowly and hurry away. *What courage,* they said, looking over their shoulders. *What a pity!*

Yet Molly was docile, sweet to the adults as always. Her resting expression was that of a blind Madonna, a wise half smile playing on her lips as if she were immersed in a world that had only become visible after Lyle Pax pulverized her eyes with a hand spade. She was beyond the membrane. I was fascinated.

It was Molly who came to me, though how she discovered I was there I still don't know. I was in my chair by the window, where I'd been for the better part of a week, silently watching the wind move through the treetops and the people outside scurrying down the patchy sidewalk. I heard her cane tapping along the wall and watched her round the corner and cross the carpeted living room.

She had grown taller, of course, in the four years since I'd last seen her. Unlike me, she'd developed a woman's body, slim and lithe, with a lovely flared hipbone and long, slender fingers. Her body should have redeemed her beauty in some way, but somehow it only made her ravaged face more disconcerting—like a Lladró figurine with a chipped goblin's head glued on top.

Molly patted and crept her way into the chair across from mine, settling back with her legs pulled up to her chin. She unfastened a braid and began to pluck it apart.

"Alice," she said as if in explanation.

"Molly," I said, so we'd know where we were.

"You weren't going to say hello?"

"Vow of silence," I said. My voice was hoarse with disuse.

From down the hall we heard a fight begin between a patient and one of the nurses: *Get off me! Get your fucking hands off me!* Yelling was common among the lunatics; we barely noticed it.

"I thought you'd write me," she said.

"I did. But there was no place to send the letters."

"M. Jinks," she said. "Care of nooooobody."

"Care of the state of Washington."

"Exactly." She smiled, her face turned to the light. The scars radiated from under her black glasses like a child's drawing of the sun. Her fingers twitched at her braid. "I'm surprised to find you here, Alice. I thought you had better survival skills."

"My skills are fine. I am surviving."

"I see. Got tired of being the good girl?"

I thought about this. "I'm exploring my options," I said.

"Oh, right. Let's review. Option one: be charming and lovely. Find your forever home, become a schoolteacher, marry well and have two point five children and a house in West Bellevue."

"I'm sunk right out of the gate."

"True. Miss Congeniality, you are not. Moving right along to option two: lay low, eighteen and out. Learn to play the guitar. Develop a heroin addiction—not there yet, are you?"

"No, but I'm not ruling it out."

"Right? You could end your days like a rock star, face down in vomit on the floor of a seedy motel."

"A rock star with no musical talent. Unprecedented."

Molly laughed. "Option three: perfect the art of the snarl. Bite the hands that feed you."

"Now you're talking."

"Get jiggy with a bullwhip. Become a jewel thief in a leather mask, the next feline fatale."

"I'd look terrible in a catsuit."

"Go bald," she said. "You could be—"

"Lex Luthor."

She nodded, leaning her head back on the chair. I could see the bottoms of her empty eye sockets from under her glasses. It was like seeing a man with his zipper undone.

"It's good to have options," she said softly.

When it was time for dinner, Molly folded up her cane and took my arm. I was startled, and awkward as I led her down the hall to the dining room, but she didn't seem to notice.

"You're beautiful," she said, "aren't you? I always thought you would be."

It felt like an accusation.

"Aren't you?" she said again.

"It doesn't matter what I look like."

Her head swiveled toward me.

"Really," she said. "I can't think of anything that matters more."

Late that night, I heard someone crying. This was not unusual; a lot of crying went on at the PNC, though usually it was a morning or late-afternoon activity. I tried to ignore it and focus on my book, but the sobs went on and on. Muffled at first, then with a long-drawn sound: *ayy, ayyyy...* Soothing professional voices joined in, offering comfort, but those two long sounds rose to a scream, and after a minute I realized they were words.

"My eyes. My *eyes!*"

With mine closed now, I try to imagine a life in darkness so complete that even the noonday sun couldn't penetrate it. There would be no waiting for the dawn. No hours of daytime safety. Only darkness and the fear of drifting away.

A wave of exhaustion ripples through me. I tip back my head and let my body sway in the wind.

Without warning, Jack appears beside me, his hand like a manacle around my upper arm.

"Jesus, baby, step back. What the hell are you doing?"

I look down, surprised, and realize how close I have come. My toes are one tuft of grass from the cliff's edge. If the ground were to crumble, we would fall fifty feet to the rocks below. I take a few cautious steps back and manage a smile.

"For a minute there, I imagined I could fly," I say.

Jack puts his hand on the top of my head and turns me around, takes my hand and leads me back up the path to the motel. The room is small and beautiful, with pale blue walls and snowy bedding, and a tufted headboard of yellow silk damask. I close the striped drapes and he runs a shower. Silently, he undresses me, laying slow kisses upon my breasts, sweeping his hands over my chilled skin as though to reassure himself that I'm still in one piece.

"Don't go to the edge without me," he says. "You might fall."

He pulls me into the shower and washes my hair, slicks my body with soap, sips the river that streams between my breasts and over my nipples. I kneel before him and take him in my mouth. He tastes clean, almost sweet, his cock gliding across my tongue and easily back, while the water slips like summer rain over our skin.

I trace his body with my hands. The flattened ripples of his abdomen, like the sea-pressed patterns on a sandy beach; the ridge above his hip, and the firm curve of his ass; the long ropey sinew at the backs of his knees, his thighs rough with hair. I cup my hands over his forearms as he smooths the water from my face. This is where his power is, in the clever strength of his fingers, in the fat-veined muscle on the underside of his arm. His body fills me with pride.

Mine. He wants me, he's mine.

He presses into my mouth and I sink lower before him, tilting my head, waiting with my tongue out like a child in the rain. Instead, he tugs at my arm and lifts me to my feet, slides me up the wall and buries himself inside me with one clean, complete stroke. My back slips along the tile, my legs lock around him. I drink the water from our kiss, gasping and crying out from the sweetness of it.

★ ★ ★

For dinner that evening we have seafood at a small restaurant on the edge of the pines. Below us is the beach we've just left, where the tide is rising over the rocks, opening fans of sea-spray-tinged orange from the setting sun.

I devour a tangle of salmon-pink crab legs, dripping with butter, while Jack attacks a plate of raw oysters.

"Mmm-mmm," he says. "Like eating a mermaid's pussy."

"So crude."

"The mermaids have nothing on you." He gives me a lopsided smile, one that reminds me of how he must have looked as a boy. His hair is still tousled from the beach and there are fine grains of sand clinging to his eyebrow. He dabs some wasabi cream on the last oyster and slurps it into his mouth. "So, I was thinking."

"Always good."

"We should do it again."

I crack apart a shell and draw out a tender chunk of crab meat.

"You liked it, too," he says.

I don't answer. I'm thinking of the scent of the leather man's house, the texture of his blanket against my cheek and the landscape of crumpled bedding, a foreign mountain range viewed from the side—and Jack inside me, all the way inside me, his hands splayed over the welts on my ass that lasted through the next day, his fingertips circling, making me come.

I shift in my seat, roll the seam of my pants over my clitoris, cross my legs to press the ache away. I watch his face. The power in his jaw as he eats, the width of his hands.

Light streams over his hair, flashes on his teeth as he grins at me. He knows.

I want to do it again.

After dinner I ask Jack to take me to a bar.

"You can get me drunk and take advantage of me." I link my arm through his as we leave the restaurant.

"I don't need to get you drunk for that."

"I've been known to say no."

"Not to me."

"Then you've been lucky so far."

"Mmm. You playing a game, baby?

"No games. I just want a beer and maybe a game of pool."

He looks at me. "Sure you do."

The bar is arranged like an Irish pub, with some random seating, an L-shaped bar with a worn brass rail, and two pool tables at the back of the room. We claim one of those and Jack proceeds to make good on his promise to kick my ass at the game, which is not difficult since this is only the second attempt in my life and I can't figure out how to hold the cue. Jack tries to demonstrate, but the cue is too big for my hands.

"I can't hold my finger closed," I say.

He circles to my side of the table and leans over me.

"Cock your thumb," he says, "and slide the cue along the back. You want to make a bridge of your hand with a notch on top."

He demonstrates, and I follow along. It still feels awkward, but my hand is more stable and I'm able to get off a solid—though poorly aimed—shot.

I look at Jack doubtfully.

"Better," he says.

"You shouldn't let your opponent teach you," says a voice behind us.

I straighten and turn to see two men about my age, each with a mug of beer in his hand and wearing a Seahawks T-shirt. The blond in the baseball cap introduces himself as Tom, and says his heavyset friend is L.J.

"We stink at pool," Tom says in the flat nonaccent of the Pacific Northwest. "But we're bored and the other table's in use."

Jack rubs some chalk on the end of his cue. At first I think he's going to refuse.

"As long as we're not playing for money," he says.

"What money?" says L.J.

We decide Jack and I will play together. Tom orders another round of beer and L.J. breaks, scattering the balls with a sound like a toy machine gun.

"We're being hustled already," Jack says good-naturedly.

"You've just seen my only move," L.J. says.

It really is, too. L.J. is almost as bad as I am, and Tom almost as good as Jack. We play three games in a row, chatting idly. From the jukebox, a favorite song seduces me into motion, just a little, a rock of my hips and a slide, following the beat.

"Where are you two from?" Tom says.

"Seattle," I say.

"Vashon," Jack says at the same time.

"Hey, I used to live on Maury, near the lighthouse," says L.J.

"Why did you leave?" I ask.

"To meet women," he says, round belly bouncing once with a grunt of laughter.

"And how's that working for you?"

"All the good ones are taken," he says, eyeing me regretfully.

Jack is leaning over the table, lining up his shot. He throws a glance over his shoulder at L.J., draws back his cue and sinks the eight ball neatly in the corner pocket.

"Damn, that's two out of three," Tom says.

"We should've played for money, after all," I say.

"What money?" L.J. says again.

"Everyone's got something to gamble with," Jack says. He straightens and looks L.J. in the eye. Though there's nothing overtly threatening in Jack's tone or body language, a frisson of unease passes through me.

Jack hangs up his cue and heads off to the men's room, while Tom pays for another game and begins to arrange the rack.

"So what do you do for a living, Alice?" he says.

"I'm a writer."

He glances up.

"Is that right. Anything I would know?"

"I doubt it."

He assumes an expression of offended dignity, one hand over his heart.

"I read."

"Oh, I believe you."

"No, you don't," he says, laughing.

I place the cue ball on the table and try again to perfect my bridge. Tom moves to my side of the table and stands next to me. I move a half step closer, a slight shift from left to right, and look up at him.

"Spread your fingers more," he says. "And lock your elbow."

He bends over me, takes hold of the end of the cue to show me how far to draw it back. His scent fills my nose, an unfamiliar blend of beer and aftershave, and I feel the heat of his body.

"You're hesitating," he says. "Push through, think of it like a tennis stroke."

I lock my elbow and let the cue slide over my thumb. The ball shoots down the table and zips straight back.

"That was good," he says.

His eyes are on my mouth, quickly to my breasts, back again. I've read that men don't fantasize about the *idea* of a woman the way I do with men. They think of someone they've actually met, some real woman they've seen and wanted. And I know from Tom's quick glance at my mouth, down my shirt, that this stranger will be using me tonight. When he's home alone and the lights are out, he'll have me bent over this pool table, and may even have ideas about the wooden cue I'm holding in my hands.

It's an insult and a compliment at once. But I don't have time to think about it. Jack has returned to the table.

"Time to go." He takes my cue and hangs it on the wall rack. He shakes Tom's hand. "Good to meet you."

"Yeah, you, too," Tom says. "Sure we can't talk you into another game?"

Jack's expression never changes, but his eyes are fixed on me as he answers.

"No, I think we've had about enough."

He follows me to the door, one hand lightly on the back of my neck. I begin to turn slightly, to say goodbye, and feel his fingers tighten to keep me moving forward.

At the motorcycle, Jack hands me my helmet.

"You might want to keep that on when we get back to

the motel," he says. He buckles his helmet in place and lowers the tinted shield over his eyes. He swings his leg over the bike and starts the engine, revving it gently, and jerks his head at me.

From the bar, light bursts into the cool blue darkness as a couple opens the door and goes inside. The door eases closed, and we are alone again. Jack's helmet frightens me. There's no way to gauge him. I can't tell whether he's amused or angry.

I scoot onto the bike behind him and wrap my arms around his waist. He leaves the parking lot with a swooping curve like a big shark flicking its tail. Gravel clatters to the pavement behind us.

The streets are clear and dry. But even so, Jack is going much too fast along the unfamiliar road, which winds like a snake through the pines. He leans into the turns, hugging the center line like he's on a rail, never deviating, never slowing down no matter how sharp the curve. The trees flash by in a blur, and I am clinging to him with both hands locked around his waist, sure he's going to crash, that we'll hit a pothole and sail off the bike, that a deer will leap into the road and Jack will lose control. I call his name but can hardly hear it myself over the engine and the rush of wind. I clunk my helmet against his, tug at his shirt. But he won't slow down. Instead, he accelerates, which feels like a punishment against my protests, so I give up and hold on and pray.

At last we pull into the parking lot of the white motel. Before he can even kill the engine, my helmet is on the ground and I'm off the bike and running. My legs are trembling and weak with relief, and I have no idea where I'm going—I only know that the last thing I want is to go inside with him.

I'm on the path now, headed into the forest, where earlier today I noticed a couple of stone picnic tables nestled
in the pines. The sea is churning at the bottom of the cliff
and my footsteps and breath are coming fast. Then Jack is
behind me, two or three heavy thuds of his boots on the
ground, and his hand is around my arm.

"Where are you going?"

"Get away from me." I shake him off. "Are you trying
to kill us?"

"If I wanted to kill us, we'd be dead."

"What the hell is your problem?" I turn to face him. My
voice is shrill with fear.

"I think you know the answer to that."

"What, I can't have a conversation now?"

"A conversation. Is that what you call it, when you're act-
ing like a fucking pole dancer, letting guys hang all over
you, while you stick your ass in the air and pretend you
don't know how to play pool."

My face grows hot. "I *don't* know how to play."

"Bullshit. What you wanted was a lesson, and an excuse
to piss me off."

"That's not tr—"

"Bullshit." In the darkness, Jack's face floats like a mask,
his cheeks and eye sockets blotted with shadow. "You think
I don't know when I'm being played? How many times did
you smile tonight. I lost count. And you never smile."

"What, I can't smile now? Did we enter a no-charm zone
I was unaware of?"

He steps forward and slaps me once, hard across the cheek.
I stumble back, disoriented. He has never hit me in anger.

"The problem here," he says, "is that you haven't figured

this out yet. You think you know what you want, but you don't know shit."

He advances on me, and I'm scurrying backward, trying to get out of the way. I glance back, see I'm about to run into a metal barbecue grill and try to change course. Jack hooks my elbow and pushes me against the picnic table.

"You wanted to play a game tonight, you wanted to make me jealous." He throws out his arms, palms up. "So I'm jealous. Now what?"

"I wasn't—"

"Didn't think that far ahead, did you."

He leans forward, both hands on the table, so far that I have to arch back. I turn my face aside, gritting my teeth. Far below, the sea hisses and creams over the rocks, breaks and subsides.

"Stop, you're—"

"Scaring you?" His voice boils at my ear. "But you like to be scared, don't you."

"No, not like this—"

"Yeah, just like this."

He reaches down and unbuttons his jeans.

"Fuck you," I tell him. My voice is small and breathless and lost in the wind.

"Oh, I will." His hand is at my waist and he's got my jeans undone and my zipper down.

I push hard against him, try to twist away, but he pushes back and there isn't a contest between us. Nana's advice echoes in my mind.

You're a clever girl, Alice. Use what you have.

I won't listen, though, because Jack is right about me and this gimmick. I'm full of fear, lusting for pain, and he knows it. I push so he'll grab, I claw so he'll hit. He won't back off, even when my fingernails graze his cheek, even when my fist connects with his chin. He is unfazed and his power ignites me.

Take over. I don't want to be in control. Take this, take me, take over.

I am alone with a man twice my size, in a game run amok. This is his game now and I am locked inside. A nightmare—when the normal rules don't apply and you are trapped within your prison, still trying to make it all make sense. He could have killed me tonight and I want him. His eyes are lit with fury and I want him. With my ear still ringing from the palm of his hand and my cheek on fire and a voice of caution screaming to be heard, I want him. It's a nightmare.

I need him, I need him, I want him. It's a nightmare.

I let him lift me to the cold cement table and press his tongue into my mouth. His hand closes over my breast, a shock of cold against my skin, and he bites my lip as his warm cock plunges inside me, easy and slick.

He groans, puts his mouth to my ear and insults me even as I open myself and let him in. "Knew you'd be wet... fucking whore, aren't you...aren't you..."

I'm ashamed but I don't care—not with his mouth over mine, not with his hand tearing at my shirt and the hard, unforgiving stone holding me fast beneath him. My breasts tighten under his fingers and then under his tongue, and the abrasive pain of the table and of Jack's anger seem to feed my frenzied desire to take all of him, to make it hurt from the inside.

He pushes me down, rips again at my shirt and pulls my breast to his mouth. He finds a rhythm, a long, fast stroke, and strikes hard to the depths of me. He clutches my wrists with one hand and slides his fingers into the space between us, unerringly to the center of my clitoris.

"How's this game," he says against my lips. "Let's finish it baby, come on."

He kisses me again, with deep strokes of his tongue against my teeth, his mouth angled over mine, and I know he has won because I can't stop now. His dick has torn me open and his hand is on my wrists and I am naked under him, helpless under him, and there's nothing I want more than to stay here and do exactly what he says. He pinches my clitoris between his two fingers, forcing words down my throat, and I am crying, begging, apologizing, coming again and again. The waves of pain and pleasure collide against him but I am trapped inside my climax, inside my body, too tightly bound even to rise to him. He comes then, too, with savage glee and insults, as full of his triumph as I am full of him.

He shudders. His hips snap against me like the slamming of a door.

CHAPTER FIFTEEN

Late at night I can sometimes see the patterns. I see myself standing still and Death rushing past me to claim someone else. I understand my self-inflicted pain as a spike in the ground, a means of holding myself in place.

In the shadows on the wall I see the ghost-faces of my mother and grandmother, of an eyeless girl with hair like cobwebs and a boy whose face dissolves into mist before it's ever fully formed.

I see myself at a distance as a child of thirteen, and the door opening with a particular creak, a strange dry creak that pinches my eyes and draws my body tight as a bow, a tiny screaming creak of the door and the bed beside me sinking, heavy.

By the time I was sixteen, the state of Washington had all but given up on me. After leaving the PNC, I was placed in four or five different foster homes with stops between at the Center, which had come to feel like an airport or a train station. I knew the routine, the cloying smell of the place. I had figured out how to avoid attention by sitting quietly aside and casting my eyes down, by keeping my hair short and my clothes baggy and my voice out of the conversation. I strived for invisibility and for the most part I succeeded.

I was nobody, a ghost in the machine.

Carla had exhausted most of her options in trying to place me. She was exhausted in general, always with an armful of folders and her hair like a bird's nest, wanting so much to do some good. When she came to me with Verity Cruz, I knew she was scraping the bottom of the barrel and I felt for her.

"She's a little eccentric," Carla said. "An artist or something. I think she does pottery. That might be fun, right? She could teach you about it."

I hesitated. Nana used to say that most choices were between the devil you knew and the devil you didn't, and longevity favored those who kept to the former. But I was young and still hopeful that the next devil might prove to be one of my own.

"Sure," I said. "Pottery."

Carla closed her folders and laid her hands side by side over the top.

"Just try, honey. She lives out in the country where it's nice and quiet. You'd like that, wouldn't you?"

I shrugged. "Where exactly?"

"One of the islands. Vashon, I think."

She drove me out there a few days later, along a narrow road through whiskery fields and thick stands of pine trees, to the north end of the island where the homes were scattered and the tourist money never seemed to penetrate.

The house itself had a threadbare appearance, with small gaps in the siding and a peeling front porch that listed slightly to the left and seemed to be the repository for an overflowing collection of potted plants. The windows were

covered with printed dish towels, and there was a chicken
coop in the front yard and a soft chorus of clucking, which
I would grow used to as part of the sound of the place.

As we got out of the car, a young man came out the front
door and down the steps.

"Michael," said Carla. "I didn't know you were still here."

He had a rag in his hands and was working it around each
long finger, drying them off.

"Verity's letting me stay until I get some money saved
for a place of my own."

Carla frowned. "She should have mentioned it."

"Maybe she thought you already knew."

Carla looked as if she had something else to say, but at
that moment there was a cry from the side of the house,
and a woman came around the corner with her arms open
wide. She was short, olive-skinned, with hair as black as
mine but long and curly and threaded with gray. She came
immediately at me and enfolded me in a damp, solid hug.
She smelled of clay and her hair scratched my cheek.

"Alice," she said. She put one arm around my shoulders
and steered me up the front porch steps as if we were alone,
as if I were her long-lost sister. "Be careful now, this old
place is near to falling down."

She linked my arm in hers and led me into the house,
from room to room without stopping, except to call back
over her shoulder, "Michael, give Miss Carla something
to drink while I show Alice to her room." And the tour
continued: kitchen, living room, bathroom, bedrooms, with
Verity's voice beside me and her hand gripping my shoulder
as if to keep me facing forward. "It ain't the Ritz, but—
watch your step—but then you know what they say about
beggars and choosers. And we're pretty comfortable. Got

a couple of buckets here and there 'cause the roof leaks—
we're gonna see to that next year—so if you see a bucket's
getting full, go on ahead and empty it. All hands on deck,
right, sugar?"

We had come to my room. Verity opened the door with
a flourish and gave me a little push inside.

"Miss Carla says you like to write," she said, "so me and
Michael fixed up a place for you, what do you think?"

I set down my duffel bag and looked around. The closet
was full of boxes, but the bed had a flowery sheet and a
scarlet blanket over the top, and there was a small desk with
a lamp on it and a chair. The window was hung with one
leaf-green curtain and one yellow, but they sort of matched,
and the sun was spilling through them and right across the
surface of the desk. I traced a circle with my finger where
someone's coffee cup had left a mark. On the desk were a
spiral notebook still in its wrapper and a plastic Hello Kitty
tumbler full of pens.

"It's great," I said.

Verity beamed.

"Well, now, that's fine. I'm going downstairs to talk to
Miss Carla, and you go on ahead and get settled in."

She bustled out the door, then stopped and put her head
back through.

"You ain't vegetarian, are you?"

I shook my head.

"Good," she said. "One of them hens has stopped laying." She grinned and drew one finger across her throat.

Then she was gone. I heard her down the hall, still talking, the stairs squeaking under her feet.

I pushed the curtains aside and looked out over the small
square of backyard and the fields beyond. It had been six

years since I lived on Vashon Island, but I remembered the smell of the place and the lay of the land; on the way here from the ferry dock, I'd noticed some familiar landmarks—stores where I used to go with Nana, the empty lot where they held the weekend farmers' market, the turnoff to the cemetery where she and my mother were buried. I felt as if they had been waiting for me.

I turned back to the room and started to unpack. There were two empty drawers and some hangers in the closet, more than enough space for me. An image flickered in my mind, of myself in two years' time, eighteen and out, re-packing my bag and going…somewhere. The fantasy always broke apart at this point. Where I would go when there was no place left to go was unclear. But if I could make this one last, if I could get my feet under me in Verity's house, there might still be a chance for my future.

"Hey." A voice spoke from the door. "Can I come in?"

I waved my hand and sat down on the edge of the bed. My duffel bag was open to a small jumble of underwear and bras. I tossed a pair of jeans over the top to hide them.

"So I'm Michael Keeling."

"Alice. Croft."

He shoved his hands into his front pockets.

"Weird, huh? Coming into a new place?"

"Always."

He looked out the window, at his feet, back at me. He was tall and thin, but had a gentle stoop like a professor, a posture I'd come to associate with the boys from my background; it was a way to appear smaller, an attempt to dis-appear.

"So, what's the story?" I said.

"With what?"

"Verity. What's the deal? Why's she fostering?" I felt it was better always to know the score from the outset, the better to stay the fuck out of the game.

"Oh, she's…" He seemed to think it over. "I think she's just lonely."

Lonely. I should have known then that this would end badly. Anyone looking for emotional fulfillment from a collection of broken teenagers was clearly misguided.

"Foster kids," I said. "A laugh a minute."

"She was a prison pen pal for a while. I'd call us an improvement."

I couldn't tell whether he was serious. But right away I knew I would like Michael Keeling.

"Hey, I can give you a ride to school if you want." He had a way of looking around me, past me, addressing his conversation to the objects around the room. Now he seemed to be talking to the lamp. "The bus is late half the time, you can be standing in the rain awhile."

I got up and started refolding my T-shirts, laying them in a drawer. "I don't go to school."

He looked surprised. "Oh, I thought you were like sixteen, or—"

"I got tired of switching schools all the time, so I signed up for online classes a while back. Graduated two months ago."

"Huh. So what are you going to do now?"

"I'm going to write."

That night I sat at the rickety desk and listened to the raindrops on the roof, stared up from that smeary window to the soft, shrouded glow of the moon and thought for the first time, *Would you kill for me?*

But Michael Keeling was a gentle boy. I knew without asking that the answer would always be no.

The notebook he left me is the one I'm sitting with now, at another table by a different window, the same question running through my mind.

In the bed next to me, Jack grumbles in his sleep. His fingers twitch and curl inward. Jack always sleeps lightly and seems even when dreaming to be uncannily aware. He turns over as I watch him. His shoulder rolls forward and the line of his muscled arm forms an undulating pattern against the wall.

I touch my cheek. We came back to the room a few hours ago, bringing the struggle from outside with us. He slapped me again, twice.

Go on. Go ahead.

I lifted my chin, willing myself to face him.

Instead, he pulled off my clothes and shoved me to the floor. But this time as he moved inside me, I saw fear begin to take hold. He's afraid of hurting me. Afraid, really, of how much he wants to.

For the second time that day, he backed us away from the ledge. His orgasm was tender. His hands cradled my face as he checked for damage. *Sorry, I'm so sorry....*

I look back at the pages I wrote at Verity's house. My wrists, now crossed over the battered notebook, are scraped and ringed with bruises. But that first night under Verity's leaky roof, the empty pages gleamed white and full of promise, and I couldn't fill them fast enough.

When I first arrived, I thought Carla was right to suggest the placement at Verity's house. My new foster was a potter who had converted an old detached garage into a studio. Her worktops were old doors set on sawhorses and caked with clay and flecks of dried paint. She had experimented at first, she said, to find out what would sell. Now she had it narrowed down. She did coffee cups using molds made of Styrofoam cups, and she did bowls. Palm-sized bowls that she said could be used for anything: spoon rest in the kitchen, ashtray by the couch. If you cooked, they could hold spices or salt. You could use them for facial scrubs, or to soak your nails, or for condiments at dinner. The bowls were her best seller, she explained, though you had to have a spiel to make people see why they were so useful.

Every week Verity took her bowls and cups to the street market and set them up on a folding table under a tent. She took me with her—to learn the business, she said. She gave me a bag full of saltwater taffy and I walked around the market, handing out the pieces one by one. Each piece was wrapped in waxed paper printed with her logo: *Verity's Got Bowls*. If you brought her the taffy wrapper, she'd give you a second bowl for half off.

"Now that you're here," Verity said, "we can expand. You could do bonsai, maybe. Or soaps, soaps are good sellers. Not jewelry, though, you can't make a dime with jewelry. People help themselves to the five-finger discount."

She ran happily through the possibilities: dog sweaters, purses, handmade stationery. Eventually she ran out of ideas, and decided to have me embellish her coffee cups with sayings she'd copied from a website: Shh, This Ain't Coffee; How About a Nice Warm Cup of SHUT THE FUCK UP; Thanks a Latte; and my favorite charmer, Coffee Makes You Poop. She gave me some stencils and a set of brushes and told me to go to town.

The profits would go to the household, for expenses.

I joined in with a spirit of bemusement. It was not loneliness that led Verity to the foster kids, as Michael had said; Verity was an entrepreneur, she was in it for the free labor. And I was perfect for that. I fit right into the assembly line and didn't complain. There was nothing to complain about, anyway. I admired her resourcefulness. I liked the way the paint felt under the brush as it went on, and the magical alchemy of firing the pieces to set the glaze, the heat of the kiln. It was quiet work, like writing. It soothed me.

Of course she was crazy. I found that out the very first week. But it was the kind of crazy I thought I could handle.

Verity was a drunk. Not a drinker, not an alcoholic. She was big-time.

She'd start in the afternoon, when she got home from her shift at the supermarket where she worked as a checker. Always it was red wine, which as she pointed out more than once was actually good for your heart. She had a special glass she carried around, with a short, thick stem around which she'd thread her fingers to cup the wine in her palm. The glass made her gestures more theatrical, more expansive, the wine sloshing around inside and sometimes over the edge, leaving small pink puddles on the countertops and floor, lines of sticky maroon down the back of the couch. She would set the glass on the table without removing her hand, as if she thought someone was going to take it away.

Often she had friends over in the evening, bearded men with thin ponytails and flannel shirts who laughed and slapped her butt and knew she was good company until around midnight, when the alcohol hit a critical mass. In the early hours she was raunchy and fun, her T-shirts cut in wide, ragged circles around the neck and tied with a rubber band at the waist, long horsey teeth stained with wine. Sometimes I could hear the men in her bedroom, the headboard rapping like knuckles on the wall, and Verity's voice rising in a sexual delirium: *Yes, yes, oh, honey! Yes!*

On the nights she was alone, she usually slept in the living room, exhausted from screaming at the politicians on TV or repeating loud amens and hallelujahs along with the kind of congregants who would shiver and roll their eyes in a religious fervor before falling out in a trance at the miracle of forgiveness. Also, she shopped. She knew all the TV salespeople by name and had strong opinions about which of them could be trusted: "Lisa's on tonight, she's doing a cooking show with Cody, and I really do need a new frying pan." Lisa and the gang sold her on dolls and gadgets and spandex underwear, on Popsicle molds, egg slicers, pinking shears and jewelry, producing a steady stream of UPS boxes and an ongoing flirtation with the delivery man. Verity never remembered what she'd ordered, so every box was a surprise. She said it was like having Christmas every day.

Definitely, she was crazy. But we all have our thing.

I tried to stay out of the way. At night, I would bundle up in layers of socks and sweaters, and go down to the garage to paint that day's collection of bowls, or experiment with new glazes on the ceramic coffee cups. A space heater buzzed at my feet, and a bare bulb swung overhead, pushing the shadows around the room like dancers. The garage was quiet and damp and uncomfortable, but the silence drew me almost every night.

Sometimes it drew Michael, too.

He was teaching me to play backgammon. He had a beautiful set with red and white checkers made of polished stone that he would rub with his thumb as he surveyed the board. He knew all the variations from Russian backgammon to acey-deucey; he said he'd learned the game at the Center when he was fifteen and used to play with his friends in the yard, or even by himself if no one else was interested.

I liked the patience of backgammon, the interplay of skill and chance. We played most nights when Verity was asleep on the couch or watching the shopping network for late-night deals. Michael kept a tin of weed in the shed, and we would pass the pipe back and forth as we tried to psych each other out, filling the cold room with skunky smoke that mixed with the steam from our breath, mingled over the board, then settled like a cloud bank at the ceiling.

It was easier to beat him when he first taught me the game. Later, as I learned the ropes, I found it almost impossible.

"You were letting me win," I said.

He grinned. "You wouldn't have wanted to play if I beat you every time while you were learning."

"And now?"

"Now you're hooked. You'll keep playing whether you win or not."

"You're like a drug dealer. 'First time's free…'"

"Very perceptive, young lady."

I looked up. "Really? You're a drug dealer? What do you sell?"

"Just weed, mostly. Used to push some coke, but that was a pain in the ass. People would buy a little, go away, come back again in the middle of the night for more. And more, and more. A pothead is just gonna take his bag of weed and leave you in peace."

"Huh. Is this a big deal?"

"Does it look like I'm a big deal? It's a sideline when I have extra." He moved a checker, lining them up to beat me again. "When I get my own place, I'm going into business for myself. A buddy of mine said he'd get me some seeds and help me set up a grow house. Really, you just need a room and some lamps to start with, but once the crops are rolling it'd be easy enough to expand. Just takes time."

"And money."

"Yeah, money. But not as much as you'd think."

He went on to describe his plans. He had the whole thing all worked out, with prices and timelines, details about licensing and semilegal sales channels he'd already worked out. It surprised me that he had such a well-thought-out agenda. Michael had always seemed a little lazy to me, unambitious. But as he talked, I began to realize how much work he actually did. Often it was Michael who drove me around Vashon, who did the grocery shopping or the laundry, who collected the hens' eggs and made dinner for all of us. He was so quiet and easygoing that I had never given him credit for his initiative.

I imagined him prosperous, bright and warm in his greenhouse, with all his plants around him.

"This probably sounds like a pipe dream," he said, grinning at the weed in his hand. "But I'm really going to do it."

"I know you are."

I have a picture of Michael in my box at home. Just a snapshot I took one night when we went out for pizza. He's got a slice in his hand, such an ordinary thing. But sometimes I look at the picture and search his face for some hint of knowledge—an orb of light floating near his head, some haunting double image or regret in his eyes.

Sometimes I even think I see it.

At dawn I'm still awake, curled in a chair by the window of the white motel, the notebook Michael gave me lying open on the table. I thumb through the pages, reading bits of work I did years ago at that rickety desk in Verity's house. Much of it is unfamiliar to me. Writing exercises, poems, assorted fragments from whatever I was working on at the time, none of which went further than the notebook in my hands. The fact that the pages are written in my handwriting unnerves me, as though my past self is trying to send a message through the void.

Lonesome is a quiet man
who leads you from the crowd, whispers in your ear
that you are not okay.
Lonesome is an open sky: a far-off birdcall to a fallen mate,
repeating; a curled-up
chick inside an egg, freezing.

It's the scent of a stranger's house, the lure of the unknown,
the deep, damp base note of
skin and sweat and semen.
This is where his spirit lives, here
amongst the dying plants, whose leaves
lay crisp and fragile on the floor,
where weed is left in a kitchen drawer, and thick shoes sit
beside the mat, encased in mud that breaks like glass and
crumbles by the door.

Here is his mind,
exposed: in the bills, stacked or scattered,
the carpet, clean or torn; in the leftovers, the aftershave, the
kitchen knives, the porn.
Within these walls there lives a spirit.

Just inside the door.

I look over at the bed and see Jack is awake, watching me. His hair is rumpled and his wide shoulders are curled lazily forward. One long arm is stretched across my empty side of the bed, palm down. He looks like a big exotic cat, tangled in the sheets.

"God, you're beautiful," he says, gruff with sleep.

"Put your glasses on."

"What are you writing?"

"Just something I started a long time ago from a prompt."

"What's the prompt?"

"*Lonesome is.* Dot dot dot."

"Interesting. Can I read it?"

"No."

"Why not?"

Jack's opinion matters to me; I won't be able to dismiss what he says.

"It makes me uncomfortable. All my subliminal crap is still in there."

"I'd have thought that was a good thing."

"Not for me, I'm not that brave."

He beckons me, holding the blankets up and patting the mattress beside him. I set my pen aside and crawl in next to him, let him spoon his warm body around mine.

"Why would you need to be brave?"

"Are you kidding me?"

"No. I'm asking you."

"The more people know about you, the more powerful they become. You've got to hand that shit out in small doses."

"You think me asking to see your work is a power trip?"

"I think we both understand your desire for leverage."

He kisses my ear and the back of my neck.

"I don't want leverage," he says.

"No? What do you want?"

His voice is a murmur in the half-light.

"I want to give you what you need, and take what I need. I think they're the same thing. Am I wrong?"

I hesitate. We never discuss the things we do, and Jack never asks permission. He just knows. Somehow, he always knows. His knowledge of my body is almost supernatural, so finely tuned that he can bring me to the edge of climax and spin me there like a yo-yo on the end of a string, until I am wired and slick and pleading for release.

I'm not sure that's what he means, but the answer is the same in any case.

"No," I say. "You're not wrong."

He lifts the hair from my neck and nuzzles in, wraps his arm around me. For a few minutes we are quiet, and I wonder whether he's gone back to sleep. I close my eyes and begin to drift.

"Why don't you ever sleep at night?" he says softly.

Silence creeps into the room.

"Is it just since your mother died?"

"Yes."

"Since you went into foster homes." His voice rumbles behind me like distant thunder, a vibration at the back of my neck.

I don't open my eyes. The sun filters through a chink in the curtains, pinkening my eyelids. His arm is solid and heavy around my waist, his palm cupping my breast.

"Yes."

"I see," he says.

What he sees, he doesn't say, and for that I'm grateful.

We lie together quietly and after a few minutes Jack falls back to sleep.

I wish it were as easy for me.

Even with my eyes closed, I feel the presence of the door across the room.

I hear the long-ago creak of another door, one that always opened—even when I'd locked it, even when I'd jammed it with a chair, with a desk, finally with my pink lacquered dresser, which I'd dragged across the room.

Even when I'd sealed it up with an entire roll of packing tape.

Even when I gave up on the bed altogether and slept behind the clothes in my closet.

The door always opened.

Eventually I stopped trying.

Don't hide from me, Alice, you know I'd never hurt you. I only want to make you feel good.

The horror was that it did feel good. Big hands, strange acrid male smells. Huge invasions that stretched and burned but also, shamefully, brought with the dread an inexplicable excitement, a helpless itching pulse between my legs that utterly devastated me.

You like it, honey, doesn't it feel so good....

I prayed that it would not. When the terrible thrill rose in me, I tried to absolve myself with nicks and cigarette burns as if a heady dose of suffering would mitigate that awful moment of acceptance, that horrifying onslaught when orgasm rushed through me like a demon and left in its wake a craving for sensation I couldn't bear to feel. I tried so hard to carve it out of me that the pain and pleasure and shame and fear became inextricably linked in the process, and any one of those sensations could trigger any other.

Later I would fuck other men. Terrifying men who recognized the addict in me, whose perversions mirrored my own. One of them dug a copy of *Lolita* out of his glove box and sent me away with it. I was flattered at first—Lolita was my age, the source of an older lover's obsession—but after reading the book I realized he'd meant to be ironic. Humbert's nymphet inspired love. I inspired at most a fascinated infatuation. With my black hair and clothes, flat chest and filthy mouth, I was a sinner's nightmare. Men fucked me quickly, looking over their shoulders. They fucked me and skulked away.

It seemed I was not the only one trapped in this nightmare; we were all afflicted. I began to feel a sort of nauseated tenderness about the whole business, which I brought back into line with firm swipes of the razor.

Too firm, on more than one occasion.

In the aftermath, as I walked the halls of the PNC with the night nurses and cleaning crew, past doors with names and numbers on the side, I found myself sometimes opening Molly's door, slipping between the cool sheets as she had done four years earlier when my mother died.

"We are so fucked up," she would say, but we'd twine together for comfort and I'd stroke her milk-white hair, and sometimes I'd stir at daylight and realize I had slept.

Jack's breath is heavy now and his hand is warm around my breast.

Doesn't it feel good, honey, doesn't it feel so nice....

CHAPTER SIXTEEN

I wake up one afternoon not feeling right. My body is heavy, and there is an unlubricated stiffness in my joints that makes even the smallest movement seem like an enormous effort. I get up and sit with my pages, but the words have become hieroglyphics, devoid of meaning, a collection of sharp and painful letters on a glaring white page. It's three o'clock. Jack is supposed to come over after work; we have plans to check out the new Italian restaurant up-island and maybe go for a drive along the coast. But after a long hot shower and a mouthful of acrid coffee, I decide I'm coming down with something. I call him, leave a voice mail and crawl back into bed, shivering uncontrollably though my face and chest are prickly hot.

I wake again to the sensation of the bed sinking. I am startled, rolling forward, but my eyelids are heavy and almost impossible to open. Through the curtain of my eyelashes I see Jack sitting beside me. His hand is wide and cool on my forehead.

"I think I'm sick," I tell him as if imparting valuable information.

"I think so, too. You need to see a doctor."

I shake my head, and the room seems to tilt as though I'm going to slide out of the bed. I clutch at the sheets and close my eyes, muttering that he should go home and let me sleep it off. But he lifts me, blankets and all, from the bed, carries me through the front door and lays me across the backseat of his truck. The engine starts up and I fall asleep again, shuddering with cold, listening to the sound of the tires on the wet pavement.

The next time I awaken, Jack is leaning into the truck— *Put your arm around my neck, baby, there you go*—and carrying me through the open door. Raindrops sting like BBs on my face, the top of my head, my eyelids. Then I am inside, still wrapped in my blankets. I know this clinic and the doctor. His drawl seems even deeper and more languid than I remember, as though his throat is full of oil. Hands at my neck, fingertips gently prodding, a swift professional touch, a wooden tongue depressor that makes me gag. The doctor asks questions and Jack answers. He shifts the blankets around my feet, takes off my socks, puts them back on. I am given a shot, something to swallow, then I am gathered up and we go back into the rain.

Bed. I bury my face in the pillow and recognize the scent of Jack and know he's brought me home. His home.

It's dark the next time I open my eyes. Jack is at the side of the bed again, with a mug in one hand and three pills in the other. I struggle to a sitting position. My muscles ache, and my head is buzzing as though several vital connections have been burned away.

He hands me the mug.

I take a tentative sip. It tastes like hot, hard lemonade. "What is it?"

"A concoction. Drink it up and take these."

He puts the capsules on my tongue, presses the back of his fingers to my forehead.

"You have the flu," he says.

I choke down the pills. "I feel like shit."

He smiles. "You've looked better."

He takes the empty mug from my hands. I collapse against the pillows and curl onto my side. He goes around the bed and climbs in with me, his big warm body fitted to mine at the hips and knees, his lips pressed to the back of my neck.

I fall asleep with his arm wrapped around me.

Over the next few days, he stays home with me. He helps me to the bath, washes my hair, feeds me broth and ice cream and pills. He buys a heating pad and tucks it around my feet. We play cards in bed, watch movies, listen to an unabridged version of *The Stand*. I urge him to go to work but he refuses.

"I never get sick," he says, "so I'm going to take advantage of your flu and score a few days off for myself."

When I remind him of the project he's been worrying over, he silences me.

"I'm not leaving you."

I remember previous illnesses, the social workers who made sure I saw the doctor, then redeposited me at whatever shelter or home I was living in at the time. No one has ever stayed with me this way, not since Michael.

A week before Christmas at Verity's house, I went down with a bad cold, exacerbated by the fact that I refused to stay in my warm bed at night and instead spent the hours coughing and sniffling in the garage. The holidays had sent Verity into a binge of drinking and shopping, and all I wanted was to be out of earshot and alone with Michael, who took one look at me and left without saying a word. He returned a half hour later with a sack full of medicine and a new space heater.

"I should have thought of this earlier," he said as he plugged it in and aimed the fan at me.

I rubbed my hands over the warm air.

"You don't need to baby me," I said. "I'm a big girl."

But he had the bottles lined up, all the proper dosages measured out, and a big cup of soup to wash down the tablets.

"Thanks, Dad," I joked.

He grinned and pulled my hat down over my eyes.

A couple of days later, he brought home a tree from the lot he'd been working in Burton. He hammered two slats of wood to the bottom and dragged it inside, and sat next to it all evening, stringing popcorn and cranberries for garland. He'd bought lights and a box of twelve ornaments at the drugstore, plus a white plastic angel for the top.

For a while, I watched him silently from the kitchen table. His fingers were stained red and he'd been a few days without a shave. But I liked the nimble way he used his hands. Like a musician, deft and sure. After a while, I set my pages aside and went to join him.

"I didn't know people actually strung cranberries," I said, threading a needle. "I thought it was just in books."

"My mom did," he said. "She did all that stuff. Presents, sugar cookies, big turkey dinner. She said Christmas was for kids, and she always made a big deal of it."

I hesitated. "You've never said…"

"Car accident. I was twelve."

I pushed a cranberry onto the needle. It made a small popping sound, and a drop of red juice swelled at the tip.

"You must remember her pretty well, then."

He waggled his head. "I remember her, but I didn't really know her."

"What do you mean?"

"Well, I mean I knew her from a kid's point of view. That's not the same as knowing her as a person."

I frowned. "I think it is. Kids see more than adults give them credit for."

"Maybe. But my mom was at twice the legal limit when she died, and she was driving. I wouldn't have thought she'd do something like that when I was a kid. I didn't think of her as a person. She was my mother. I always kind of thought she was infallible."

Verity came downstairs then, in her stretch pants and sequined T-shirt. She laughed and said our tree wouldn't make the cover of *House Beautiful.*

"Maybe not," Michael said. "But Alice should have a Christmas."

She raised her glass of red wine.

"Well, I ain't her mother, so you go on ahead."

On Christmas morning, I found a stocking by the fire and in it a small box wrapped in brown paper and trimmed with hemp string and tiny pinecones. Inside the box was a fine silver chain, with a sterling pendant shaped like a heart.

I looked up to see Verity's face, sallow and puffy, the creases from the sofa cushion in a pattern across her cheek. She was looking at me as though she'd made a sudden and unpleasant discovery.

She had saved herself a couple of UPS boxes to open

that morning. I found them in the garbage the next day, the seals still intact.

There was knowledge between the three of us after that.

Though I was quiet and stayed carefully out of the way, Verity must have known on some level that I was a threat. She tried to think of ways to keep me out of the house. She'd already gotten me a job as a bagger at the market and now found me another at a secondhand clothing store owned by a friend of hers. She collected the money I earned—for the household.

"I expect you to earn your keep, missy. We got no room for slackers around here. You don't pull your weight, back you go. You remember that."

I looked at her steadily.

"I'll remember," I said.

Verity went away, muttering under her breath.

Michael and I talked things over during the long, cold nights in Verity's garage.

"Maybe you should leave," he said.

"Go back to the Center?" I said. "What's the point? And anyway, who are you to talk? You're twenty years old, why are you even here?"

He looked at me across the backgammon board, the light threading through his eyelashes, laying shadows like spiders on his cheek.

"Why do you think?" he said.

But I didn't know what to think. Michael had friends in Seattle; he could easily have found a place to stay while he got on his feet. Everyone liked him; it was impossible not to. I didn't understand why he wouldn't leave. His reluctance made me impatient.

"I don't get you," I said. "You keep talking about saving

for a place of your own, but you're handing over almost your whole paycheck every week. How's that going to help?"

"It's not, I guess. But I feel sorry for her."

"Why?"

He moved a checker. "Well, look at her. Married and divorced four times, living in a house that's about to fall down around her head—"

"She'd have more money for repairs if she didn't send it all to the Home Shopping Network."

"Alice, come on. She's grabbing at things because she's fucking drowning, and all of this—" He waved his hand at the teetering stacks of half-finished cups and bowls on the tables around us. Verity had stopped taking a booth at the market weeks ago. She never said why, and I never asked. "The guys, the booze, the shopping. She's drowning, and all she's got to hold on to are a thousand rubber duckies."

I had to smile. "And you think you're a lifesaver?"

"No. But I can't help—" He looked at me. "I want people to be happy."

I reached across the table and put my hand on his. He turned it over, pulled off my glove, held my hand to his face. My fingers curved around his cool cheekbone. His beard tickled my palm.

"I want *you* to be happy," he said.

"I know you do."

He pressed his lips to the inside of my wrist. The skin there tingled with cold.

"You're underage," he said.

"Overexperienced."

"I want to do the right thing. I don't know—"

I laughed. "The right thing. Okay, Michael."

He turned his chair and pulled me into his lap, and he

swallowed up my laughter, already burrowing through my layers of clothes with fingers so cold they seemed to burn. He uncovered slivers of bare skin, his hand inside my jeans and the slippery warm center of me, two fingers reaching up and his lips like a brand on my neck.

"Stop me," he said.

Michael was like a brother to me, the closest thing to family I would ever have. But I had no faith in brotherly love. I took off my jeans and opened myself over him. His breath rose in a cloud around my face, and through this haze I watched the house at the top of the yard, the bright yellow window in the corner.

The next morning, a quiet storm settled over the Sound. The sky thickened and sank into the trees. Snow bloomed in the air, floating as if through water to the ground. An eerie silence crept in. A breathless hush, and everything suspended, waiting.

I dressed and went into the gauzy stillness, past the garage and the small stand of trees to the field beyond, and I stood there alone, turning in slow circles to see my tracks like stitches behind me and the dark smudge of trees through the fog. I tilted my face to the sky to catch the snow on my lashes and the tip of my tongue, to watch my breath disappear into the mist.

Michael came out of the forest silent as a shadow, right to me without stopping. He slid his cold fingers under my cap, pressed them to my scalp, opened his chilled lips and pulled me inside to the warmth of his mouth. The silence was so complete that I could hear my own heartbeat and the soft fan of his breath on my cheek, and almost the snowflakes themselves as they drifted to the ground.

"I'm leaving," he whispered. "Come with me."

The untouched snow lay smooth and clean on the field before us. Beyond that, the small quiet road, the patient ferry. A whole world waiting for us to step into it. We could have kept walking across the snow. Maybe we'd be walking still.

Instead, we retraced our steps and went back to Verity's house.

I shiver now in Jack's bed, thinking of the enveloping cold, the empty stillness of that morning. Jack pulls the covers around me and his hand moves over my body without lingering, long firm strokes of friction to warm me. I turn to him gratefully, my head tucked under his chin. His hand moves over my back. His erection rises between us, then softens, unacknowledged.

After four days I am finally able to eat solid food. My body no longer aches, but I'm thinner and weak as a child. I look up as Jack comes out to the back porch, into the low morning light, his cheeks freshly shaved and a mug of coffee in each hand. The sunlight catches in his eyes, skates across the line of his jaw. His sweater is pushed up to his elbows and he has a book under his arm. I feel my body's response, the slow warm stirring, heat moving down the tops of my thighs, and know the illness is over.

"Thank you," I say.

He sets down the coffee next to my chair and kisses my forehead. He strokes my cheek with his cup-warmed hand.

Jack and I find the flower man in the farmers' market two weeks later.

We've stopped for lunch after seeing an exhibit of the

work of Julius Shulman, the photographer who immortalized the work of architects like Neutra and Frank Lloyd Wright. Jack has several of Shulman's books at home and has been looking forward to the exhibition for weeks.

"They thought they could change the world," Jack says as we stroll through the market. Spring has melted into summer, and the city is fresh and sparkling under a flat blue sky. "It seems almost painfully naive, these days."

"Oh, I don't know. Maybe not the world, but is it too much to think you could improve one corner of it?"

He smiles down at me, his cheek bulging over a bite of soft pretzel. "Sometimes I forget how young you are."

"Why is it young to want to change things? Great men do that all their lives."

"Great men think they have some insight the rest of us lack. They think they understand other people. Which is bullshit. And naive. No one has a fucking clue what other people are like."

I accept this in silence, given how little Jack knows about me. Maybe he's right, and the unknowing is a part of life. The architects Shulman photographed tried to dictate how their clients would live, down to the shape and placement of every chair and light fixture. But in the end, I suppose, people lived in those sternly designed homes the way they wanted to, sprawled this way and that across the hard-backed chairs, rearranging the sofas around the TV, dragging an old quilt in from the bedroom. It's what I would have done.

"Do you miss it? Designing?"

He wobbles a hand back and forth. "Well, it wasn't a calling or anything like that, not for me. It was a job I trained for, so it pisses me off to have wasted the education. I miss the life I thought I was building. I miss the money." His voice sounds different, wistful under the breezy confidence. "I miss my mom."

He rarely talks about his family. I know Jack was a wild teenager who fought almost constantly with his father, and I get the impression that his father was an abusive man. Jack has called him "hardhanded" and "pigheaded" and, with a little liquor in him, "an arrogant fuck." His mother seems to retreat into the background, a gentle soul under her husband's thumb.

"Can't you call her?"

He shakes his head. "She won't pick up. I sent a couple of letters. They both came back unopened. So that's that."

"Sounds pretty final."

"Yeah. I think it is. But there are compensations. Fewer responsibilities means greater freedom. My dad was the one who insisted I study architecture. But actually I prefer carpentry. Being outside, working with my hands. I like assembly better than design, it's more tangible."

Ahead is a wooden cart inset with plastic buckets holding hundreds of flowers, a parade of color marching across our path. Daisies, roses, masses of tulips and frilled pink peonies. The scent draws me like a honeybee.

Jack crumples his napkin and brushes the salt from his hands.

"And I still have a couple bucks to buy flowers for a pretty girl."

The vendor grins at us. He's small, thick, with a fringe of dark hair and matching mustache. His smile is so sunny, so full of joie de vivre, that it's almost a cliché.

I press my nose to a bouquet of lavender roses.

"Mmm… That's what a rose is supposed to smell like."

"Blue Moon," the flower man says. "Nothing like it."

Jack smiles, already reaching for his wallet, and the vendor takes the roses to his bench. With a wickedly sharp knife, he cuts a fresh end on each stem and wraps the bouquet in white paper. I like the quick precision of his blunt fingers, one firm strike through the fibrous stem. The sharpness of the blade seems like more than a respect for the tool and a wish to make the job easier; it's a kindness to the flower.

"The lavender rose symbolizes mystery," he says, waggling his eyebrows.

"Perfect," Jack says. He's looking at me with an expression I am coming to recognize.

Later, when I get out of the bath, I find that Jack has plucked the petals from the roses and strewn them over the bed. The room is heavy with fragrance.

"I've always wanted to do that," he says, and lays me down.

The flower man's house is not as I imagined. The tan carpet is matted and stained, and the furniture is cheap laminated stuff, peeling around the edges. There's not a lot on the walls, but in one corner of the living room is a beautiful antique clock, half-hidden behind the tweed drapes on the front window.

It's not a place I would associate with the cheerful flower man at the fair. It hurts somehow, to imagine him here. It's disorienting.

The house is in an older neighborhood on the south end of Seattle, where the houses are huddled together in clusters as if for protection. Safety in numbers. Jack couldn't find a key in the front yard, but we discovered a warped window where the latch doesn't hold. By pressing the glass and lifting the pane, Jack was able to get the window open, and hoisted me through ahead of him.

I walk up the staircase with Jack on my heels. The walls are lined with photographs of young people in old clothes. I recognize the flower man in some of them, with a full head of hair and a dark mustache. There is a woman with him, and a young girl with hair so long and straight it looks as though she's been dipped in water. Her nose is covered with freckles. In most of the pictures she is laughing, her head tipped back.

The flower man's bed is small and rumpled on one side. I stare at it from the doorway, imagining him in it, reading and sleeping, alone at the end of a dark rainy day. The room smells strongly of cigarettes, so cold and depressing I don't want to go in. Instead, I cross the hall to what looks like a child's room. There's a small bed with a pink quilt and next to it a white desk with brass pulls, and here the walls are covered with posters. Shawn Cassidy, the Bee Gees, other young idols whose faces are not familiar. They are the heartthrobs of decades past, faded and curling on the walls.

I recognize the imprint on this house. It's a home where someone died young and took a living soul with her. Unsettling to imagine the flower man living here. If I hadn't seen his face in the pictures on the wall, I would have sworn Jack brought us to the wrong place.

We return downstairs to the kitchen and I turn to Jack. His eyes are glassy and there is a hectic flush across his cheekbones. He traces my jaw with his fingertips, runs his thumb across my lip.

Then he takes off his belt.

His hand on top of my head, he gives me a push and sits me down on a wooden chair at the flower man's kitchen table. As he binds my wrists to the back of the chair, I stare at the glasses on the counter, the crumbs around the toaster, the pale areas on the cabinet doors where the varnish has worn away. There is a water stain on the ceiling. A paperback, facedown. Envelope by the phone with writing on it. Magnet on the refrigerator. Cobweb, spoon, tomato, vodka. My eyes dart around the room. My heartbeat thrums in my ears. The grandfather clock ticks softly from the living room, then chimes the quarter hour: 2:15 a.m.

Jack leans over me, his hand in my hair, and pulls my head back as he kisses me. Softly at first, then slanting, deeper. His lips are hot and dry as if with fever. He runs a hand down the length of my neck and cups my breast through my shirt, passing his thumb across my nipple.

"What do you think about all this," he says, unbuttoning my shirt and drawing the two halves aside. "What are you thinking when you look at me like that."

I don't answer. My face is carefully still. A thick, heavy pulse throbs between my legs.

He circles the chair, slipping through the shadows. He pulls my shirt over my shoulders, as far as it will go down my arms. I shiver when he stops behind me and traces the edge of my bra, along the swell of my breasts.

"So cool, aren't you." His face is pressed to the top of my head. My breasts sink heavily into his palms and my nipples draw up tight. He weighs them, considering, then moves away. He returns a moment later with a dish towel. I watch him fold it diagonally, then around and around to form a long strip. He lays it over my eyes and ties it behind my head.

My lips part. I sigh and inhale again. The dish towel

smells richly stale, of old water and detergent. Of someone else. Another shiver breaks inside my chest, icy and sharp.

"I want you to think about where you are, sweetheart," he says. "Spread your legs."

His voice is deep, seductive. But I can't do what he says. I can't, though I want to. My body is wound too tight, and opening myself would take more strength than I have. I don't know what I need. I don't know how to explain.

Please.

I hear his footsteps cross the room, and a familiar sound: a chilling shush of metal on wood. Then he is back, my hair in his fist.

And he has a knife.

He presses the blade flat against my throat. My heart leaps and heat flashes over my skin. A searing ache begins between my thighs.

"Let me make it easier," he says. "Spread your fucking legs."

The fear and heat release me, as though he's burned through a hinge that's been holding me together. I walk my feet apart until they are planted on either side of the chair. Cool air licks at my inner thighs.

The tip of the knife trails down the bones of my arched throat, slides under a bra strap. He cuts one, then the other. He unhooks the clasp between my breasts and pulls off my bra, lets it drop to the ground beside me.

My breath has grown swift and shallow. My heart is tumbling like a rock down a barren cliff. The scent and vibration of another man's home crowd my mind, drive home the incomprehensible wrongness of what we're doing.

Criminal, I think, and the word clicks into place. This is criminal behavior; we are criminals.

"Oh, you like sharp things, don't you," he says. The knife traces a pattern around my breasts, the outline of my missing bra. The dull side of the blade clicks against my nipple ring. He inserts the tip into the ring and tugs gently.

I shudder and turn my wrist against the edge of the belt.

He twists the knife and whispers in my ear. "I'm gonna cut you."

My entire body freezes—breath and speech and even my rolling heartbeat. Every cell is awash with fear and longing. For a second I can see us from someplace outside myself, as though I'm looking at the scene through the wrong end of a pair of binoculars.

He kneels between my knees, the knife pressed to my throat. He hikes up my skirt and runs the backs of his fingers over the fabric between my legs, the last flimsy barrier.

"You think I don't know what you are," he says. "Like I didn't know the first time I laid eyes on you."

A choked cry lodges in my throat. I want to hide my face but the knife is hard against my skin. When his thumb slips under the fabric, I press my lips together, ashamed at the slickness he discovers. I want to close my legs, cover my breasts, conceal my reactions, and am perversely glad that the choice is out of my hands. Jack is here. He's in control. I don't have to figure it out, don't have to decide; I couldn't turn back if I wanted to. His hips are between my knees; his belt is around my wrists. I am not responsible.

The blade leaves my throat, and a thrill of fear rises like a zipper up my spine. He cuts the straps of my underwear. Muscles deep inside my vagina begin to open, up and out, already contracting, already weeping.

Please. Oh, please.

The knife is back, under my chin. He sweeps his four

fingers up my folds, then slides them into my mouth, hooks them around my lower teeth. I taste myself, my salty tang, and the sleek texture of my fluid on his skin, now a cool wet trail from my mouth to cunt.

"Look at you," he says, pushing my thighs apart. "Spread your legs. I don't want to tell you again."

He rocks the heel of his hand over my clitoris, and I moan. *Please, please.* He presses inside me, two fingers, then three, and four, muttering threats and insults into my open mouth. *Whore, bitch, slut, mine. Think where you are, Alice, think what I could do.* I inhale the venom in the words, grinding upward as he forces me down. The ache is so intense that I begin to cry, a long inarticulate plea for something, something. The blade bites at my throat. A quick, fiery snap of pain under my chin, and I am coming, in burning convulsive waves that lift me to a crest of agonized pleasure. I would die for him now; I would die for him willingly, gratefully, because he knows. He knows, somehow—

He nicks me again along the inner curve of my shoulder, and as his mouth closes over the wound, I hear the knife clatter to the floor. His hands slide beneath me and he lifts me to him and pushes inside.

"Oh, fuck," he groans, and he sounds like someone else. "Oh, you don't know."

He reaches up and slips off the blindfold. I open my eyes and see his expression, so wild and primal and male, and I watch the climax gather in his eyes—the inevitability, the fracture. His thrusts grow ragged, so deep and so relentless that I can only be swept along with him, bound with the leather man's belt to a stranger's chair, and when Jack comes I don't even recognize him. I don't recognize myself.

We are strangers, too, faceless and frightening.

All this time I have asked myself the question: *Would you kill for me?* Now I see the answer in his eyes.

Before he withdraws, Jack unties me. He soothes my nicks with soft strokes of his tongue and murmured apologies. I take his face in my hands and kiss him. His mouth tastes like blood.

"Let it burn," I tell him.

CHAPTER SEVENTEEN

I can't sleep. A cat is hidden under my front porch, meowing. I walk around outside, peering under the newly painted floorboards, trying to see if I can get her out and take her to the vet. I see a pair of jade-green eyes, but can't persuade the cat to leave the shelter of the porch. I coax, cajole, offer a can of tuna and a bowl of water. In desperation, I poke at her with the end of a broom. But she won't move and she won't stop crying.

I return to bed and lie there listening. The cries blur into a thick, continuous yowl, muffled by the rain but inescapable. The sound becomes eerie, stretched, the auditory version of Edvard Munch's *The Scream*. A shiver sweeps over my skin and prickles at the nape of my neck. I put on my headphones and go to the living room, try to ignore the cat and get some sleep. But the noise goes on. Every time there is a break in the music, I can hear her—even with the volume turned up, it seems the cat's voice is embedded under the electric guitar. There is something ominous about her persistence, something witchy and foreboding.

The sound reminds me of my mother, the night she died. The cries are almost indistinguishable.

I was ten the last time I heard my mother's voice. I'd been listening for hours with my cheek pressed to the pillow and a blanket wrapped tight over my head. Earlier I'd heard my mother fighting with Ray through the open window on the back side of the gray house, and after he was gone I had crept inside, through the back door to my room, while my mother sat alone in the living room, crying. Crying, on and on.

I lay there in an agony of indecision. She didn't like to talk when she was upset; she wanted to be left alone. But surely she knew I could hear her—would she think I didn't care?

I got out of bed and went to the door, drawn by my mother's sobs to the living room down the hall. All the pictures had fallen or been thrown to the floor in the hallway, and I picked up a shard of glass in my heel as I passed. It bit into my skin and hung there, but to remove it I would have needed the light and my mother. I crept closer, hovering at the end of the hall. Her crying frightened me. Adults didn't run in street clothes, they didn't wipe their mouths on their shirts and they didn't cry. Not this way, not with this kind of ferocious abandon. Her voice had grown tight and hoarse. There was no sign of Ray.

I walked to her on tiptoe, keeping the weight off the glass in my heel.

"Mom?"

Her face looked ugly, twisted and swollen with tears. I realized immediately that I'd made a mistake; she didn't want me there. She waved me off with one hand, flipping her wrist. She had a photograph of Nana in her lap and was picking away the chips of glass inside the frame.

"Go back to bed."

It's the last thing she said to me.

The cat's cries are growing feeble. She must be under the porch again, but the meows have grown so faint it's hard to tell. I sit up, listening. Nothing.

I grab a flashlight and go outside. Moving around the porch, I sweep the light back and forth, looking for the glowing pair of eyes. I have almost given up when at last I see them. The cat is lying against the side of the house, eyes half-open. She is very still and doesn't respond when I thunk the end of the flashlight against the wooden rail.

I set the flashlight aside. The damned cat has died under my porch. I need to bury her, or there will be one hell of a stink in the weeks to come. With a shovel from the shed, I dig a cat-sized hole at the tree line, then return to the porch with an old burlap sack.

The ground is muddy, cold and wet on my belly as I crawl under the porch with the sack in my hand. There's a little more room near the house, though, and when I reach the dead cat I'm able to sit up. I lay a hand over her ribs, just to be sure. Her fur is still warm but she's not breathing and her face is unmistakably vacant. I shudder and begin to gather up her limp remains when I see a small movement from the cat's flank.

A kitten, struggling under the weight of its mother's dead body. Its eyes are shut tight, its lips drawn back in a tiny unknowing grimace of effort. I lift the mother cat's thigh. The umbilical cord is still intact, so I find a sharp rock and cut it, lift the kitten by the scruff of its neck and cradle it against my chest. It wriggles against me, weak and bloody and fiercely alive. I search the area carefully but can see no other survivors.

With the kitten curled in my palm and the mother cat's

body draped over my arm, I struggle out from under the porch into a fine mist just beginning to gather into rain. I lay the kitten at the front door, wrap its mother in the burlap sack and carry her to the grave. Her body is still warm inside the sack as I lay her in the damp soil.

When I return to the porch, I find the kitten squirming in a vaguely circular motion across the mat, looking for its dead mother, its head moving side to side. I scoop it up with both hands and carry it to the kitchen, where I give it a gentle bath with a warm washcloth, working carefully around the umbilical cord, trying to get the blood out of its fur. The kitten's small body curls with pleasure, and I feel a soundless ticking vibration in its throat.

When I have rubbed its fur dry, I wrap the kitten in an old T-shirt and feed it warm milk from a dropper. It has a healthy appetite, surely a good sign.

"You're a fighter, you are."

The kitten opens its mouth but no sound comes out. I place another drop of milk on its tongue.

Late afternoon. The sun is sinking over the roof of the gray house, casting long shadows that reach across the street to the park where I've been waiting, rocking gently, with the kitten tucked inside my shirt, its velvety head under my chin. It's been a while and I'm ready to give up, when finally my patience is rewarded. Big sister comes out the front door, looks both ways from the sidewalk of Cooper Street and crosses the road.

The girl is dressed in a pair of sturdy jeans, a little too short, and a Minnie Mouse T-shirt with a stain on the front. She's the most beautiful child I've ever seen, all legs and spindly arms, and a new haircut that makes her hair look like a cartoon drawing, each curl separate and springing out from her head.

She sees the kitten in my lap, and gives me a sloe-eyed glance before plopping down into the swing next to mine. I catch her eye and wave the kitten's paw in her direction.

She croons. "Oh, he's so little."

"He's brand-new, his eyes are still closed. Do you want to hold him?"

Her face lights up. We sit on the grass in the sunshine, cross-legged, our knees touching. I give her the kitten and she accepts him gingerly, cradling him against her chest.

"What's his name?" she says.

"He doesn't have one yet."

"Well, you should give him a name before he opens his eyes, or he'll run away."

"Hmm, you may be right. But I don't know what to call him."

She cranes her neck to look at him. "Smokey?"

"Every gray cat is a Smokey."

"Well, maybe Cloud? He's soft like that."

"In Vashon? Don't we have enough of those?"

She laughs. "How about a person name. Jasper?"

"There you go. Jasper. I like it."

She cuddles the kitten to her chest. She's humming something I don't recognize, a lullaby.

"What's your name?" I ask.

"Amanda."

"I'm Jennifer. I used to live on this street when I was your age."

"Oh, really?" she says, clearly uninterested in this fascinating bit of information.

"Yeah, down at the other end." I scoot back a few feet,

light a cigarette and take a long drag. "All my friends used to say your house was haunted."

Her head springs up. "Haunted?"

"Yep. Apparently someone died there or was murdered or something. My friend said she saw a woman in a white dress one night, looking out the window. But when she asked who the lady was, nobody knew who she was talking about."

Amanda is at full attention now, still rubbing absently at the kitten's ears.

"Another person told me he heard someone moaning late one night. Or crying, maybe." I begin to worry that I'm laying on the ghost story a little too thick, but she answers me honestly, wide-eyed.

"I've never heard anything like that."

"Good to know. So what's it like inside? Creepy?"

"Not really. It's just a house."

"Mmm. And you live with your mom?"

"My mom and my little sister, and Ray. My mom's boyfriend."

"Awkward," I say, putting on a voice.

"Yeah. I mean, at first."

"Not now?"

"No." She lifts the kitten to her cheek. "It's okay now, everything's calmed down."

I'm not sure what to make of this.

"So, things were weird at first, huh? New house, new boyfriend and all that."

"Yeah. But Ray's really nice and my mom says I'll like the school."

The kitten's nose twitches and he sneezes. Amanda

laughs, and the sound rings like music in the stillness. "Do you think I'll see a ghost?"

"I don't know. Do you want to?"

She considers this, her eyebrows drawing up like ribbons toward the bridge of her nose.

"No," she says. "Dead people should get their own houses."

I look at her, at the kitten, at the gray house across the street. The fence is gone and there are flowers in the front yard and lace curtains in the windows. When we lived there, my mother didn't change a thing. We simply moved in with the clothes on our backs and a few cardboard boxes.

The thought startles me. Frightens me somehow, as if I've forgotten some piece of crucial information.

I get to my feet.

"Are you leaving?" Amanda asks, disappointed.

"Yeah."

She holds out the kitten reluctantly.

"I can't keep him," I say. "He should stay with you."

A flicker of hope crosses her face—and longing. It's a look no mother could refuse. Especially not the kind of mother who plants petunias in the front yard.

"I have to ask my mom," she says.

But I'm already walking away.

CHAPTER EIGHTEEN

One day as Jack and I are leaving the farmers' market, we see a strange black cloud moving like oil across the horizon. The cloud rolls and condenses, flattens out, trails off and thickens again, quickly and without apparent regard to the direction of the wind. Jack sets his basket in the bed of the truck and shades his eyes with one hand.

The farmer's wife looks up, as well. She shifts the pumpkin she's carrying and gives it to Jack, then rests her forearms on the side of the truck next to mine. Her fingers, curled around her elbow, are knotted and gnarled with age, and the skin on the back of her hands slips across the bones beneath it like a threadbare blanket over a row of sleeping children.

"Starlings," she says, whistling over the consonants.

"What, a flock of birds?" Jack says.

"A murmuration, that's the name for it."

Murmuration. The word slides into my mind and I am back again to a snowy field on the other side of the island, the starlings unfurling like a black ribbon through the fog, and Michael's cold hand in mine as we retraced our steps through the feathery white flakes that melted and dripped between our fingers.

We paused at the front door, looking back. The sky had lowered a veil to mask our leaving, which Michael saw as a sign. Vashon wanted us to go, he said, and on the other side of the water, the sun would be shining. It was our time.

We went inside to pack.

My duffel bag was half-filled when I heard the silence begin to break on the other side of my bedroom door. Verity's voice, sleepy at first, then rising in pitch, slurred and garbled with last night's wine.

"Where's my money?"

I couldn't hear Michael's response. His voice was a murmur drowned out by hers.

"You owe me rent, you owe me for food. I had almost two hundred dollars in my purse and it's gone. Where's my fucking money?"

I had wanted to leave without waking her, just pack our bags and go, but Michael said he couldn't do that. Verity had been good to us. We couldn't leave without saying goodbye.

"Fuck you," she said. There was a hard thump, like something had been thrown against the wall. "Self-righteous little prick."

My face had begun to sweat and itch, and my neck crawled with angry hives. Anxiety swarmed like an anthill behind my rib cage. I imagined Michael with his suitcase lying open across his bed, warding her off, trying to calm things down.

But he was a kid. A broken kid and not the man this situation demanded.

"You can call Carla," he said, and I heard the bewilderment in his voice. "Have her send someone else. Or I'll call her. I'll tell her you're great—"

"Fuck Carla! You think I'm going to let her bring some other crackhead whore's kid into *my* house?"

There was a silence. Then the sound of Michael's suitcase shutting.

Hurry. Hurry, hurry.

I grabbed up my notebooks and shoved them into my bag, then my shoes and hairbrush and my kit, where I'd hidden the money I'd stolen from Verity. I snapped it closed and stood there listening, sweaty and panicked.

"You like that tight young pussy? You take the tricks I taught you and use them on that skinny little bitch? Hey, *hey,* I'm talking to you."

"No, you're done talking to me."

They were in the hallway. I grabbed up my duffel bag and opened the door.

"Alice, wait—" Michael put up his hand.

"Oh, *Alice.*" Verity's face was a mask, a parody of itself. Her eyes were wide and wild, filled with a lemony light. "Alice, what a sweet girl."

She rushed at me with her hands stretched out, this sudden chaotic force, all hair and teeth and long purple fingernails. Michael dropped his suitcase and tried to restrain her, pushed his hand against that gaping mouth, cursing when she bit him.

"Alice," he said. "Get in the car."

He caught her arm and twisted it back, and I shoved past them through a rain of blows from her feet and her one free hand. Her nails raked my cheek and sliced like a knife down the side of my neck. But I kept going, the duffel bag banging at my shins, down the stairs and out the front door. I hit the rickety porch steps at a run, and they gave way as they had long threatened to do, with a brittle crack that sent me tumbling into the snow. I scrambled to my feet and kept going down the snowy driveway, skidding to my knees beside Michael's car.

I ripped open my bag and began to claw through it for my kit. I would throw the two hundred dollars back at her—no matter that I'd earned it, no matter that I thought it was mine. I'd give it back and stop her yelling, and Michael and I would get the hell out of there.

The house was suddenly quiet. I waited, the bills clutched in my fist. Overhead, the starlings poured out of the clouds, necks outstretched, their wings beating hard against the sky. Then the front door sprang open and Michael shot through it and across the front porch, leaping past the broken steps to the sidewalk. He was empty-handed, and distantly I registered the alarm in this. He would never have left his bag behind; it was everything he had in the world.

Then I saw his face. My breath and heartbeat and the thumping of his feet seemed to lift away, and the moment hung in place where I can see it still: Michael moving toward me with his hands outstretched as if to pull me up. His eyes open wide. So terrifyingly aware. So alive.

Like Nana, sailing down the steps.

"She's g—"

A shot cracked the air. And Michael was gone, instantly gone even as he fell, gone even before the blood hit my cheek. As if his spirit was suddenly too full to be contained, one small prick of a bullet sent him rushing from his body like the air from a torn balloon.

The world collapsed into two dimensions, images flipping past. The mud in a frozen crust around the fender of Michael's car. The tire, half-moons of ice inside the hubcap.

Michael's scarf flung out across the ground, and next to it, three red spots like strawberries in the snow.

As I crouched beside the car, a small hole appeared in the door. I never heard the shot, though, and I never looked back. I left him where he lay, left Michael alone and seeping into the ground, and as the starlings retreated into the thick white sky, I started to run.

A third bullet was fired that morning, the one that killed Verity Cruz. But by then I was long gone.

Now the cloud of birds glides toward us, a slow undulating mass, then a quick pivot as a school of minnows will do when chased by a shark. The murmuration seems to be one entity, a single, liquid consciousness, but I imagine each quick-winged bird fluttering inside the cloud, a tiny busy heart thrumming in its breast.

"How do they all move at once like that?" I ask.

She shakes her head. "Each bird is watching the one next to it, I suppose."

It's an unsatisfying answer. She feels that, too, I think.

As we watch, a larger bird appears, diving through the clouds. Its wings tuck and expand and its body swivels, adjusting, but its eyes are locked on a single starling that trails behind the rest—struggling, wounded, or maybe just distracted.

"Hawk," Jack says.

The murmuration is almost directly overhead. A long ripple passes through the flock, and the cloud of birds divides and reforms behind us, while the last starling, sensing danger, plunges toward the mass of black bodies. But it's too late. The hawk's wings open wide and the starling is plucked from the flock. Its wings flap desperately and we hear a small, shrill cry.

The starlings glide away, and the hawk sinks with its prize into the trees.

"Poor thing," the farmer lady says.

Jack turns to me, a strange half smile on his lips.

"The hawk has to eat," I say, and hand my basket to him.

The scent of Jack's house has become as familiar to me as my own: coffee and soap and wood glue, warm linen sheets and the earthy musk of Jack's muddy leather work boots, the astringent scent of his rosemary shampoo in the bathroom, a trace of last night's weed from the pipe on the mantel.

I lie next to him for an hour or two before he leaves for work in the morning, watching his chest rise and fall, listening to the clean sweep of air that fills his lungs and empties in a long steady draft, tickling across my skin. My head fits into the dip between his chest and shoulder, and I nestle into the warmth of him, the lid of his chin on top of my head.

After he leaves, I sleep for a while, then get a shower and something to eat. Sometimes I vacuum or do the dishes while the coffee is brewing, or toss an armful of laundry in the washing machine; a month ago, in a fit of activity, I dragged his leather rag rug outside, draped it over a tree branch and beat the dust out of it with a wooden broom, then scrubbed it down with a dry brush. When the rug was clean, I laid it back in the living room, opposite side up and turned ninety degrees to the fireplace. I expected Jack to correct it and was surprised to find the rug lying the same way for a week, before eventually I moved it myself.

Neither of us comments on this increasing domesticity, the roles we are beginning to play.

Today I notice that the Ansel Adams calendar in the kitchen needs to be advanced. I flip the page and realize the date is something of an anniversary: a year ago today I learned about Jack and set this plan in motion.

No, that's not exactly true. I had been watching the gray house for years, whenever I could get to Vashon Island from whatever foster home I was living in at the time. Most of those homes were in Seattle, so I would sometimes skip school and take my bike on the bus across town to board the ferry. I always went straight to the Red Ranger in the tree. I would sit gazing up at it, thinking that if only I could figure out how to separate the metal from the hemlock, everything else would seem easy.

And leaving the tree, I would visit the gray house.

In the early days, I would circle behind the yard and watch from the shelter of the woods. I never saw much because the curtains were usually closed, but the slices of life I did witness were enough to feed my obsession. There were a lot of women at the house. I saw one scurrying through the rain to her car in the morning, another propped inside the dark rectangle of the door frame with a cigarette dangling from her fingers and a phone pressed to her ear. I once saw a pale face at the window, on the inside looking out, her fingers twitching along the edge of the bedroom curtain; years later, when I was old enough to venture there alone at night, I found that window belligerently open with a woman leaning over the sill while a man who was not Ray fucked her from behind, her arms clutching at the window frame and a strange rapt expression on her face.

It was around that time that I decided to go inside. If there was a reason in my mind to propel me over the threshold, I've forgotten it now. Getting in just seemed necessary. Logical, as a step along a given path, a paving stone set in the grass. I needed to get inside the gray house, and

I knew it would be easy; the key was still under the crumbling flower pot next to the gate.

I went in by the side door and passed through the laundry room, stepping over piles of crumpled T-shirts and stiff
socks, and one nauseating pair of gray underwear with tracks
in the crotch. The laundry room led to a small dark hallway.

The house stank of cigarette smoke and moldy carpet.
It was worse in the living room, which was furnished as if
for a cheap rental, with a sagging tweed couch and tables
encased in peeling, grainy veneers. The dining room table
was chrome, the chairs plastic, the miniblinds crimped and
covered with oily dust. There were fast-food wrappers everywhere I looked, and beer bottles, and ketchup-crusted
paper plates. On the wall hung a picture of Jesus in a gold
plastic frame.

I opened the door to the master bedroom. Like the rest
of the house, the bed had an unwashed look about it. Tan
sheets, flattened pillows. A black comforter, pilled with tiny
balls of lint. A couple of discolored blankets. The dresser still
took up most of the back wall, its surface covered with junk
and a thin fur of dust. I stopped in front of it, opening and
closing the drawers. At the back of the lowest drawer was
a shoebox. I took it out, set it on the bed and lifted the lid.

The box was mostly full of debris. Receipts, a couple of
old lighters, a pad of rolling papers, a faded Polaroid of a
nude woman I didn't recognize, who sat open-legged on the
edge of the bed, pressing her breasts together as she simpered
for the camera. Nothing in the box about my mother. Not
a photo, a note, a matchbook with her name on it. Nothing. It was as though she'd never been there at all.

But I did find something else.

A small, folded square consisting of two newspaper photographs. The first was a business portrait of a confident young man standing in front of a construction site, one hand in his pocket and the other holding a rolled-up blueprint. In the second, the same man, clean-shaven and unsmiling behind his heavy-rimmed glasses, sitting at the defendant's table with his head bent as his lawyer spoke in his ear.

Now I imagine a third photograph, as if from a video surveillance camera. That tall young man with a knife in his hand, kneeling beside a kitchen chair.

I go to the ship room to gather up my work. There are some notes I've left at home, the framework for a couple of new scenes that need to be finished, and a DVD Jack said he wanted to watch tonight. As I sit down and put my legs under the table, something flops onto my knee. At first it seems that I've dropped some papers, but when I reach to collect them and put them back on the table, I realize this is something else. I scoot my chair back to take a look. A large manilla envelope is taped to the underside of the table, and on one side, the tape has come loose. I pull the whole thing out and set it in my lap.

The envelope is filled with pages. My pages.

I once found Carla reading my journal. She'd clearly been unhappy with the way our conversation with the rag doll had gone and was looking for some kind of toehold, something to explain my moody silence and reconcile it with whatever information she had gathered elsewhere. And although on some level I understood her frustration, when I replayed the incident later it had shrunk to a still-frame of the foolish look on her face with the journal laid open across her knees. The memory exists for me now as an indignant, half-finished sentence in my mind: *Of all the people…*

I no longer keep a journal, but Jack has been undeterred.

The hidden envelope is thick with the scraps on which I have scribbled and discarded odd bits of writing: paragraphs from my work in progress, notes about characters, meandering plot ideas, failed poems. All collected by him, carefully smoothed and pressed flat and gathered into this envelope that has finally become too heavy for the tape he used to hide it. Some of the pages have Jack's notes in the margins, question marks and cryptic queries; some are stained with coffee or smeared from rainwater. He's even found a paper deli bag with a half-finished verse from a poem I'd been working on. All the pages are dated in fine blue ink at the upper right-hand corner. At the bottom of the stack is the page I wrote and crumpled at the coffee shop, the prompt about faceless men. I took that home, I remember, and threw it away. He must have gotten it from the trash can outside my house.

These are my failures, my saddest attempts at transforming thought into workable writing, my unguarded descriptions of places and people—of Jack. Over and over, though never by name, the phrases and quotes and scraps of erotic imagery clearly allude to him. Reading them now feels strangely voyeuristic; though the papers are covered in my handwriting and I recognize some familiar fragments of language, the writing voice and the depth of the author's obsession seem to belong to some other woman, having nothing to do with me. I've delivered the accumulated evidence of my own infatuation into his hands, but for me, this stash is all about Jack.

As I spread the papers out before me, a strange mix of sensations creeps up my breastbone: dismay, at first. Then a thrill of pride, swelling in my throat. A freakish enchantment.

He has taken me over. There is nothing left of me that does not belong to him.

★ ★ ★

When he comes home hours later, I am still at the table, gazing out the rain-smeared window with the pages in my lap and scattered across the table. The front door opens and closes, and there is a familiar swish as he hangs his nylon jacket by the door, a harder brushing sound of his boots on the sisal mat, then his footsteps on the floor and his voice calling my name.

He stops at the door, his grin fading as he sees the envelope in my hands. His gaze flickers from the table to my hands to my eyes and back again to where I've spread the papers around me as if sorting evidence. I keep my expression impassive. I want to see what he'll say.

He crosses the room in three strides, gathers the pages from the table and pulls them from my hands.

"Been snooping again," he says.

I shrug. I've searched his house many times. Every drawer, cabinet, cubbyhole. I've hacked his computer and his phone. I've been through his truck, his garage, his closets. The fact that I found these pages after I'd given up is irrelevant— and since we are both guilty of the same crime, it seems pointless to argue.

He straightens the papers, shoves them back into the envelope. He won't look me in the eye.

I rise to my feet. "I was just leaving. I need to get home."

"Look," he says. "I know this seems—"

"Creepy?" I say, to diffuse the tension. But my flippant attitude has the opposite effect on Jack. He lifts his chin and barks out a laugh.

"Oh, that's perfect." He jerks off his glasses and tosses them on the table. "*I'm* creepy now. *I* am."

"What the hell is that supposed to mean?"

"It means you're not fooling anyone, sweetheart, with your sneaking around." He drops the envelope and stands between me and the door, hands on his hips. "Where do you go when I'm at work? Because you're sure as hell not at home, finishing that book. Due last month, wasn't it?"

Heat floods my face. "And what exactly does that have to do with you?"

He stares at me. Raises his arms and lets them fall.

"What does it have to do with me? Jesus fucking Christ. What the fuck are we doing here? What does *any* of this have to do with me? You're practically living in my house, doing my laundry, washing the goddamned coffee cups. You're in my bed, I'm *fucking* you every night—"

His voice has risen to a thunderous pitch, vibrating hard against my ears.

"You're on my mind every fucking *second* of the day. God-damn. And you want to know what it has to do with *me?*"

"Hey, I don't know what you think—"

"Well, that's the point, isn't it? You don't tell me a god-damned thing. You've got me creeping around like some lovesick little schoolboy, because you won't tell me what the hell is *up* with you."

I hold up a hand, palm out. "Please. Don't act like you were driven to it. Clearly you started collecting this shit long before 'we' were anything."

"Really," he says. "Remind me again how this started, I've forgotten the details. When exactly did 'we' become something? Was that before or after I found you in my bed-room?"

I sling my computer bag over one shoulder and push past him to the door.

"Where are you going?"

"Leaving."

"The hell you are."

He grabs my bag. I'm holding on, but when my hand slips off the strap, the bag swings out and knocks against a shelf. Two of the ships come crashing down and shatter on the hardwood floor. The sound explodes inside my ears. Shards of glass fly up at me, biting like a swarm of insects across my bare legs.

Jack steps toward me, his boots crunching on the floor, a swift flash of concern on his face. But I am beyond slowing down. I dive for my bag. Jack yanks it aside and flings it across the room. This time an entire shelf comes down, and all the bottles with it. I feel the loss of them immediately, a knifelike pain at the base of my throat. All the beautiful ships, with their tiny masts and decks and cannons, the carefully painted hulls, perfectly knotted ropes—gone.

I am incoherent with rage. My voice deepens to a stuttering growl, tripping over the first word: *You, you, you...*

He plants his feet, brings me on with both hands fluttering at the ceiling. His expression is so exasperated, so unafraid, that I draw back my whole arm and swing for him like a man, straight from the hip. My fist slams into his jaw and I feel a vicious stab of pain in my knuckles.

His head snaps back and he falls away a step. He gathers himself as if in slow motion. When his eyes return to mine, they are ablaze with fury. Blind, graceless, unswerving. Deadly.

He wants to kill me. He could kill me right now.

Galvanized by fear, I abandon my laptop and spring for the hallway and the front door beyond. But my feet get tangled in the wreckage of the pirate ship. I lose my balance and fall to my knees. Jack grabs for me but I scramble backward, regain my footing and try again to get through the doorway. As I round the corner, he grabs a handful of my hair. He yanks me sideways, half off my feet, and spins me by the shoulder, slams me to the wall across the hallway with one hand flat against my chest.

"You want to start that shit with me?" he says. "Who do you think you're fucking with?"

I shove him away with both hands.

"Psycho fucking sonofa*bitch*—"

"That's right. I'm *psycho* now. I'm *creepy*."

I duck my head aside and try to get under his arm and out the door. My heartbeat roars. A white-hot pressure builds behind my eyes.

Jack takes my chin in his hand and forces my face forward. His nose is inches from mine.

"How about you tell me what's up with you," he says. "How about you explain why this gets you off."

I knock his hand away from my chin. "Or how about we figure out why it gets *you* off. You got no problem pushing me around—"

"That's right. I don't."

His hand opens flat against my chest, moves up to circle my throat. His fingers clench and release, allowing air and taking it away. Outside, rain sluices down the gutters, dribbles to the sidewalk under the window. Down the street, a dog barks three times, then goes silent. My strangled breath is the only sound in the room.

I reach between us, slide my hand into his shirt pocket and pull out his lighter. With his fingers still tight around my throat, I flick the lighter, raise my arm to shoulder level and hold the flame beneath my wrist.

He frowns. "What the fuck."

I don't blink or look away. My eyes remain locked on his face as the flame begins to burn my skin. Pain drives into my wrist, shoots up my arm and down the center of my body like a superheated drill through the top of my head, setting my whole mind afire.

"Stop," he says.

Ripples of heat rise in the narrow space between us. I watch his face: oval beads of sweat spring from his upper lip, gather at his hairline and slither into his eyebrows. Pain rages inside my head, a dull roar at the base of my skull. My hand begins to shake.

Jack isn't watching the flame. His stare is nailed to mine, and in his expression is the depth of our shared perversion, this mutual need to locate the line. His eyebrows knit together as his head tips slowly to one side. A drop of sweat slides off a strand of his hair and lands like a hot coal on my elbow.

"Stop," he says. "Jesus Christ—"

I purse my lips, blow a slow breath of cool air across his flushed, damp face.

I smile.

He grabs the lighter and throws it sidearm down the hall, spitting my name like a curse.

"You have not come close," I tell him.

I raise my hands above my head, stretched to the ceiling, waiting. I lift my knee, press it to his groin, pass it back and forth over his erection to prove my point.

He stares at me as though I am a stranger to him, but he's jerking his own boxers down my thighs, unbuttoning his jeans, lifting me up the wall with his hands around my ass. He pulls me down on top of him and slams his hips against me. The pressure forces a gasp through my teeth.

"How do I get close, then," he says. He frees one hand and clutches at my hair. "What's enough for you?"

He pushes my chin aside with his thumb and lowers his mouth to my neck.

"You want me to choke you," he says, and his teeth graze my skin, "beat you, fuck you up the ass, what is it..."

I open my legs, tilt my hips to accommodate him. I let my eyes drift closed, relieved finally to have relinquished control—or demanded that he take it from me. For a few seconds, a few precious minutes, I am helpless. My body is not mine—it belongs to Jack until he's through.

He moves his hand down the front of my body, over my breasts. He bites my shoulder, my neck, my lower lip. His incisors are sharp against my tongue.

"What happened to you," he says into my mouth.

He cups one hand under my thigh, wraps the other around the burn on my arm and pins it to the wall next to our faces. The pain is so intense that it feels as if my body is a lightning rod, gathering volts of wild, sudden, massive energy. I pull him closer with one leg around his hips. His thrusts get smoother, deeper and I spread my thighs until my clitoris is pressed to his groin. I cry out, clinging to him, arching back for more, and feel his response inside me as he begins to lose control.

"Say it, say yes, say it..."

Tears spring to my eyes and just as quickly I am coming, riding a crest of agonized pleasure, grinding against him, my ankles locked around his waist.

"Yes." I sigh, and let go.

Jack carries me to the kitchen, sets me on the counter and brings an ice pack for my wrist. The skin is blistered, furiously red, insulted. Jack slathers it with ointment, lays a square of gauze over the burn and covers it with an enormous Band-Aid. He smooths it down and presses a kiss into my hand.

I lay my forehead in the bend of his neck and draw a long, shuddering sigh.

CHAPTER NINETEEN

I'm in my car. The engine is ticking, cooling down, and I'm chain-smoking weed from a glass pipe while I watch people come and go from a club in downtown Seattle. The music thumps softly at my windows, careens into the night air every time the door opens. A neon sign flickers against the rain-streaked side of the bar: Cherries. Next to it is a pair of nubile cherries in a polka-dot bra, flashing on and off, painting my windshield with pink and green light.

I've been here before. Last week I waited down the street from the gray house and watched Ray Burbank drive away in his long-nosed sedan, then rode behind him on the ferry, across the silent Sound, filtering down from four-lane roads to two, until he pulled into the back of this lot, parked and went inside. This is as far as I've gone. Always before tonight, I've given up and gone home, knowing nothing more about him than I did to begin with.

But the conversation with Amanda has unsettled me. I feel vaguely in need of reassurance, a refueling of the hatred I have always felt for the man who let my mother die.

I close my eyes, call up my decade-old memories, the sound of my mother crying the night the glass broke and lodged in my foot, that last terrible night when at ten years old I lay dry-eyed and tense, wrapped in the sounds of my mother's grief. From the next room, for hours after she sent me away, I listened to her sobbing, coughing, the agonized tightness of her breath, like air through a crimped rubber hose. I had pried the glass from my foot earlier, but dug it out of the trash to use it again—the first wavering lines of my lifelong addiction, the only way to get close enough to her pain to understand it. The only way I could think to punish myself for not knowing what to do.

At 1:13 a.m., I heard Ray's car pull into the driveway. The door opened, closed. Then, nothing. Not my mother's wheezing, not the sobs or moaning. No yelling or cursing as I'd expected.

Something about the silence unnerved me. I limped to the door and listened, twisting my cotton nightgown around my finger, waiting. Ray began to snore.

I gnawed on my thumbnail. My mom had made it clear that she didn't want me around. I understood that; it had always been our way to steer clear of each other in times of stress. But maybe she was asleep in her room. Maybe I could sleep, too, knowing it was over. I would pretend I needed to use the bathroom. If everything was okay, I could go back to bed.

I opened the door. The house was filled with a thick silence, through which the soft sounds of Ray's snores vibrated like a foghorn from a distant vessel. I crept down the hall. Past the couch, where he was sprawled with one arm trailing to the floor, still wearing his shoes, his face repellently slack-mouthed and vacant.

"I hate you," I whispered.

I passed him, crossed the living room to their bedroom.

The door was ajar, so I pushed it and looked inside. My mom was not there. Not in the bathroom, either. The worm of apprehension that had brought me out of my room swelled and wriggled in my throat, deep inside my chest.

Why could I not hear her?

I retraced my steps, then checked the kitchen. The dining room. Nothing.

"Mom?" I said. And, louder, "Mom?"

I decided to go outside and look for her car. That's when I found her.

She was huddled by the front door, propped in the corner with her knees drawn up to her chest. Her arms hung awkwardly at her sides as though they'd fallen there. One hand lay on the floor, palm up, the fingers curled and gray and locked in place. A deep blue color had settled in her lips to form a halo around her open mouth.

Don't call an ambulance.

My mother's long-standing admonition flashed through my mind. Always since Nana died, my mother had warned me in no uncertain terms not to call an ambulance for her.

"We can't afford it," she said. "One ambulance ride would bankrupt us. If I have an attack, just bring my inhaler. I'll be fine."

I knelt beside her. The muscles of her neck stood out like pillars along the column of her windpipe. Her breath was quick and shallow as a bird's.

"Mom!" My voice sounded hollow. "Mom…"

Her eyes were open, staring. As I shook her, the careful arrangement of her limbs came undone. She crumpled under my hands and slipped sideways to the floor.

I leaped up and ran to the kitchen drawer where she kept her medications.

But there was nothing there. The drawer was full of junk—Ray's junk. I put both hands in and pulled the contents out, right to the floor. Her inhaler should have been there, at the front, in a plastic bag. It should have been there, right there, right at the front. Ready to use. It should have been right *there*.

And it wasn't.

I abandoned the drawer and scrambled around the corner to where her purse was hanging from the back of a dining room chair. I jerked it down and turned it over, spilling the contents over the chipped plastic tabletop.

"Come on," I muttered. Feverish tears flooded my eyes and clouded my vision. I swiped at them impatiently, looking with disbelief at the items on the table: lipstick, keys, old receipts, powder, nail clippers, checkbook… I put my hand into the bag, all the side pockets. Nothing.

I backed away. The light seemed to fade from the edges of the room.

"Ray," I said. I went to him, shook him hard with my fists balled up around the front of his shirt. "Wake up! Ray—Ray—"

He opened his eyes, smacked his lips. His breath rushed up at me, a nauseating stench of cigarettes and an acrid, medicinal smell I couldn't place. Hatred rose in my chest.

"My mom's inhaler, where is it, *hurry*—"

He stared at me with no expression on his face. Not worry, not terror, not even anger at being awakened. Nothing.

I screamed at him, my voice sharp as glass in the quiet room. "*Where* is my mom's *inhaler!*"

He blinked.

I ran to the phone and dialed 9-1-1.

But even as I hovered over my mother with the phone in my hand and the voice on the line calling, *Hello, hello,* I knew she was already gone. I knew it from Schultzie. From Nana.

My mother's face was a cold blue husk, dry and empty. Not a face anymore, not a person, not my mother.

All the blood seemed to slide from the center of my body outward, pooling in my feet and the tips of my fingers. My limbs were ropes, with heavy stones at the ends where my feet and hands used to be. Everything seemed far away, at the end of a dark tunnel, and my mind was a pinpoint of light rushing through.

From a distance came a high-pitched scream. A siren. Feet and legs trampling, a commotion, a bag, a bed with wheels that squeaked. Voices and hands, my feet moving, numb.

And Ray, upright at last, still and silent. Our eyes met for the last time over the body of my mother.

The lights are flashing now behind my eyelids, pink and green. When I sit up and look around, I see the parking lot is almost full. A truck pulls up next to me, and two young women spill out and scamper through the rain toward the flashing sign.

I hit the pipe until I'm numb, let the weed lift me from the car and carry me into a small crowd of night-dressed couples at the front door. I show my ID to the guy at the door and allow myself to be shuffled inside.

The music strikes my ears like a freight train bearing down, all whistle and weight. I am momentarily disoriented by the crowd and shrieking laughter, the flashing strobe lights and the damp musk of closely packed bodies. I grit my teeth and try to find a bubble of peace inside my buzz as I set off for the bar.

The bartender is a young blonde in a pink leather bustier. She points at me.

"Seven and seven," I say, because it's the only cocktail I know.

There is no sign of Ray. But this is a big place. I take my drink upstairs, walking with as much purpose as I can muster, as if I have friends to meet. I look straight ahead, avoiding eye contact. At the top of the stairs, I see a free corner against the rail, and scurry to claim it.

Now I feel better. Safer. Backed to the wall, hip to the rail, with a drink in hand, carefully expressionless as I look out over the throng of dancers on the floor below. I see a man who looks like Jack, passing through the front door, and feel a pang of longing.

If Jack were here, he would take all this in hand. He would know what to do, how to find Ray, how to solve this unsolvable problem. But I've been lying to Jack since we met, and it's too late to turn back now. Nana would expect me to finish what I started, and I'm very close.

"Hey, are you here alone?"

The voice at my shoulder jars me back to the present. My drink sloshes inside the glass and drips over the rail. A man is beside me. He's short and wide, a brick of a man, with mottled cheeks and a blond brush mustache.

"No," I tell him, collecting myself. His breath smells like stale beer and I turn slightly aside.

"Really? Where are your friends?"

"Lost them." My voice is nearly inaudible over the music.

He leans back, as if I've told a whopper, his mouth a comedy of disbelief.

"What are you drinking?"

It takes me a second to remember.

"Seven and seven."

"You want a refill?"

"No, I'm—"

"Looking for your friends. I know." He winks and retreats into the crowd, weaving a little. I'm glad he's gone, and go back to searching the floor below for Ray Burbank.

Not for the first time, it occurs to me that there's nothing to be learned from following him here. What am I hoping to discover? What can possibly be gained by a further accumulation of knowledge? This reconnaissance is a stall tactic and nothing more. I can almost hear Nana scolding me.

"Lovey," she would say, "sometimes the medicine is too bitter, and all the sugar in the bowl is not going to sweeten it. You've got to hold your nose and drink it up."

I drain my glass and push back from the rail. My head aches, and my eyelids are dry and scratchy. Even in the darkness, tonight I think I could sleep.

Halfway down the stairs, I encounter the man with the mustache, on his way up with a drink in each hand.

"Where are you going?" he says.

"Home."

"But I just bought you a drink." He holds up the glass as evidence.

I'm confused, swimming through a haze of weed and alcohol. I don't remember asking for a drink.

"Sorry," I say, since he's looking wounded.

"Stay for a while. Just to talk."

"I can't, my friend texted me and she's ready to go."

"Text her back, tell her to wait."

"No, I can't, she's—"

"This drink cost me ten bucks," he says. "And you won't even have a fucking conversation with me?"

Now I'm annoyed and increasingly certain that I never asked for a drink in the first place.

"Drink it yourself," I tell him. "I'm going home."

He shakes his head. "Fucking bitch."

As I pass him on the stairs, he throws a shoulder into my path, which catches me midstep and knocks me off-balance and down the last three steps. I land hard on my knee and then, as I turn, flat on my ass. He tosses the drink out on top of me. Ice-cold liquor splashes all over my neck and arms. Now I'm sticky-wet, sore and thoroughly pissed off. I leap up and spring for him. But before I go a step, a hand catches me by the collar of my jacket, hauls me sideways and hustles me through the crowd toward the front of the club.

"Hey," I'm yelling, over and over. "Hey!"

We reach the front door, and I am deposited on the front step. Right behind me is the guy with the mustache, who fires a couple more insults at me, then weaves into the parking lot, followed by another guy yelling at his back, "What happened?"

I turn around to protest—because though I'm leaving, anyway, the unfairness of it rankles. But even as I turn, the words stall on my lips. I know who I will see.

For the first time in a dozen years, I'm looking into the face of Ray Burbank—the man I am going to kill.

CHAPTER TWENTY

For a moment I am ten years old, looking up this mountain of a man, up his T-shirted chest to the eyes of the man my mother loved. His face is more deeply lined, coarse, but aside from that unchanged. Same close-set eyes, same snub nose, chipped tooth. Small gold cross in his ear, folds of skin under the lobe. His eyelids are fleshy, the lashes almost invisible.

He's talking, something about how I need to go home. He's waiting for an answer.

"Do you?" he asks.

I blink. "Do I what?"

"Need a cab." His tone is impatient, professional and slightly bored.

I shake my head.

"You need to leave," he says.

I stare at him, and feel the numbness retreat dangerously, like the waves on a beach, and behind them a tsunami of laughter. The sound breaks loose from my chest—*ha ha ha ha ha*—and within seconds I'm consumed by it. *You need to go home, you need to go home.* It's the funniest thing I've ever heard, considering the source.

I'm sure he's perplexed, I do feel the absurdity of my reaction, the inappropriateness, but the laughter has claimed me.

Go home go home go home—

"Okay," he says, "come inside. I'm gonna call you a ride."

He pulls me back into the bar. The noise and lights and the ridiculous neon pinkness of the place add fuel to my hysteria—*go home, go home, go home, ha ha ha*—and for the moment it's all I can do to hold myself upright and let him lead me through the crowd. We pass the dance floor and the restrooms, and he puts a key in the lock and opens the door to a small office. He motions to a chair and I drop into it, hiccuping, wiping my eyes while he makes the phone call.

By the time he hangs up I am quiet. The night has taken on the quality of a dream, and I am dizzy and off-kilter, trying to remember how I came to be in the back room of a bar with the man I've been plotting to kill since I was ten years old.

"Better?" he says.

I nod, take a steadying breath.

He's looking me squarely in the face now, under flat fluorescent lights, and his expression holds no hint of recognition. Though my mother and I lived with him for almost a year, though I've thought of little else but the destruction of this man, he doesn't know me. I feel as I did with Amanda at the park, as though I've successfully combined the ingredients for a bomb but the fuse keeps going out.

"You don't remember me." It's not an accusation. My voice is flat, wondering.

"Should I? It's a busy place."

I nod, and keep nodding.

He leans against the battered desk, arms crossed in front of him. I remember that, and the way he rubs his nose, a nervous tic that reminds me he still has a problem with coke. I think of Jack—and Rosemary, wherever she is—and feel the anger begin to reassert itself.

"That's a giveaway," I tell him, jerking my chin.

"What?"

I imitate his gesture, that pinch around his nostrils, and point at his nose.

"Yeah?" he says. "And your eyes are bloodshot because you had a long day."

"Actually, I have."

"Well, join the crowd, sweetheart."

The blood races up my neck, suffuses my face. That's exactly the way he used to talk to my mom.

I am up, heading for the door. I don't want to have a conversation with this stupid fuck, I want him dead.

You need to go home.

"I'll wait outside," I tell him.

And the crowd sucks me back in and spits me out, through the open doors to the dark, wet parking lot. I don't stop, though. I keep going through the rain to the far corner where my car is parked. Ray is behind me, calling out.

"Hey."

I turn back, my hand on the car door.

"Hey, I know you. I remember your walk," he says. "You're Annie's kid."

Annie's kid. Well, what else would I be?

"Very good."

"Why didn't you tell me that in the first place?"

His tone is bewildered—and honest. Again I have this strong sense of something being wrong. Why is he not afraid? Or at least uncomfortable. I don't understand.

"You don't remember the last time I saw you? It was the night my mother died."

"Yeah, I'm—Jesus, yeah—"

"The night you killed her."

He backs up a step, but although I've shot my arrow, his expression is still completely baffled.

"What the hell are you talking about?"

"You *let* her die. You had a fight, you threw out her inhaler and you let her die. I heard it all. I was there."

"Jesus, you were nine years old—"

"Ten."

"Okay, ten. You were a little kid."

My lip curls into a sneer.

"Big enough to call 9-1-1 while you were passed out on the couch, though. Big enough for that."

His face collapses and his shoulders roll forward as though I have suddenly placed a heavy weight on his back. I carry on more confidently, gloating, reassured that my hatred is not misplaced.

"You were horrible to her. Out drinking every night, pissed off, always yelling. I *heard* you. I heard all of it. You threw her medicine out the window and you *let* my mother die."

"Now wait a minute—"

"And *me,* you don't even remember. Did you give a single thought to what my life became after that? You murdered my mother, and you *wrecked* me. You fucking *wrecked* me."

I splutter to a halt. My hair is soaked and my eyes are burning hot.

"Look," he says, pinching his nose. "I don't know what you think you saw or heard. But I didn't throw any medicine out. Christ, she probably did that herself. Your mother was a fucking lunatic. Totally batshit."

My head is full now, flooded and coursing with rage. I open my purse and find the cold hard handle of the gun, pull it out and flip the safety. I hold it in front of me, level it at his chest. The trigger is solid under my finger—one tiny door to break through, one little squeeze, and all of this will be over.

His eyes and mouth spring open, his whole face round with fear. "Wait," he says, hands stretched out in front of him, palms out like he's trying to calm a fractious young horse. "Wait—"

"Say that again, about my mother. Go on. I fucking dare you."

"Wait," he says again. "Just—"

I cup the gun with both hands. It feels so heavy. The hammer resists as I cock it.

"Wait, I didn't mean that." His voice has gone up an octave, skittering fast. "I meant, you know, she was sick. Ill, I mean. She was—"

"Sick! Yes. And you threw away her medicine."

"No, not the asthma. I meant the bipolar thing. She was sick."

I feel the blood drain from my face. I must have heard him wrong.

Ray seems to sense this. "You didn't know?"

"I know what I saw! I found her inhalers in the bushes the day after she died. After you *wished* she was dead. You threw them away and left her to die. I know what I saw!"

"But you didn't see me throw anything away. You were a kid, just a little kid, you—"

"Shut up, just shut up."

I raise the gun until I'm looking down my arm, down the hard steel of the barrel, into his face. I swipe the rain out of my eyes. The gun is shaking like a fish on the end of a line.

Pull the trigger, lovey, your mother is dead because of him.

My mother is dead, and Nana is dead, and they are both so long gone.

You were a little kid.

All at once I want my mother, so desperately it feels like a kick in the chest. He took her from me. This stupid, hateful man. He robbed me of my mother and sent me into this hellish existence, this un-life. Unloved, unwanted—

Unwanted.

The word makes me think of Jack. How many times, in how many ways, have I been wanted by him. Love is not mine; it isn't an emotion I'd engender. But need and desire—that's something else. He does want me, has wanted me all along.

Homeless, then.

But I've made myself a home. I've built a life of sorts, on my own. A lonely life, until Jack.

I blink hard, licking the rain from my lips.

"You don't need to do this," Ray says. "Go home, sleep it off."

I don't need to do this. I can go home, to my home, to my bed and my lover and my life.

I am very tired. My arm aches. The gun is too heavy to hold.

"Go back inside," I tell him.

He backs away, slowly at first, then quicker, finally turning his back on me as he shouts to the other bouncer.

I get into my car and rest my head against the glass.

I'm tired.

★ ★ ★

Under a streetlamp in front of a long white building, I open my umbrella and take a two-year-old magazine article out of my pocket, unfold it and try to smooth the paper flat.

On the page is a photo of a painter and his canvas. From the article it's clear the man is a famous artist, but his name is unfamiliar to me and my attention as always is riveted on the painting itself and the girl beside him who inspired it. A colorless, eyeless girl, painted in a red shawl, with her hands at her braid and an enigmatic tilt of the head. A strange, singular light skims across the canvas, and she is turned toward it, her lips half-parted, as if the light itself is an interruption to her train of thought.

I went to the artist's gallery after the article came out, and found myself standing before the painting with my jaw aching in suppressed fury, grinding my foot against the bottom of my shoe. It seemed to me that something had been misunderstood. I couldn't reconcile the girl in the painting with the voice screaming from inside the tunnel of trees, or later from her room at the mental health ward. This artist, this handsome, successful man, couldn't know shit about Molly's life. *At the Window,* he'd titled his painting. Either he had missed the point altogether, or was using her to make a point of his own. But Molly couldn't see the portrait for herself and so had no means to argue. The injustice of this infuriated me.

I fold up the paper now and tuck it back in my pocket. The front of the building is mostly dark but there is a light in the entryway and another at the end of the building. I walk up the sidewalk and close my umbrella under the portico. The door is unlocked so I go inside.

At the front desk is a young man in scrubs with his feet

up, playing video games on his phone. He looks up, surprised, and asks if he can help me.

"No," I say, and keep walking. I hear him calling after me as I pass through the double doors and head down the corridor. There are rooms right and left, each with personalized name tags and braille markers below them. I turn right at the end of the hall, pass a small rec room and stop at the door next to it: M Jinks.

I knock on the door. "Yes," she calls, and I go inside.

She's sitting in the corner, knitting. The room is dark except for the flickering light of the TV beside her, but her silvery hair makes a mothlike outline against the wall. She turns her head when I close the door behind me, and I see the two puckered sockets in her pale skin. She lowers her needles and the yarn piles softly in her lap.

I shrug out of my jacket, come around the end of the bed and sit down across from her.

Her snub nose twitches.

"Well," she says. "Hello, Alice. It's been a while."

"I know. I met someone…." I kick off my shoes and push them under the bed, out of her way. "How've you been?"

She gestures around the tiny room. "Never better."

A commercial comes on, and the TV flashes with the image of a woman who's explaining how she's been transformed: *I lost fifty-five pounds and got my life back, and so can you. The secret is—* I slap the power button and the screen goes dark.

Molly raises her eyebrows. "Make yourself at home."

"I'm sorry. I know this is…" I light a cigarette and take a long drag. She holds her hand out, and I put the cigarette between her fingers. The light from the cherry warms her skin, rakes across the scars on her cheeks and the crumpled, empty eyelids.

"Look, I need to ask you something."

"Boy trouble?" She waves the cigarette. "You've come to the right place."

I lower my gaze from her mangled face and tap out another cigarette for myself. On every previous visit, she's had an ashtray near to hand. This time, nothing. I get up and search the kitchenette for a saucer, bring it back and set it on the table beside her.

"I just need—" I hear myself, my own voice saying to this poor freakish wreck of a girl: *I need*. I clear my throat and start again. "Back when we first met at the Center. Before—before what happened with Lyle. You were stealing things."

"Yeah, well, every kid needs a hobby."

"Right. But I think you did more than that." I take her cigarette, flick off the ash and hand it back to her. "You had a copy of your file from Drummond's office. You had all the pages folded up and taped to the back of a drawer, remember?"

"Sure."

I take a deep breath. "I need to know. Did you ever pull my file?"

Her mouth curves upward, and I remember the sly little girl in straggling braids, with her greasy paper bag of treasures and her childish arrogance. I remember the feather pillow, all the grubby trinkets she brought me in a spirit of collusive friendship. She and I understood each other then; we understand each other now.

"You want to know about your mother," she says.

"Yes."

"What do you remember?"

I think of my mother's face. It's almost lost to me now. It's a collection of watery images, a glide-by memory. An impression of her is all I have left. A constellation of freckles across her nose, a tumble of blond hair. It occurs to me that my physical memories of her are never from eye level, but from a child's height, looking up. I remember her breast against my cheek and the smell of her cotton sweater, a golden dragonfly charm at her throat. Her hand on my cheek once when I was sick, her voice crooning, *Poor baby!* How fiercely I clung to those words.

She belonged to me then. I was her baby, but she belonged to me.

I try to describe these things to Molly.

"She had this really loud laugh, kind of goofy, you know? You'd want to keep being funny to keep her laughing."

She nods.

"I always think of her as being really young. Even to me, she seemed young. Struggling. Overwhelmed, maybe."

"She sleep a lot?"

I swallow. "She worked a lot."

"So she worked a lot, laughed a lot. Cried a lot?"

"She had reason to cry."

"Cried in bed, maybe?" Her voice is quiet. "Didn't want to get up? Didn't want to eat sometimes?"

I get up and go to the window. Outside, the rain has stopped. The sidewalks are glazed with water and the tree branches slump toward the ground. My mother used to say that Vashon was an exhausting place to live. Rain and more rain, low gray skies pressing down. She wanted to live in San Diego, where it was sunny all the time. *No one could be*

*sad in San Diego, sugarplum. We'll move there someday. We'll
lay on the beach and get fat and suntanned, won't that be the life?*

But she was so pale when she died.

"You don't need to know what was in the file," Molly
says. "Words the medical people tell each other, labels, di-
agnoses. That's their language, you don't need it."

I turn back, and allow myself a closer look around the
room. The tiny refrigerator is covered with a child's col-
orful drawings, decorated with glitter and dried macaroni,
each one signed with blocky letters in the corner: *SUNNY*.
There are flowers on the table, crammed to overflowing
in an old mason jar. A dreamcatcher over the bed, and on
the bedpost, a winter cap adorned with jaunty pom-poms.

Signs of friendship, of an outdoor life. I wonder whose
scarf she is knitting.

"What do you *know?*" she says.

What do I know. What do I want to know? If I understand the forces that brought me here, if I begin to parse
the blame, I might stumble to an unavoidable forgiveness.
Toward Ray, but more dangerously toward myself.

I want to do the right thing.

Oh, the right thing. Okay, Michael.

I stub out my cigarette, then hers. I bend to kiss her
cheek. As I move away, she grasps my forearm and pulls
me back. Her fingers are surprisingly strong, the way an
old woman's can be sometimes.

"Alice," she says. "It wasn't your fault."

There are no streetlights in the cemetery—no lights at
all, as a matter of fact—but I know the way. Through the
curved wrought iron gates and the weathered brass lettering
set into a large stone rectangle. Past the stately trees, down

the pale gray path that winds like time from old to new. My shoes crunch against the gravel and my breath rises in small, smoky clouds from my nose.

How many times have I circled this graveyard since Nana came to rest here? Nana, then my mother. I've never been here after dark and it feels like illicit behavior, but also as though I am seeing things clearly for the first time. I look up to the night sky. The bare branches rock like fish bones on the surface of an inky sea, and beyond them a fish-hook moon. The gravestones rise up to meet me—old friends whose names are dear and familiar, though most of them had been here for decades when that football player caught my mother's eye. I've written entire stories based on these names, populated books with the people I imagined them to be, given them life again, and passion, and death. The dead are more alive now in my mind than they ever could have been when they were walking, as I am walking, under the moon.

I wonder how much of my life is real and how much make-believe. I have imagined since I was a child that my mother died because of Ray, that he all but murdered her by throwing out her inhaler in that last, terrible fight, then lay there as she suffocated trying to get to the door. But his face tonight—a hated face, unintelligent, clumsy—was full of confusion when our eyes met. Nothing of what I understood about my mother's death was present in his expression. I had expected fear from him, an acknowledgment of guilt for what he'd done to my mother. But there was nothing. Just a blank white space where the information should have been.

The rain is back, a delicate patter on the gravestones and gravel path. I recite the names of the dead as I pass, though the letters are smoothed to illegibility by time and darkness: Sylvia Rosen, whom I immortalized as a murderess; Zacharay Filch and Francine Turner Wolfe, two characters from *Zebra Crossing;* Charlotte Aberdeen, the protagonist from my first unpublished short story. I pause at her grave for a moment, pluck away some pine needles and wonder again about who she was and how she died, eighty-seven years ago, at the age of twenty-five. My mother's age, too, on her last day.

At the end of the lane, tucked aside like an afterthought: Michael John Keeling. No epitaph, no embellishment, just a name and two dates on a small brass plaque.

Not your fault, Molly said. But she doesn't know me really.

"I'm sorry," I whisper. My voice is lost in the thrum of the rain.

I leave Michael and continue on, past a wall of shrubs, to the newest section of the graveyard, where my mother and grandmother lie side by side under the manicured turf. I clear their headstones and sit down on the iron bench where I have sat so often before.

Juliette Larimer
April 9, 1954–November 2, 2000
Safe in the hallowed quiets of the past.

Anna Jane Croft
June 16, 1976–July 25, 2001
Where there is much light, the shadows are deepest.

My mother's grave has tilted a little since the last time I was here. The top no longer lines up visually against the boxwood shrubs behind it. I wonder abstractedly how to correct it.

I'm lost. I don't know what to do, how to fix this and make things right.

I take a lighter from my pocket and find the stub of a roach. I smoke the last couple of hits, watching the flame pop in the darkness, disappear, flicker back to life. I graze my fingers through the light that springs up between them, slide the flame over my palm, down my arm and hold it to the inside of my elbow. The pain is a long time coming— a slow itch, a creeping hurt, then at last the burn and my body snapping apart, asserting its instinct against my will. I turn my arm to see the faint, rosy circle in the blue-veined whiteness of my skin. Another point tallied in my favor.

As the pain continues to smolder, I think of the foster system, that nightmare world where things fell apart and got lost, where bones were broken, and promises, and innocence. Seven years in hell, and after that a hollow aloneness where my stories have spun like wind chimes in the desert.

This is where I've been, all this time, but what part of it is real? What have I understood correctly and what is imagined?

Bipolar...

Ray's word flashes before me, slithering white at the corners of my mind. A frightening word, one he'd clearly assumed was understood between us. He had offered it as an elaboration to something already understood.

Bipolar. It's the word more than anything else that shakes me, because it's not something he'd come up with on his own. It's a medical term. A diagnosis.

What else don't I know about my mother? Michael would have said she was no different from any of the other souls who rest here. She was human. Flawed, maybe angry. Certainly she had cause to be. Knocked up at fourteen, a mother at fifteen, a daughter who'd been forced by Nana to live with the product of her sins. She was moody. Quiet for months at a time, then full of sudden wild energy. But I was wrapped up in my games, immersed in my own small world, and I never saw the patterns in hers.

You were just a little kid.

I was. Just a kid, and so was she. A child thrust prematurely into an adult world, ill-equipped for what she found there.

Bipolar disorder. Batshit. A fucking lunatic.

She probably tossed the inhaler herself.

A finger of cold air creeps under my collar and trails down my spine.

She probably tossed it out herself.

But if that were true, then it meant—

I stare at her grave and feel the cold crystallize in my chest.

She wanted to die. She left me deliberately. Took herself away and left me here alone. She didn't love me enough to stay here and give me a home. She didn't love me enough to live.

I sit with this thought, and the truth of it claims me like an icy sea—inescapable, vast, a truth so big and dark and bitter that for years I've clung to the nearest of the debris with the tenacity of a drowning man.

Now I understand why Amanda failed to rise to my prompts about her home life, why there are flowers in the front yard when for years there was only decay. I understand my mother's habits and Nana's protectiveness—and the absence of knowledge that a crime had been committed on the night my mother died. I saw nothing in Ray because there was nothing to see.

He is innocent. Ugly, stupid and mean, but innocent of this particular crime. The only one that matters to me.

And I almost—

Jack is so close now to the man I wanted him to be. A killer. I sought him out, wound him up, made him dependent on me, sensitive to my opinion. I could say to him, *Look what this guy has done to you. Look what he's done to* me. *How can you call yourself a man and let this miscreant live?*

There was a moment during that last fight when I almost said that very thing. The words had hovered in the space between us, an expectation had been raised. Jack had stood there wired with his hand on my throat, searching my face like a soldier waiting for orders. But again...I couldn't pull the trigger.

Relief floods my body, so strong I have to wrap my arms around my stomach to keep from vomiting. I rock forward and back, gulping the cold air, remembering the weight of the gun in my hand and the smooth expanse of Ray's chest. The trigger felt so small under my finger, the juicy flow of humanity so easily pierced. I almost killed him.

Almost.

But not quite. Michael did save one of us, after all.

I get to my feet, stiff and heavy with cold. I stare down at my mother's tilted headstone, and Nana's, straight as a pillar.

I want to go home.

By the time I close the front door behind me, it's been forty hours since I've slept. A bone-deep weariness drags me toward the earth, as though Death himself has wrapped his fingers around me and begun to tug.

I go to the bathroom and run a tub. Peel off my clothes a layer at a time: sweater and shoes, jeans and socks and T-shirt and bra and underwear. I stare at my reflection, my grandmother's silver cross hanging silent and heavy between my breasts. The weight of it has always comforted me, but tonight it clings to me like a slug and the chain around my neck feels repellently sticky. I grab the pendant and jerk it over my head, not bothering with the clasp. I toss it on the counter. Then, after a minute, take the wooden box from my closet and lay the necklace inside.

When I drag myself out of the tub half an hour later, I'm so tired I can barely move. Dawn is hours away, I won't make it.

I lie down and pull the covers over my head.

CHAPTER TWENTY-ONE

I dream that I am drowning. I've been standing on a riverbank, but it's not like any place real, more like the edge of the cliff at the white motel. Far below, a brown river seethes and roils, bristling with flotsam. In the dream, it's been raining for years and though I know the bank is unstable, I keep edging closer, looking for something in the river. Something important.

Without warning, the ground beneath my feet begins to slide, as though the whole riverbank has turned to oil. My stomach heaves. I feel the drop, the inexorable fall, the inevitability—and I am in the river.

The water is filthy, warm and coated with thick bubbles. A snake floats past. I'm not sure whether it's alive or dead but I know it's poisonous. I aim for shore but the water is so thick and full of debris that I can't get my limbs moving through it. It's all so heavy. As I look across the surface to the distant bank, another realization hits me. The flotsam choking the water is not wood.

The river is full of bones.

My body begins to sink. I am underwater, drowning in a river of blood.

I open my eyes.

Someone is here. A man. He's on top of me, a wall of muscle lying on my chest. My legs are pinned under his feet, my wrists shackled by his fingers. His hand is over my mouth.

I draw a shallow breath and scream. The sound is strangled, muffled under his hand as though I really am underwater. My heart leaps. I begin to buck and kick.

"Where have you been?" he says against my ear.

I close my eyes. Jack. Relief pours though me, rinses the strength from my limbs. I wait for him to roll away and let me up.

But he doesn't do that. He rises to his elbows, a faceless silhouette in the dark. His shoulders loom over me; his legs against mine are bare. When he speaks again, I smell whiskey on his breath, thick as gasoline.

"Where'd you go, hmm?"

I shake my head. He's asking a question but won't let me answer. Like he knows, like he already knows.

He releases my wrists and slides his free hand between us, jerking at the hem of my tank top, groping for my breast. His cock is hard against my hip. When I try to pry his fingers from my mouth, he grabs my hand and holds my arm in place with his elbow. He forces my thighs apart with one knee.

"This is how it is?" His voice is a sibilant hiss, with a drunken softness in the consonants. "You won't even lay here and spread your legs for me?"

With his other knee, he digs into the bed, working his way between my thighs. He pinches my nipple and clamps his hand over my cry of pain.

"Tell me where you were tonight," he says. "But you better tell me now, because I'm not going to ask again."

He leans over me till we're nose to nose. He lifts his hand from my mouth.

"Five seconds," he says.

Relax, I think. *This is Jack.*

"Wait—"

"Tell me now."

"Just wait—"

He slams his hand over my mouth. My teeth tear at my lips.

"I don't want to fucking wait," he says.

It's Jack, I think again, as if this will save me. This is Jack, it's okay for him to be here, he's been here before, it will be fine, this is Jack…

He reaches between my legs and yanks my underwear aside.

"We never talked about this, did we?" he says. "But I bet it's in the repertoire. You won't even have to get your hands dirty."

My heart careens against my ribs. My stomach sinks, then lurches upward as though we are riding a roller coaster in the darkness.

Jack has always known the way when he leads me to these places. But tonight he's lost, bluffing, clumsy with need and anger. He's too heavy. His hands are too hard. Under the weight of his body, I begin to struggle for air. I want him to get off, let me get a breath, slow down and give me a chance to follow.

He does none of those things.

He spits on his fingertips, smears this over his dick, and plunges inside me.

This is Jack, I think helplessly, *this is Jack, this is Jack…*

"Always playing, aren't you. You think this is a game?" His head has been turned but now he looks at my face, my wide-open eyes. "Stop looking at me, fuck you—"

He lets go of my mouth. Withdraws for a second to flip me over. Then he's back, between my legs, back inside me with his hip bones sharp against my ass. I sob his name, plead for him to slow down.

"Wait, wait—"

He cuts me off, his hand back in place to silence my cries and keep me from scrambling away. I curl my arm at my side, push up hard, trying to find some space for myself beneath him. It feels as though I'm trapped in the rubble of an earthquake, pinned beneath a collapsed wall. I can't breathe, I can't breathe.

"I waited all day. Waited for you to call. Waited for you to come over. But you had someplace else to be, didn't you. Some other game to play."

His thrusts grow harder, a bludgeon against my cervix. There is no room to adjust. No slowing him down, no pleasure in this pain. He is everywhere, crushing me. I can't get my knees under me, can't get a breath. In full panic mode, I gather my strength for one final push to get him off me. I bite, try to buck, reach back to rake my fingernails along his flank.

He crushes my forearm with his hand, presses me into the bed.

I can't breathe.

This is Jack…this is Jack…

The room begins to spin and collapse. Pinpoints of light burst in my eyes. I can't fight anymore. He is huge, monstrous inside me, his nose at my cheek, one hand over my breast. It's like a dream, a nightmare.

This is Jack, this is Jack, this is Jack...

He releases my mouth and I gasp. The air brings me the sweetest high, warm and liquid, an instant balm inside my aching chest. I gulp it like tequila and feel a similar flush of relief.

"That's it," he says as if to himself.

His thrusts lengthen. He pushes my thigh aside to give himself more room.

"I saw you tonight. Didn't expect *that,* did you? What were you doing in my house that day, sneaking around?"

He pushes my hair aside, but small tendrils cling to my tears and fall into my mouth. The pain takes my breath away.

This is Jack, this is Jack...

"And what...the fuck...were you doing with *him.*"

His voice breaks, he's crying. His cheek is wet, feverish against mine. He buries his nose at the side of my neck and inhales, wraps his arm around me as if one of us is drowning.

"I'm sorry, I'm sorry," I tell him, but my voice is only a whisper and he's too far gone to hear.

He comes inside me, crying, calling my name.

CHAPTER TWENTY-TWO

Jack's arm is heavy as a door across my chest. I lift it away gingerly so as not to wake him. But his breathing is thick and drunken, and he doesn't stir when I swing my legs over the side of the bed and pick across his discarded clothes to the bathroom.

The darkness is lifting, the pines outside faintly outlined against the sky. I close the bathroom door behind me and lower myself to the toilet. My urine burns as it trickles over me, and the tissue is tinged with pink. An ugly bruise is blossoming on my inner thigh.

I know where you were—

With my head in my hands, I replay the night before, trying to sort out what Jack knows and what he doesn't.

I saw you.

I imagine the scene from Jack's point of view, as though we were characters in a book. He must have followed me to Cherries and seen me there with Ray. Clearly he never saw the gun or he would have said so.

So he saw—what? Me and Ray, together.

It comes at me in a rush. Jack believes I'm with Ray, romantically.

The first time Jack and I met, I was breaking into his house. Now, after seeing me with Ray when I was supposed to be at home working, he surely knows there is a connection between the two events. Jack is too smart to believe in coincidence. He must think Ray has it in for him somehow or is still trying to get his hands on some money. He thinks I've been playing him.

Which I have. All along. Just not the way he thinks.

I get up and look in the mirror. My eyes are huge and glassy. The nicks on my throat and shoulder are scabbed over, ugly, and my mouth is swollen from Jack's teeth. The tattoo around my arm looks more like a circle of thorns than a dandelion chain. The fatigue that's been building since yesterday is thick and woolen around me.

I open the cabinet and take out my kit, sit at the edge of the tub and lay my left foot across my knee. The blade flashes and lays a delicate etching in my skin, but there is no corresponding fire. I lay three stripes and feel nothing, so I add three more, then three and three and three more, each cut longer and deeper than the one before. They begin to weep and bead and drip, one into the other, and still I'm waiting to feel something.

My throat closes up—not in pain but terror. The razor has always been my friend, my ally, the stimulant I need to focus and snap myself awake. And today there is nothing.

The blood is running so freely now that the towel is soaked red. I pivot around so my feet are in the tub, and watch the thin red line move like an editor's pen across the porcelain, imagining the way Gus would react to a scene like this if he read it on my pages: *This is hyperbole, Alice, pull it back. Less is more.*

I trickle some water over my foot, dump some peroxide

on for good measure, pad the whole mess with gauze and wrap it around and around with an Ace bandage.

I won't be able to hide this from Jack. But maybe we are beyond the point of hiding.

In the living room, I build a fire and stare into it as the morning light seeps across the window. I'm numb with cold and the silence is unnerving. For company, I turn on the TV and listen to it with half an ear, twirling my hair around my finger, trying to think what to say to Jack.

I could feign coincidence, tell him I went to Cherries to meet a friend.... No, not that, I have no friends. I could say that Ray contacted me for some reason. Or maybe I went to Cherries for a drink, and—

A familiar name snaps me to attention. A newscaster is on location, standing in front of a building that I don't recognize at first. But as the camera pans out, I see that the door behind her is the very one I spent an hour staring at last night. She must be standing almost exactly where I stood next to my car, in the far corner of Cherries' parking lot.

I sit forward and turn up the volume.

"...body has been identified as that of Raymond Burbank, an employee of the nightclub. Police say he was found by two patrons leaving the club, the apparent victim of a beating. He was taken to Harborview Medical Center and was pronounced dead.... Janet, back to you...."

The colors seem to leach from the room, then spring back to life, vivid and sharply outlined, the edges of my vision fading to black. My head turns slowly, eyeballs sliding ineluctably sideways.

Jack's shoes are by the door, where he left them last night when he came in after me. I pick them up and carry them into the light. They are thick leather work boots, caked with damp mud. I've seen them dozens of times—in my doorway or his, on the front porch, discarded next to the bed. I've stubbed my toes on them, scolded Jack for leaving them underfoot. And once, when he came over late at night, I stood with bare feet on these wide brown laces as Jack danced me around the living room and eased me to the floor.

But I have never seen the fat, dark red spot on the toe of the right boot.

Oh, Jack.

This is where we are, where we're going. Two days ago he said it himself, while I lay facedown on the bed as he smeared ointment over the cut he'd laid across the small of my back:

"You want this as much as I do. Sometimes I get the most insane hard-on, thinking about the blood on your skin, the way it tastes, the way it makes you come." And later, nose to nose on the pillow: "I'm scared, baby, I'm scared."

He's been waiting for me to stop him. But I don't think I can.

I want it. I've wanted, all this time, a killer.

My killer.

Would you kill for me?

Would you kill me?

Are the two so very different?

As I drop into a chair with his boots between my feet, my fingers begin to buzz and tingle. My scalp prickles, creeping up from the nape of my neck like a swarm of ants marching through my hair. I blink at the spot of blood on

his boot, which swims out of focus and back to sharp defi-
nition. I feel as if I'm waking from a long sleep in a strange
place. None of this seems familiar—not the nubbly rag rug
under his boot or the view from the wooden chair or the
shabby brick fireplace. The house has taken on a feeling of
impermanence, as of a motel room or the inside of a stranger's car. The air is heavy in my lungs.

I get up and go to the bedroom doorway.

Jack's breathing has grown more shallow. He has turned
over and is lying with one long arm flung across the bed,
palm up as though he's waiting for a gift. His dark hair is
tousled and soft against the sheet, his eyelashes like a spar-
row's wing against his cheek. He has never looked so child-
like, so unbearably dear.

If I stay, he will kill me.

And I can't bear to let him be punished for it.

CHAPTER TWENTY-THREE

I take his clothes to the living room, along with a pair of poultry shears from the kitchen. I cut the buttons, zipper and rivets from his jeans and shirt and put them into an empty canvas satchel, along with his boots. Then, a piece at a time, I feed his clothes to the fire, stirring, adding wood, until everything he was wearing last night is reduced to ashes. I empty the writing from my safe and add my notes and journals, tens of thousands of words, all the pages and pages I've labored over, and watch them flare and curl inward and disappear.

The buzz sweeps over me, that odd tingle, sharpened now to pins and needles along my arms, tightening across my breasts. A dull ache has begun in the sole of my mangled foot, but I'm moving quickly. I'm dressed and have packed a second satchel with my laptop, wallet, a few items of clothing and a supply of gauze and ointment. And the wooden box.

I know I'm making mistakes, leaving things behind that I should be destroying or taking with me. But I can't stop. I can't face Jack.

If I see him wake in the pink morning light, soft with

sleep and blinking into the blurry distance, I won't be strong enough to do what I need to do.

I step out the front door. The morning air is cool and damp, laced with the scent of the things I have burned. I'm a prisoner at the gate who wants nothing more than to stay in her cell, to be caught and held and maybe even executed in due time.

Jack, Jack...

I swallow around the knot in my throat and step off the front porch, pausing at Jack's truck to find what I expected: a claw hammer. Stained with blood, wrapped in an old T-shirt. I drop it into the satchel with what's left of his clothes and boots, sling the straps over my shoulders and set off into the forest.

CHAPTER TWENTY-FOUR

I didn't think to bring a spade. I'll have to make do with the bloody hammer.

The earth between the graves of my mother and Nana is cool and damp. The claw sinks in easily, with small sighs of friction, as I loosen the soil and pile it beside the hole. The trees overhead are damp with morning dew that weeps down onto the back of my head and drips into the hole. The gap widens slowly, a mouth in a slow-motion scream.

When the hole is big enough, I lay the box inside. The burnished wood is smooth and fine against the rough-textured soil; the scent of lemon polish rises from the earth, mixed with the odor of soil and decaying leaves. Nearby is a cluster of yellow wildflowers, clinging to the leg of the iron bench. I pluck one and lay it on top of the box.

I fill the hole with my bare hands and return the hammer to my satchel.

By the time I reach the ferry dock, my left foot feels as if I'm stepping into glass. To avoid the main roads, I've been walking for two hours along the hiking trails that crisscross the island. I've met no one, and am fairly certain nobody has seen me. All they would notice in any case is a small figure in a waterproof jacket, her head covered in a dark hood. Nothing anyone would remember.

Despite the pain, I would like to keep walking. The motion soothes me. One foot in front of the other, it's so simple. The trees against the sky, a moss-green path, pines rising like sentinels into the fog. But now I need a different form of transport.

I veer off the path near the parking lot at the water's edge, and watch from the forest as the morning commuters park their cars or get in line to board the next ferry. For now the dock is empty, but in fifteen minutes the next boat will arrive, and I will be on it.

In my bed at home, Jack will be waking up. He'll see that his clothes are gone, that I am gone, but my car is still in the driveway. He may assume I've gone to get a cup of coffee or am out for a walk. He'll probably search my belongings for further clues of my betrayal. He'll pace the house and eventually come looking.

I sit down on a fallen log, curl forward with my elbows on my knees and let the satchels fall to the ground. The air is thick with mist, and for several long seconds there is a plenary silence in which no birdsong or engine or voice can be heard. There is only absence.

On the other side of the island, the Red Ranger bike continues its inexorable crawl skyward, lodged in the throat of the tree, which I see for the first time as another victim of the tragedy. The bike rolled into its branches and stayed there, and the sapling, rooted in place and unable to halt its own growth, has spent the prime of its life choking on the abandoned wreckage. The bike and the tree are victims of their own natures. Freakish conjoined twins, hopelessly fused.

I take my cell phone from my pocket, pull out the battery and dig a hole. I drop in the pieces and use a stick to arrange a few vines of poison oak over the top. My trail will end here.

The ferry approaches through the fog, its light bobbing gently over the water. The silence is cut by the sound of the bell, a single clang, stern in its clarity. I get to my feet. Dimly I am aware of pain. Hunger. An ominous fatigue that will overtake me if I don't keep moving. I try to ignore my body and concentrate on the ferry. Strange that I've never really looked at it closely before. How dirty it is, streaked with algae, the red stripe along its side peeling away in places, windows crusted with salt. In my mind, the ferry has always seemed a magical thing, bearing me across the water and home again; all it is really is a tired old bus.

As I start down the slope to the parking lot, I hear a familiar rumble. I sink into the undergrowth as Jack's truck swims past, through the ribbons of silvery fog. Inside the cab, his profile is the sharp prow of a boat, sweeping back and forth.

I hesitate. If I get onto the ferry he might follow me. But the next ride is half an hour from now. I am not strong enough to be still that long. Thirty minutes of reflection would be more than enough to send me back to him. Even now, knowing he's near, probably still furious, a newly minted murderer with a witness to deal with, even with my mind full of fear and a frisson of animal wariness like a blanket of needles across my back, the overwhelming impulse from my body is desire. I want him, so badly that I have to steady myself against the damp bark of a tree as a dizzying tide of longing sweeps up my limbs, gathers tingling behind my breastbone and slides to the base of my belly.

I think of the blade at my throat and imagine what it might feel like to be awash in my own blood. To drown in it or simply seep away. The possibility beguiles me like the yearning for sleep at the end of a long winter night. How blissful to rest, to gaze at the sky and weep into the earth. To give up, give in, to let the life trickle out of me, to die in my lover's arms. To close my eyes. But none of that is possible. Whatever the release or deliverance for me at the tip of the knife, whatever murky wish it might fulfill, for Jack my death would mean a lifetime of suffering.

He parks his truck at the end of the line for the ferry. I slide down the hill and head for the dock, crouching low behind the line of cars to keep out of sight. When the next group of pedestrians starts up the ramp, I step in front of them and allow myself to be carried along. The fog slides like a curtain behind me, and underfoot is the blacktop, the cement edged in stripes of black and yellow, the wooden dock. The ferry at the end, and the door open with the light shining through. One foot after the other. Unhurried, afloat, I hand my pass to the ferryman and hear his voice ring out, close beside my ear:

"All full!"

Jack's truck is still on the ramp. He'll have to wait for the next ferry, and by then I'll be long gone.

I make my way to the stern and take a rain-beaded seat with the two satchels in my lap. The pins and needles, the numbness, the chill of adrenaline are all gone now, and my body feels curiously soft and empty, a waterlogged husk on the banks of an ancient river.

There are mostly men making the commute this morning. The young guy in the seat next to me is staring fixedly ahead, but I feel the eager maleness of him, and know he'll speak to me once the ferry gets under way. The space between us is slick with the knowledge, as though we are two magnets laid the wrong way together, gliding along a space that cannot be breached.

The boat unmoors and prepares to separate from the loading dock. I sit narrow in my seat, one knee pressed to the curve of the other. The men around me seem unnaturally large, silent and menacing in their dark wet jackets, steam rising in clouds around their faces. In this forest of men, I am blind and lost, unable to distinguish good from evil, unsure after all that there is anything to choose between them. My eyes shift from face to featureless face. These men are unknowable, unmovable, solid and wooden as the pines.

For them, I am as much a mystery. As Jack said, no one knows anyone else. To believe otherwise is an expression of innocence and arrogance.

As the ferry pulls away, creaming the sea behind it, I see Jack standing at the edge of the dock, scanning the crowd with his hands slung low on his hips. He shrinks to the height of my thumbnail and smaller, until the air between us grows too thick and the distance too great, and he is gone.

I close my eyes and take a deep breath.

★ ★ ★ ★ ★

ACKNOWLEDGMENTS

I discovered early on that writing is best undertaken in the company of fellow sufferers. It didn't take me long to find them; we gravitated to Betsy Lerner's blog like moths to a streetlamp, with occasional burns ensuing that never deterred us for long. Through Betsy I acquired a circle of fascinating though somewhat imaginary friends who beguile me every day in our online conversations, who have allowed me into their minds and whom I accept with deepest gratitude into mine.

Of all these, it's the man behind the curtain who has helped me the most. More than the scads of practical advice—and actually, this book was his idea in the first place—August has given me something I never dreamed I could possess: confidence. What he's done for me and for so many others is beyond my ability to articulate. I can only give thanks for a life transformed, possibly saved. You're a good, kind man, you are.

Thanks as well to my agent, Jeff Kleinman, for his commitment, his skill and his great speedy-speed. The grass doesn't grow under your feet, my friend.

My undying appreciation goes out to Erin Craig and Tara

Scarcello, who designed a cover I'd like to paper my walls with, and to the marketing, public relations and sales teams for their enthusiasm and all-around badassery.

Thanks especially to my lovely editor, Michelle Meade, whose wisdom and guidance have helped me understand what I was trying to say and decide how to say it.

And how to finish when I've said enough.

ALICE CLOSE YOUR EYES
AVERIL DEAN

Reader's Guide

HARLEQUIN® MIRA®

1. Discuss the recurring theme of mistaken assumptions, the idea of each character's tragic misreading of the people around them. How is Molly's blindness relevant to this theme?

2. What's the significance of the character of Lyle? Why do you think the author chose to give him a disability? Why does Molly taunt him, and what does she mean when she says to Alice, "*I'm* the kid."

3. What do you think of Alice's mother? Grandmother? What do you imagine their lives were like before Nana died? And after?

4. Upon hearing that Alice is being taunted at school, her grandmother says, "Learn to use what you have." How did you feel about what Alice did with that advice? What did her actions reveal about her character? About the person she would grow up to be?

5. Alice spent a major part of her childhood in foster care. Have you, or anyone you've known, been in the

foster system? Can you relate to any of the experiences or relationships that Alice had while moving from home to home?

6. What was your initial reaction to Jack's character? Did your impression of him change as the novel progressed?

7. Discuss the intersection of pain and pleasure throughout the novel, both in the physical and emotional sense. How do these two conflicting sensations play off each other throughout the story? How do they work against each other?

8. If Jack had caught Alice before she got on the ferry, what do you think would have happened between them? What do you suppose Jack meant to do when he followed her there?

9. Where do you think Alice will go when the ferry lands in Seattle? What do you think the future holds for her? Do you think leaving silently was the right decision, or should she have stayed to confront Jack or report him?

What was your inspiration for Alice Close Your Eyes? Did the story end up the way you first imagined it or did it evolve along the way?

When I was brainstorming ideas for this book, I happened upon a low-budget neo-noir film called Following, directed by Christopher Nolan. In the film, two men break into a London flat for no particular reason other than curiosity, a voyeurism of objects. This idea hooked me immediately, and I began to imagine the erotic possibilities and play with some ideas for how to incorporate this strange habit into a psychological thriller.

In some ways, though eccentric, this seemed like a playful, relatively innocuous activity. But as I revised, the story got progressively darker, more claustrophobic, and the break-ins began to take on a sinister significance even as they moved slightly off-center from the main story line. Instead of being instigated by Alice, as I had planned, they became Jack's idea—a clue more to his character than Alice's. This change shifted the balance of power in their relationship, and infused the story with a sense of danger and deviance beyond what I originally envisioned.

Can you describe your writing process? Do you create an outline or dive right in? Do you write consecutively or jump around? Do you let anyone read early drafts or do you keep the story private until it's finished?

Most stories begin for me with other works of fiction. When I'm starting work on a new story, I spend a good amount of time watching movies, reading and listening to music. I'm looking for something that generates a particular reaction in me, something that evokes a mood or sparks an interesting line of thought.

From there, I decide where the story begins and jot down some ideas for where it might go. It's all rather nebulous at this point, and utterly disorganized. I actually prefer it that way. Writing can be intimidating, so when I'm starting a new project, I make a concerted effort to take the pressure off. I write the raw stuff longhand, with a cheap pen in a fat spiral notebook. My handwriting is awful, and the pages are covered with angry scratch-outs and incomprehensible notes up the margins, but beginning this way keeps me from having to face a blank computer screen unarmed.

My thought processes are equally messy. I hop from scene to scene, trying not to deny myself any wild idea at this stage, whether or not I understand how it relates to the story. I carry on this way until I've assembled quite a scrapalanche—maybe 30,000-40,000 words. Then I go through the scenes one by one and organize them into a new document, using only the ones that seem to matter to the story.

Beyond this point, it's rare for me to write anything extraneous. I've figured out what the story is about and have developed an understanding of the characters. All that remains is to keep adding material until the book is complete.

I don't share my work until it's as good as I can get it—and even then, only with one or two people I really trust. I'm terribly suggestible, and would head off on any number of tangents if too many people were involved in the revision process.

Alice's dark and damaged life clearly shaped her adult personality and the relationships she becomes involved in. How do you develop your characters and what is it like to write about people with such intense, painful stories?

I think characters come to life through a process of refinement, especially refinement of their outlook—the things they notice in the world around them, their reaction to what they see. Alice is essentially a beautiful soul repeatedly confronted by ugliness. She has a wistful outlook, which shows itself particularly in her interactions with children and in some of her early encounters with Jack. Her dialogue serves as counterpoint to this outlook and underlines the dichotomy between her inner life and the distance she maintains between herself and the other characters.

Though I'll admit the story took a bit of a toll, I'm not sure a writer has much choice when it comes to subject matter. Joyce Carol Oates has said that we tend to write what surprises us. I think that's true. I prefer to write about people and situations I don't understand very well, because those are the stories that hold my interest during the long and sometimes tedious process of writing a book. Emotional pain can be overcome. Boredom, for me, cannot.

What kind of research, if any, went in to the writing of Alice Close Your Eyes?

I'm not big into research. I probably should spend more time at it than I do. But I've found that concrete knowledge tends to dim the mental images I form about the setting or situation, and often creates problems I would much prefer to avoid. For instance, I discovered that the ferry schedule to and from Vashon Island does not include night runs. But I needed them! It was painful to ignore that bit of knowledge, so for a time I gave

Vashon a fictional name and considered the problem solved. It was my editor who convinced me that readers would probably forgive my lapses in verisimilitude as long as the flavor of the place was intact.

I hope she's right about that.

You've written erotic fiction before, and this novel also incorporates erotic elements in a complex and crucial way. Can you talk about how erotic scenes can be used in service to the larger story?

I'm fascinated by the psychological dynamic between sexual partners. Most people hold their fantasies and predilections secret, often with some element of shame attached to the secrecy. But in a sexual relationship, one either comes to trust another person with those secrets, or—more interestingly from a story point of view—is driven by need to reveal them to an untrustworthy partner.

These psychological plums are too juicy to resist. I love to find out what will happen between the characters when they're alone in the bedroom: what kind of power struggle will ensue, how each person will decide which secrets to reveal and which to withhold, how the characters' insecurities will manifest physically during the scene. A person's sexuality exposes his or her character in a unique way, from a different angle as it were. It adds another layer to the story.

This is the first time I've tried to incorporate fully developed sex scenes into a novel of a different genre. As I wrote, I began to think of the erotic elements as character development; I wanted the reader to be right there with Alice as she experiences first the pleasure, then the intoxicating pain and fear that lead her to realize what kind of man she's dealing with. Hopefully, each scene provides a new insight into one or both of the characters.

The novel is set mostly on Vashon Island in Puget Sound. What made you choose a small, rural setting for this story? How do you feel the setting enhances the story?

First, let me apologize to anyone who lives on Vashon Island. I wrote this story from my home in Las Vegas, and though I did my best to understand the geography, I'm sure there are plenty of discrepancies. To some extent, the setting is fictionalized—a desert rat's romantic notion of what the Pacific Northwest would be like for the residents. I was looking for a dark, slightly claustrophobic setting, definitely rural, in which Alice's isolation would be literal. An island in Puget Sound seemed like the perfect choice.

What drew me to Vashon particularly was the little Red Ranger bike in the tree. I loved the strangeness of that image and thought it was something young Alice would be drawn to. It wasn't until much later in the revision process that I understood the metaphor and was able to work it into the story.

What was your greatest challenge writing Alice Close Your Eyes? Your greatest pleasure?

At the beginning of every new piece of work, I go through an extended period of what feels like shyness, as at the start of a new romance, or the first hour of a party where you don't know any of the guests. This is a tough thing to power through. The temptation is to leave this awful situation and go back to daydreaming quietly in an armchair. I haven't found a way to make the beginnings easier. It seems to be a matter of perseverance and caffeine-fueled jags of free writing. Anything to get something on the page.

My happiest moment came at the end of the first draft. I have a writing mentor whose opinion I respect more than anyone I know. He had offered to read my manuscript. I was terrified to send it, and avoided it for a few weeks—moving the mashed potatoes around on the plate, as he would say. Eventually, with the help of a couple of strong margaritas, I worked up the courage.

His response was almost immediate. He said he'd read it in one sitting, at the computer, and he was so warm and generous in his praise that I sank to the floor next to my bed and cried for an hour. Big, ugly, messy sobs, followed by an outbreak of joyful hives. It was a hideous, wonderful night.

How did you know you wanted to be a writer? Can you describe your first piece of writing and the journey to publishing your first print book?

I started writing on my father's birthday in 2010. He had always talked about how much he wanted to write, but he passed away without ever having given it a try. I found myself in a similar state of inertia. I have always been an avid reader, a collector of words and phrases. I enjoy the beauty of language. But writing a novel—or even a short story, for that matter—was something that had never occurred to me. I'm a high school dropout, and that fact has always been a source of shame for me, and a barrier to my aspirations.

However, a story idea had been tugging at my mind, and on that day I remembered my dad and decided to write a paragraph. Just to get it out of my system, really. I liked the paragraph, so I wrote a page. The page expanded to a scene, then a chapter, then a book. Followed by a second book. I sold those novels for the princely sum of $100 apiece to an independent e-publisher.

They did not earn out.

By this time, I had become involved with an online circle of writer-friends, most of whom were blogging or commenting on writing blogs. They encouraged me to start a new book and keep at it, and when I'd finished Alice Close Your Eyes, they gave me practical advice on things like pitch lines and query letters. The quick response I received from Jeff Kleinman, the wonderful man who would become my agent, is due almost entirely to the help they gave me. I wouldn't be writing without them.

Can you tell us something about your next novel?

My next book is a psychological suspense novel called Blackbird. It's the story of a triple murder told in reverse, beginning with the crime and working back through the characters' tangled relationships to discover where it all went wrong. Like Alice Close Your Eyes, it's sexy and intense and very dark.